Ryan

ICEAPELAGO 3

Climate fiction, or...

Climate fact!!

Either way a

scary read

Peter.

(**Iceapelago** / *n. (pl.* **-os** or **-oes***)* 1. A group of islands surrounded by ice. 2. A frozen land mass with many islands.

Gk **pelagos** sea (orig.= island of Ireland post the collapse of the Gulf Stream)

ICEAPELAGO 3

THE THIRD GENERATION

DR PETER BRENNAN

ISBN (Print): 978-1-8380639-4-8
ISBN (Ebook): 978-1-8380639-5-5

To The Fourth Generation

CONTENTS

MAP OF ICEAPELAGO

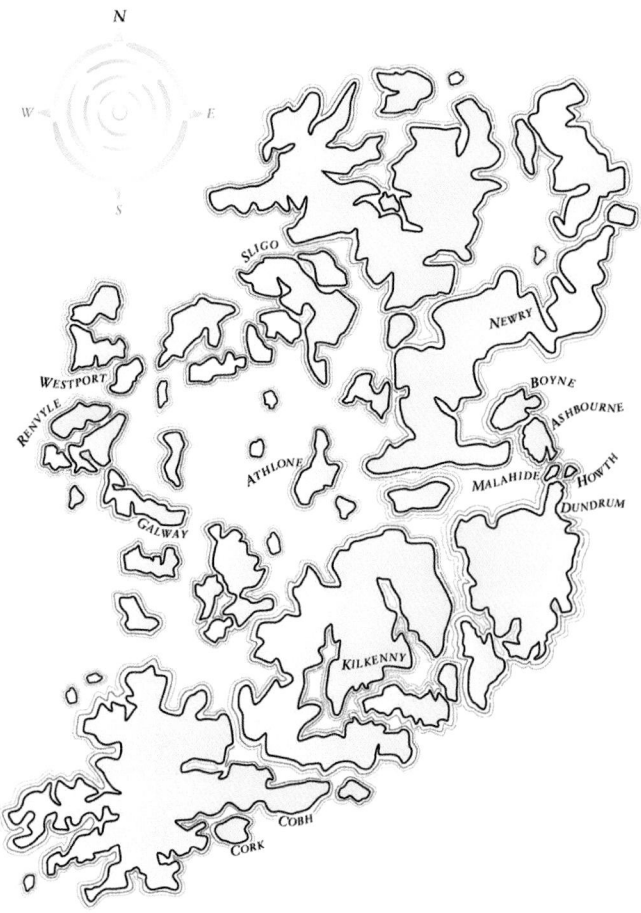

PROLOGUE

THE COMBINED IMPACT OF the tsunamis from La Palma in the Canaries and the Eriador Ridge off the Continental Shelf, and the complete collapse of the Gulf Stream, created Iceapelago – thirty ice-covered islands that were once Ireland. This climate episode was known as the Eriador Event. The widespread flooding and the sharp rise in sea levels killed millions, shattered the landscape, and destroyed critical infrastructure across the Northern Hemisphere.

In the early years, the Iceapelago survivors eked out an existence in pre-medieval conditions. The priority was to secure basic essentials such as shelter, food, water and medicine ahead of the arrival of Winter Day when severe arctic conditions locked down Iceapelago for months until the spring thaw.

An order of sorts was put in place with the appointment of the Commander of Iceapelago who ruled from Dundrum Island. Individual communities elected a leader known as the Six and also a sheriff to maintain law and order. Shortwave radio was the only means of communication. A fleet of refurbished river cruisers provided transport between the islands.

As resources grew scarce, the commander over-stepped his authority. He brought in mercenaries from Cymru to impose his wishes on fractious communities. He was not successful, and was overthrown. Ruth Henry from Cork Airport Island was appointed by the Iceapelago Sixes to replace him.

In 2091, thirty years after the Eriador Event, the Big Storm arrived. Ruth Henry received a radio warning from her Canadian contacts who, at that stage, had access to weather satellites of two catastrophic storms that would arrive within days of each other – a cyclone direct from the tropics of offshore Africa and a deep low depression from the high Arctic. The meeting of these two extreme weather systems was unprecedented. Armed with this stark warning, Ruth Henry arranged transport for her family and some friends from Cork Airport Island to the safety of the Old Head of Kinsale.

The Big Storm started with the arrival of monsoon-type rain, hurricane-force winds and dramatic thunderstorms. The sea crashed inland morning, noon and night destroying most buildings. All coastal areas across Iceapelago were under water. Days later, the weather switched as an arctic storm combination of force-twelve gales, driving ice, snow and sleet lashed onshore. Severe arctic conditions prevailed, and everything was frozen solid for months. Then, without warning, a deep thaw started as high pressure built up from Southern Europe. Within months everything had defrosted, rapidly melting the sea ice.

In the decade after the Big Storm, conditions improved as Iceapelago benefitted from more temperate conditions. The few remaining communities were self-sufficient, and none more so than the twenty-strong ageing population of Malahide Castle Island. Led by Rory, the erstwhile Commander of Iceapelago, the residents were settled in their ways. There was food on the table, and their accommodation was safe and secure. While they had no means of transport to get to other islands, being insular had become their culture, the new way of life.

The status quo would not last long. Other regions which had also suffered from Mother Nature's excesses needed to find a new home for their beleaguered citizens. Despite the grim conditions, Iceapelago became the target for climate refugees seeking a better future.

CHAPTER 1

Ria Formosa

'*Obrigado.*'

Having been thanked, the wine server withdrew from the table and quietly left the room.

The sole diner, Jorge-Paul de Sousa, drank heavily from the freshly filled silver goblet.

The Duke of the Principality of Ria Formosa had more on his mind than the quality of the Kompassus Reserva red, the best of the vineyards of Barriada in coastal northern Portugal.

He had a decision to make, one that had preyed on his mind every hour of every day for the past while. A decision that would define his reign and his family's reputation for generations.

He stared long and hard at the oil portrait of his father, which dominated the richly decorated room. The duke knew by instinct, culture, and experience what his parent would have done to protect his citizens. However, what might have been correct and proper thirty years ago was not necessarily the most appropriate choice now. He wrestled with that dilemma.

His Council of State waited patiently outside his private dining room, eagerly awaiting the outcome of his personal deliberations, not least because his decision would have an impact on them, and their immediate families. Without a partner and children, and as the last living member of his family, the duke was also aware of his responsibilities as a leader of part of a once proud nation.

The facts were stark.

In 2061, the La Palma tsunamis had wiped out the coastal regions of Portugal to upwards of a hundred kilometres inland in places. The Atlantic waters thrown ashore by the series of hundred-metre-tall waves retreated within weeks. However, everything in their path was rendered beyond physical use. Vast swathes of rubbish and bodies heaped as high as twenty metres in places delineated the barren landscape. The rapid melting of the polar ice caps over the following years raised the seashore waters by almost fifty metres, flooding areas previously occupied by the initial survivors. If that wasn't bad enough, the complete melting of the Greenland Ice Cap also caused a complete reversal of normal weather patterns. The majority of those who had managed to live through the cataclysmic effects of the tsunamis froze to death during consecutive winters as severe tundra conditions prevailed. Progressively, the situation improved. However, in the past five years Sahara-type heat pervaded all year round with midday temperatures of fifty degrees Celsius not uncommon. Crops failed repeatedly. Water was scarce. Animals died in great numbers. There were insects of all types everywhere. The population collapsed due to malnutrition, an ageing profile, and the absence of medicines. Renewable energy options were limited as most of the national grid infrastructure was under water. Portugal as a physical, never mind a political, entity was doomed to oblivion unless remedial action was taken and taken quickly.

The duke and his Council of State had debated the situation long and hard over many weeks. It was now well past decision time.

The duke rose from the table. He walked to the full-length gilded mirror that hung aloft and saw his reflection. His thick black hair was oiled and combed back, and given his young age no grey hairs were visible yet. His father had long abandoned the age-old protocol of wearing formal dress, and his son complied with that order of things. As it was always hot, and somewhat cooler at night, he wore knee-length tailored shorts secured by a soft leather belt. A light cotton shirt and worn leather sandals completed his attire.

As supreme ruler of the peoples of the region of Ria Formosa that covered much of the southern territory of old Portugal, he wore his family's regalia when significant decisions were taken, a rule his father and his father's father had set generations ago. This was one such occasion. He opened the top drawer of a dark mahogany armoire and lifted out a multi-tiered golden chain from an onyx box, which he placed solemnly around his neck.

He adjusted the heavy chain. It had huge historical significance. It contained the *Quinas*, five escutcheons in cross-azure, the coat of arms used by the Kingdom of Portugal since the Middle Ages. The chain was saved after the royal palace at Cintra was flooded. The motto *Esta e a ditosa patria minha amada* ('This is my beloved homeland') was written in small letters under the emblem of Ria Formosa – two triple-towered castles. The symbolism of wearing the chain was one of the first lessons the dying duke had taught his son. And to reinforce their commitment to the lineage, he and all his senior entourage were required by law to wear a tattoo depicting the triple towers. His discreet motif was etched into his upper chest. Most preferred the nape of their neck as it was discreetly visible.

The duke was ready, and his mind was at ease. It was decision time.

He opened the door and walked into the adjacent reception room where the members of the Council of State stood around chatting. In contrast to his private quarters, the setting was very basic. The bare walls were painted a faded pink. A small unadorned table was the centre piece. His public office desk set in a corner, devoid of clutter, was the only other piece of furniture.

The old building that was the Mercado Municipal of Loulé since 1908 had been adapted to house the duke, his followers and the region's inhabitants. It may have been the finest example of revivalist neo-Arab architecture in the Algarve, but as needs dictated, it had been converted to provide basic accommodation for almost four hundred people. The discreet side rooms, once shops selling meat, fish, vegetables, and everything of imaginable interest to tourists, had been converted to dormitory-style bedrooms. The central area was used for cooking, and as a recreational space for the children. The array of solar panels on the roof provided a limited flow of electricity for the basics, such as fans, fridges, and lighting. The Mercado Municipal building, with its thick walls and good insulation, was where the Principality was governed, where most of the remaining citizens of Loulé lived, and where its people survived.

The members of the Council of State, all dressed in cotton shirts and light shorts, stood in a semicircle in front of the duke. Each represented a specific region of the Principality – Tavira, Almancil, Quinta do Lago, Porches, Algoz and Loulé. Their wide-brimmed caps, each with a distinctive emblem, was the only way to identify which area they represented.

'Put the plan into action,' said the duke.

The Council members exchanged glances and nodded. This was the decision that had been expected.

'There is no alternative.'

'I will communicate straight away with Admiral Rodriguez,' said Counsellor Oliveira from Almancil.

'Where is he?' asked the duke.

'On board *La Santa Jorge* at the Quinta do Lago marina awaiting your command. He had anticipated your final decision and has been planning his departure for weeks. The ships of the fleet are fully provisioned for their voyage to Iceapelago.'

'The admiral will welcome the green light,' said the duke. 'He has been kicking his heels for weeks awaiting the outcome of our deliberations. Let us go to the radio room.'

The room was located in a tower above the main entrance. The floods had rendered the fixed and mobile telephone systems redundant. Cables were flooded, communication towers collapsed, and there was no electricity to power the wide network of mobile phones. Internet-based communications had stopped and were a distant memory. In the early days, the duke and the remaining leaders of Portugal had taken a quick and decisive decision to use the military's shortwave radio network as the basis for communications. As a result, each of the country's many isolated communities had access to at least a basic radio set powered by solar panels. Consequently, the duke was in personal and regular contact with the citizens of Ria Formosa, and had a keen sense of the fears, aspirations and anxieties of these very close-knit communities. Nobody was ever shy of letting him know their opinion. The tiers of hierarchy had long vanished.

The radio operator barely passed comment as the duke and his entourage entered the room.

'I will call you back,' he told a listener. 'How can I assist?'

'Get me Admiral Rodriquez, please.'

In short order, the admiral was on the line.

'Have you decided?'

'Yes, I have. I can now confirm we will proceed as the Council of State has recommended. Your fleet of ships is to sail to Iceapelago on the next high tide. Go directly to an area called Lambay, close to Malahide Castle Island. There you will support Captain Vasco da Gama in executing his plan to occupy several islands in the Dublin Bay region. Once your grenadiers have secured the islands, I will lead an armada of ships with our population to our new home.'

'Good. I have my fleet at anchor and ready to go.'

'Thank you, Admiral. I expected nothing less. You have been a loyal citizen to my family for a generation.'

'Glad to be of service, Duke.'

'By the way, Admiral, any word from Captain da Gama?'

'Rest assured, he has taken to his task with great enthusiasm. We speak on the radio most days. He is somewhere off the south coast of Iceapelago and expects to be close to Lambay Island within the week.'

'I will leave you to get on with your final preparations. Keep me posted. I expect a daily report.'

'Yes, sir,' said the admiral who was relieved the long wait was over. He and his sea captains, and indeed their crews, were eager to set sail. His troop of one hundred and fifty grenadiers, allocated across the fleet, would be especially keen to test their sea legs.

Walking back through the centre of the Mercado Municipal building, the duke returned to the reception room with the members of the Council of State.

'It is time to tell our fellow countrymen and women that the date of our departure is imminent.'

'Everyone is on notice and is expecting a radio message,' said a member of the Council of State. 'The communities of Ria Formosa have had time to get used to the idea that they can only travel with a small suitcase of personal belongings, and enough food and water for ten days. The fleet assembled at the Quinta do Lago marina is no more than a three-day walk for most of the peripheral communities. Once we get a signal to proceed from Admiral Rodriguez, we will contact our communities.'

'When might that be?' said the duke.

'The admiral has a plan to occupy the Iceapelago islands in the Dublin Bay region within one, perhaps two weeks. We expect to sail within three weeks assuming all goes according to plan.'

'Is the passenger fleet seaworthy?'

'Yes sir. All fifty vessels have been adapted and provisioned for the crossing to Iceapelago. While conditions may be cramped, the voyage should take no more than a week for the larger craft and a bit longer for the smaller sailing ships. Our citizens know what to expect, and they will not complain. All want a better future.'

'Good,' said the duke. 'If you do not mind, I would like some time on my own.'

Once alone, the duke looked out the window. Outside and in the alleyways surrounding the Mercado Municipal building were what was left of his people. The La Palma tsunamis had killed at least three million. In a way they were lucky. They died quickly. In the following decades, contrasting weather extremes had caused the deaths of another two million through acute pestilence, starvation, and sub-arctic freezing conditions that were soon replaced by an acute heat-stressed environment. He reckoned that no more than five thousand people were left, and all were at the very edge of survival. Securing a future in a temperate weather zone was the only option.

He looked up at the portrait of his parent.

'Father, I have decided to abandon the lands of the Principality due to the extremes of Mother Nature that have befallen on us. We have no option but to become climate refugees. I hope you would have made the same decision in the circumstances.'

CHAPTER 2

Healing Hamper

HAZEL CAUTIOUSLY OPENED HER mother's hamper, a worn large wicker basket that, judging by its ragged condition and frayed edges, had been well used by the family. The brand name *Findlaters* was embossed in faded thick black ink on the side. It used to be a traditional Christmas hamper packed with goodies, treats and seasonal surprises. In contrast, this basket was full to the brim with the personal flotsam and jetsam of a leader of a lost generation.

Ruth Henry, Hazel's mother, the former Commander of Iceapelago, had died of hypothermia almost a decade earlier as had most of the population of Iceapelago. She had remained in a frozen state, reposed at her favourite window seat at the family home. Her decomposed body, and those of many other souls, were placed in a large shallow communal grave with no ceremony, with two disinterested gravediggers present. The putrid smell motivated them to dig. Like so many other unmarked burial sites, it was now overgrown, the soil and undergrowth merged and largely forgotten by the few remaining survivors. She was fortunate to have had a burial. Many had not.

The hamper contained Ruth's prized personal possessions – memorabilia which included random bits and bobs, records, and documents. Long ago, she had told Hazel it was her *Healing Hamper*, a carefully constructed time capsule. She had deliberately assembled the contents knowing they would contain evidence of her testimony, her legacy. Her parents and theirs, and indeed theirs again, had used the hamper basket for many memorable family events. Therefore, it was fitting that it would have one final such use.

Knowing she was about to die, Ruth had prepared an inventory of its contents, and it was this list that Hazel held in front of her.

The Demise of Iceapelago, the page read.

It was not the first time Hazel had opened and experienced the contents of the curiously named Healing Hamper. Touching and exploring the hamper was always a cathartic experience. She was drawn to the contents, its stark revelations, jarring memories, and evidence of mournful episodes. Hazel got goosebumps every time she held an item taken from the hamper. She shivered being so close, and yet so far from her mother. Like at a séance, she could feel her mother's presence when she touched the hamper's contents, or at least she imagined she did.

Hazel sought out the hamper when she felt her emotions were beginning to overwhelm her. Her children knew the signs. When their mother got upset, she sought the comfort of the hamper. And today, as before, her son Tony was dispatched to the loft. He manhandled the precious cargo down to the living room. With a degree of trepidation, he placed the hamper on the wooden floor in front of the open log fire. As there was no electricity, an array of candles provided additional light to the evening sunbeams that filled parts of the room.

Hazel smiled on her young adult son who squatted on a ragged carpet nearby with his exposed brown legs akimbo. He wore a worn leather veston over a cotton shirt and blue denim shorts. Scavenged red knee-length football socks were tucked into football boots so old the studs were worn down. It was a long time since the boots had seen a football, never mind a football pitch. They had been transformed into comfortable and sturdy walking shoes. A faded baseball hat hid most of his mop of black hair, which Kate, his older sister by two years, trimmed whenever it grew over his collar.

Tony had an acute sense of curiosity, a trait he inherited from his grandmother, coupled with a gut instinct to test the physical and mental limits of what was deemed by his peers to be acceptable behaviour. Over many years and unknown to his mother, usually late into the night, he had examined every item in the hamper as often as he could. This treasure trove was his playground, the source of his knowledge and understanding of the past, his personal museum. He knew the purpose and relevance of every item so carefully documented by his famous relative. He knew his mother would not approve that he was so familiar with what she believed was her personal legacy. Not that she ever got angry, an emotion rarely experienced in the Henry household. What was there to be angry about?

Kate had much less of an interest in their grandmother's life and times than her younger brother, preferring to spend her spare time reading her way through the vast array of novels, books, periodicals and magazines on the high mahogany bookcases that covered the walls of their living room. With nothing published since the Eriador Event, Kate's exposure to literature was of an era that bore no relationship to the way she lived her life. But she could dream. Reading endless romantic novels allowed her to frame and consider issues, both personal and practical, from a different perspective. Tony, on the other hand, had little interest in reading about the past, whether it be fact or fiction.

Kate treated her brother as an adult who was capable of making up his mind. She knew at heart he was more adventurous and daring as befitted a young man. Informed by the stories of her many fictional heroines, she was a dreamer and optimistic by nature. As a result, she was more settled and accepting of the dull routine of daily life.

Like her sibling, and solely for practical reasons, she dressed in a minimalist manner. In this respect, Kate ignored all she read about fashion and style. She worked and lived in a one-piece work smock. It used to be blue, but the sun had faded the cheap fabric. Her dun army boots had stood the test of time despite the fact they had not been shined since the polish ran out over a decade ago. Her wardrobe was almost bare. She had never worn a dress. She had shoulder-length red hair, but always kept it tied back. She rarely let her hair down, figuratively or literally.

As the only young adults in their small community, they had not had the experience of the range of raw emotions and personal experiences that had been commonplace among teenagers in years gone by. In the absence of any other children, their upbringing was certainly unique. That did not bother the siblings. They were totally at ease in each other's company, while allowing each other their respective personal space.

Hazel's son and daughter were like twins. They instinctively knew and responded to each other's moods and needs. They often finished each other's sentences and continued their endless conversations in unison. That was quite uncanny. They worked on the farm as a team. Tony had the physical strength and Kate had the husbandry skills that kept the community fully provisioned throughout the seasons of the year. And they were clearly devoted to their mother. She knew she was lucky to have such caring adult children, especially when she felt a bit melancholy at times, as was the case today.

Hazel gently touched the rim of the hamper. She gathered herself. This was a special anniversary, Eriador Day. In 2061, the start of the destruction of what was once Ireland took place when a series of tsunami waves flattened the country, and the dramatic climate conditions subsequently transformed the land and surrounding seas into frozen ice-islands. The harsh conditions were a distant memory, at least for the younger generation. On Eriador Day, it seemed appropriate to reflect on past events, sad and distant memories, especially those of a woman who had provided much-needed leadership to the citizens of Iceapelago. Hazel unfastened the soft leather straps and pushed open the top.

'What do you think this was used for?' said Hazel.

She held up a small square white box with three small prongs protruding.

'It's an adapter,' replied Tony playing the game. 'Actually, it's an adapter for what, if I'm correct, was called an Apple MacBook Air. See the distinctive fruit logo. This laptop computer was state-of-the-art technology long ago.'

'Yes, practically everyone had one,' said Hazel. 'They were even used in schools.'

'Until there was no more electricity,' said Tony.

'And no more pupils,' said Kate.

'Yes, sadly on both counts,' said Hazel. 'Your grandmother used a MacBook Air to keep track of everything on the internet communication platform, which is also a thing of the past.'

'And did she keep a diary?' said Tony.

'Yes, but only a few short extracts were printed off in hard copy,' said Hazel. 'I told you that paper was scarce after the Eriador Event so what's left is quite precious. She printed out the narrative of her last week only. We'll talk about that later.'

'If we had electricity, we could power up the MacBook Air, couldn't we?' said Kate.

'One day perhaps, Kate,' said her mother. 'Our solar panels are beyond repair as a result of the Big Storm. I have no idea how they might be fixed. And the batteries are obviously useless.'

Tony knew exactly where the laptop could be found. It was placed safely in its original designer vellum packaging at the bottom of the hamper. His mother had never asked him to lift the laptop out of the hamper. She knew it would reveal buried secrets.

'Access to her laptop was probably password protected,' said Tony.

'I suppose so,' said Hazel.

His secret was he knew the code, *CorkHurling3**. On one of his sorties into the hamper, he had discovered a sealed envelope with the password written out on a blank sheet of paper. He surmised correctly that his grandmother was an organised person, and she knew eventually someone would find the password and open her records.

'Imagine, if all her documents became accessible,' said Kate. 'We would finally get to know what actually happened at Cork Airport Island.'

'Maybe,' said Tony. 'I've never used one of these computer devices. I wouldn't know where to start to be honest.'

This was a blatant lie, but he had no option but to pretend because if his mother knew he had read his grandmother's computer files she would get even more upset. Once he fully appreciated the significance of what they had inherited as a family heirloom, Tony's ambition in life was to better understand what had happened during the period immediately before and after the Big Storm that shook Iceapelago to its very core. Ruth Henry was a legend, but there were so many unanswered questions and the innards of the MacBook Air, once fully unlocked, would reveal all. Or so he hoped.

'And this?' Hazel lifted another item at random out of the hamper.

'We've done this before, Mother,' pleaded Kate who wanted to finish her latest Maeve Binchy novel. She only had five pages left to read.

'It's a portable battery-powered radio,' said Tony.

'And like the laptop, it too is banjaxed,' said Kate. 'Is there anything in the hamper that actually works?'

'Patience, my children,' urged Hazel, who sensed that her daughter would much prefer to get back to her book. After all, she needed time out having spent long hours since dawn tending to the animals and crops. Working a twelve-hour day seven days a week entitled her daughter to enjoy her love of books.

'Your grandmother told me she actually spoke on the radio,' said Hazel. 'In fact, once she took over as Commander of Iceapelago she did a weekly bulletin to keep everyone up to date.'

After what was in effect a *coup d'état*, the leaders of the thirty Iceapelago communities, the sheriffs who tried to maintain the law of the land, or at least gave the impression they were interested, and the Sixes who set the rules at community level, unanimously endorsed the fiery representative from Cork as Commander of Iceapelago. As there was no state to speak of, the role of commander was a head-of-state figure. Her role became one of facilitator, persuader, and encourager. She tried to foster collaboration, mutual support, and trust in stark contrast to the style and behaviour of the previous Commander of Iceapelago.

'Was that after she returned from Dundrum Island to Cork Airport Island?' asked Tony.

'Yes, and little did she know what would happen so soon afterwards,' said Kate barely raising her disinterested eyes above the remaining pages of the romantic novel.

'I know we did better than most, so don't get me wrong,' said Hazel. 'Mom's decision to move her family to this unique building in the parish of the Old Head of Kinsale saved our lives for sure.'

She paused to let her children absorb the import of her remark.

'The radio is totally useless, other than as another example of a failed and out-of-date communication system,' said Hazel. 'Even if we managed to power it up, the central radio service is long since gone. Without a radio station, antennae and announcers there are no broadcasts, no news, no music, nothing.'

Hazel inadvertently and uncharacteristically showed her growing frustration. She had hoped that another visit to her mother's hamper would, as before, improve her form. *Why in goodness did she call it the Healing Hamper?* she thought.

'I would make a brilliant radio news presenter,' speculated Tony in an effort to lighten the rising tension. 'Far better than the famous presenter Maurice O'Donnell, or the Howth Six, who had the reputation of having the most boring voice on what was left of the planet.'

'You've a nice tone to your voice, son,' said Hazel. 'But news presenters need news, and there's not a lot of that about, is there? And as we all know, no news is good news.'

'And there are hardly any listeners left in any event,' said Tony.

'Didn't grandma have her own radio transmitter back in the day?' asked Kate.

'Yes, it was located in the control tower of Cork Airport and was the biggest in Iceapelago,' said Hazel. 'The airport's technicians were on hand when repairs, maintenance, and fine tuning were needed. As commander, she was in regular and direct contact on shortwave radio with all the island communities. With no internet, no emails and no social media, shortwave radio was the only way people could communicate. She was on air almost non-stop at the end.'

'And this item is also totally redundant,' said Hazel putting what was called a mobile phone into the palm of her hand.

'Everyone had a mobile device back in the day, isn't that so?' said Tony. 'This communications enabler was a social media necessity, and an essential personal accessory.'

'…and totally useless,' said Kate finishing his sentence.

'After the Eriador Event, the infrastructure supporting the mobile phone network was obliterated,' said Hazel. 'There were hundreds of masts, tens of thousands of what were called "telegraph poles", endless kilometres of cable and dozens of booster stations across Ireland. The Eriador Event and the Big Storm put paid to what was considered to be the best of what Ireland had by way of modern communications.'

'What happened to satellite communications?' asked Tony.

'There's a report in your grandmother's hamper that reveals how that ground network collapsed irreversibly during the apex of the Big Storm,' said Hazel. 'While Iceapelago was almost flattened, and most of its population perished, she assumed the nations of the North Atlantic met the same fate.'

'Total radio silence since?' said Tony.

'Not a signal since the Big Storm,' said Hazel. 'That's what's most scary. We may be one of the few remaining settlements in Northern Europe that survived, and in our case, one that is thriving. Relatively speaking, of course.'

'What about her maps?' asked Kate, who was on the edge of her seat, totally engaged. Her mother had not previously been so explicit about past events. Kate, like Tony, wanted facts to replace fiction, hearsay and family gossip.

'Let me get the master chart.' Hazel rummaged in the depths of the hamper and pulled out a long cardboard cylinder. She extracted what she was looking for – a detailed map of what had once been Iceapelago.

Tony and Kate approached the kitchen table where their mother spread out the large black and white map. Colour printing, like so many other things that were once taken for granted, was an historical footnote. They secured the edges of the map with candlesticks.

'They may have argued like alley cats, but the Iceapelago communities knew they could only survive if they collaborated and communicated,' said Hazel. 'Look here. This was the cruiser route from Cork Airport Island to Dundrum Island. The journey took more than a day and a half along the coastline if sea conditions were favourable. Every possible detail is on the map. See the wide variety of symbols showing navigable channels, berths, tidal conditions, where stops were located, the sites of solar panels, electric charging stations, wind turbines, and the populations of all the villages along the route. Every cruiser driver, and there were over three hundred employed at one stage, had a copy of this master chart. It was updated annually.'

'There's Malahide Castle Island,' said Tony. 'It seems so close and yet so far.'

'I believe they too have a surviving community,' said Hazel. 'The castle had been reinforced in good time before the Big Storm, and it was not too badly damaged as a consequence.'

'Have they been in touch with us?' asked Tony. He was genuinely unaware that another Iceapelago community existed. There was no mention of this in any of his grandmother's diary entries. This was the first time his mother had raised the prospect of another surviving community. 'Are there other Iceapelago communities trying to eke out an existence like us?'

'Tony, don't be silly,' said Kate. 'Even if there were other people alive, how would we get to them? Or them to us for that matter.'

'All the river cruisers sank during the Big Storm,' said Hazel. 'I haven't seen one afloat since. As you know, we have access to a few small rowing boats that are used for inshore fishing, and that's about it. They are totally unsuitable for anything else.'

'Who told you about Malahide Castle?' said Tony. His level of curiosity was increasing.

'There's a family living in a nearly island that fled from Dundrum Island by yacht once the Big Storm abated,' said Hazel. 'They said the main buildings in Dundrum had been very badly damaged, but there were reports that the castle at Malahide withstood the storm.'

'Are you not interested in making contact?' asked Tony of his mother.

'Not really. Why should we bother? What's the point?'

'But why don't we start to explore, to try to find other communities?' said Kate.

'Be practical,' said Hazel. 'We don't have a seaworthy vessel for starters but more importantly, communities like ours have grown used to being self-sufficient. We are island people. Having strangers arrive to share scarce resources is not what I suspect most people want. Everyone is rightly wary of strangers.'

'We shall see,' said Tony.

'Children, this is the anniversary of the Eriador Event, and it beholds me to mark it,' said Hazel. She clutched her son and daughter tightly to her for emotional support. She needed a comforting hug, and got one.

Hazel paused to catch her breath. 'While the Big Storm raged, we were safe and warm with provisions. Wisely, Mother sent us and a few neighbours in good time to a sturdy building that had been completely refurbished. I can still remember the unending whistling and buffeting of the gales and the windows being lashed by rain, sleet and snow. We hardly slept with all the noise. We were all scared silly. Sitting around, and with too much time to think, your father and my older brother Martin eventually decided they had to try to find Mother. We all urged them to stay put and be sensible, but there was no talking to them. A brief lull in the storm gave them the opportunity to go outside. The snow was almost as high as the roof, but they still ventured out despite everyone's pleadings. The plan was to use a ski-cat to access the river cruiser that had transported us and our few possessions to the Old Head. And…' Hazel let out a low howl. 'I lost everyone I really loved that week back in November 2091.' Her whole body trembled with deep emotion.

Somewhat dazed, she stared with wide eyes at the hamper in a state of shock. The opening of the contents of the Healing Hamper usually helped to manage her grief, but not today. Today it had quite the opposite effect.

Tony let his mother sob. He knew the routine. She would be back to normal soon. Or so he hoped. 'Can I put it back?'

'Please,' was the meek response. She mopped her watery eyes with a tissue.

Once safely secured in the loft, Tony looked at the hamper with intent and heightened curiosity. There were many more items his mother could have dug out but chose not to. His grandmother's rings, for example. Why did she include them in the hoard? The contents of the printed diary of the last week had never been revealed. Having read it surreptitiously, Tony knew why. And the revolver?

He retrieved the case containing the MacBook Air and its adapter from the hamper and hid them in a backpack that he kept in his room.

CHAPTER 3

Lords Talbot de Malahide

'My turn,' said Veronica.

She approached the spit and with her gloved hands, slowly turned and basted the two large plump geese. As splatters of grease hit the fire, red sparks jumped from the iron grate. She punctured the skins with a long fork.

'I reckon they'll be ready in twenty minutes.'

Veronica enjoyed cooking for a large group and the buzz that went with it. She also liked dressing for the part. Her colourful smock, embedded with assorted juices and stains, and chef's hat were part of the show. Her grey hair flowed over her shoulders in disorganised curls. Her hairdressing skills were not at the same standard as her cooking.

'We're on time then,' said Rory to his wife. 'I'll alert our guests.'

He ambled slowly out of the vast kitchen to the great hall dining room of Malahide Castle that was set for dinner for twenty. His brown bramble walking stick gave him the support he needed. He sensed that his knees were not going to last too much longer. Heavy pounding over many years had taken its toll. There was no question of surgery. There were no surgeons, never mind hospitals. Rory was stoic about his fragile frame of seventy-plus years. He had lived a more than full life. 'What will be, will be' was his simple philosophy.

The great hall of two storeys had been built in the early sixteenth century by the Lords Talbot de Malahide. The centre piece of the dining room was a huge stone fireplace standing to shoulder height. Above the fire hung the coat of arms of the Talbot de Malahide family with a red lion and a lioness supporting a shield that declared *Forte et Fidele* ("By Strength and Faithfulness"). The upper pane of the two large-framed wooden windows had been filled in with red bricks after it had been badly damaged during the Big Storm. On the walls, the portraits of the castle's earlier inhabitants hung proudly. The largest painting of Richard Talbot de Malahide, Earl of Tyrconnell, was quite faded but through the dimness of the evening light, his cherubic face looked down on the diners who would soon benefit from the hospitality of the castle – an age-old tradition not lost despite recent events. Richard had led the Irish militia against the armies of William of Orange at the Battle of the Boyne on July 1st, 1690. He and thirteen members of the Talbot family died on the battlefield that day. They were interred with full military honours in the small graveyard beside the ruined Protestant chapel at the rear of the castle. That graveyard was now full of corpses from more recent times, as was the larger cemetery at the western end of the island.

Blackened by years of use, the fire was fuelled mainly by wood from the nearby forests but was also used for incinerating much of the small community's biodegradable waste. The stone walls were two feet thick, providing an additional layer of warmth. As the cosiest room in the castle, it was the most frequented. Today, the antique mahogany dining table dating from the Victorian era was set in traditional banquet style reserved for special occasions. A ruby red runner ran the length of the table. The tall candlesticks with three lit candles apiece provided much-needed light. Goblets of water, Waterford lead crystal glasses, linen place mats, leather coasters, serving platters, and an array of Newbridge cutlery had been laid out earlier by Veronica with the greatest care and attention to detail. Clusters of late autumn flowers in tall narrow vases added colour and aroma. As the current custodians of Malahide Castle, she and Rory made the best use of its many treasures.

'Twenty minutes, folks,' shouted Rory as he walked into the great hall. The din of happy chatter echoed around the room. The guests at his table were at peace, and it showed. They were resourceful. They were true survivors.

'Could I borrow a few grandchildren to help serve the food?' said Rory.

He got the response he expected. Two young adults immediately reacted to his calling without reference to their parents. They followed their grandfather back into the kitchen.

'Hi, Grandma,' said Jon.

At seventeen, and the youngest and only son of Veronica's boy, Mark, Jon had spent the last eight years growing up quickly, largely unsupervised, and this gave him an air of invincibility. He was tall and broad-shouldered for his age and could easily be taken for someone several years older. He had thrown caution to the wind years ago and would take personal risks where other adults would have demurred when faced with the same challenges. Veronica knew this rashness could be his undoing.

'What can we do to help?'

Helping, not just in the kitchen, was what he did from dawn to dusk. His tasks were multiple given the ageing profile of his community.

Jon and his sister Orla, who was two years older, were wise, polite and obedient beyond their young ages. Both physical and emotional maturity had come early. It had been imposed. They had witnessed levels of trauma that nobody so young should have seen. As a result, they were not sheltered or cossetted by their parents. In sharp contrast to children of earlier generations, they had been treated like adults since early puberty, behaving and responding accordingly.

They wore variations of the same mismatched and much-repaired hand-me-down clothes. The sleeves of their worn woollen jumpers were rolled back to expose the knuckles of their hands, hands that saw manual labour in the fields most days of the week. Their working chinos were too long, the ends rolled up over their soiled runners. There was no self-consciousness about their appearance as the only other people they saw from one day to the next were each other. Their heads were close-shaven for personal hygiene reasons. The insects of Iceapelago had a liking for mops of hair. Seeing them, one could be forgiven for thinking they were street urchins.

Their status in the community was acknowledged. They were the youngest children of Iceapelago 3, the third generation of Iceapelago survivors.

Given their chores and duties, schooling was a luxury, and focused on basic literacy and numeracy skills. Teaching her grandchildren was one of Veronica's many part-time jobs. She was fortunate that the castle library contained a treasure trove of books. However, despite her best efforts, neither sibling took much of an interest in studying. They had no interest in history, geography, politics and romance, or indeed, anything in written form.

'Jon, can you please prepare the salads?' said Veronica. 'You'll find the mixed lettuces in a bowl in the storage cupboard.'

Jon knew exactly where to go. After all, he had picked the green salads earlier in the day. He had washed and stored them in one of the large wooden boxes reserved for products from the walled vegetable garden at the rear of the castle. Jon took huge pride in his plants, vegetables, and potting skills. He managed to provide the freshest produce for the table almost effortlessly.

'Orla, could you kindly bring out the water ewers and fill the goblets? And I will need you to bring the starters to the table.'

'Sure, Grandma.'

Their grandmother, the undisputed boss in the kitchen, was their role model in a lady of the manor sort of way. They took every opportunity to help her.

After the main course had been served – roasted goose with all the trimmings, including Veronica's homemade red berry chutney, and an array of freshly picked garden vegetables and salads – the conversation around the table grew louder as the diners argued over all sorts of matters, with the taste of the carrots at the top of the agenda.

Over the din, Rory watched his guests with a degree of great fondness. In addition to Veronica's children and their children, the group consisted of the remaining residents of what was once the moat enclave and a handful of long-term residents, the oldest being nearly eighty. They were all lucky to be alive and knew it. This was indeed a special community even if, for some, their years were clearly numbered.

Rory's daydreaming ended abruptly when Orla, who was sitting beside him, jabbed his ribs with her elbow gently but with purpose. She raised her voice so that everyone could hear her. 'Grandad, please tell us one of your stories.'

Rory was impressed with Orla. She had his temperament and traits – she had a fiery, restless and outspoken personality. She reminded him very much of himself at the same age. As the oldest of the young adults, she was always at the fore, inquisitive, fearless, and a total chatterbox. The main difference was she managed her frequent emotional outbursts, once passed off as teenage tantrums, much better than her brother. Managing stress in an environment where daily survival challenged everyone's existence had become a personal attribute much talked about.

'I suppose I might,' said Rory.

He had anticipated he would be asked to say a few words. His stories, adventures aplenty, had been told countless times before, but never failed to astound and entertain his audience. Rory was a natural raconteur and loved the limelight. He was acutely aware his tales were not yet written down and had to be recounted as frequently as possible to be retold by the younger generation to future listeners.

'This is Eriador Day after all. We need to mark the lives of the fallen and to celebrate the lives of those at this table. Forgive me if I do not stand as my knees are not the best, as you all know.' Rory made eye contact with his guests. They all looked back, engaged. He could see sad eyes, expectant eyes, happy eyes, and grieving eyes, all reflecting the general mood of the moment.

'Grandad, please explain the history of Eriador Day,' pleaded Orla. 'Why is it called Eriador?'

'The best place to start is at the beginning, I suppose,' said Rory. 'Eriador is the name of a sub-surface ridge some five hundred metres high and a hundred metres below sea level located over two hundred kilometres directly west of Iceapelago on what was called Ireland's Continental Shelf. While it is a geological feature, the name was better known as a region made famous in Tolkien's book, *Lord of the Rings*. Eriador was a large region in the fictional Middle Earth. In the old language of Sindarin it meant "Lonely Lands".'

'How prophetic,' said Orla.

'As far as we know, a submersible from a government research vessel was retrieving underwater samples in the area of the ridge when a series of major earthquakes struck in the space of a few hours. The enormity of the seismic forces had the effect of rocking the sub-surface and that, in turn, generated a series of tsunamis. The first was just ten metres high. But when the last hit the west coast of

Ireland an hour later, it was over fifty metres high and three hundred kilometres long. It was twenty metres high when it flooded the Dublin region. Ireland drowned in less than thirty minutes. As the survivors on the highest grounds emerged from the Eriador floods, a second series of more impactful tsunamis arrived from La Palma in the late afternoon. By the time they arrived on our shores from the Canaries, the crests of the waves were over thirty metres high. I was on the ramparts of Malahide Castle when the first series of tsunamis struck. The noise is what I remember. A loud, roaring, growling noise, a sound that captured all the air, interspersed with the screams of scattering and scared birds. It was quickly followed by a wall of water blocking out the skyline. That wall was full of bodies, vegetation – bits of everything and general detritus. The La Palma tsunamis were louder, more destructive and more powerful. I will never forget that day or the weeks that followed. Total devastation is an understatement. I lost my entire family, as did many others.' Rory paused.

He could sense his emotions rising. To regain control, he started to breath slowly and deeply. The terror passed like the waves that were the root cause of his deepest fears. His guests were patient. They too had occasional breakdowns. Veronica held his hand and softly caressed his fingers. As his second wife, she was deeply conscious that Eriador Day troubled Rory many decades later. The loss of his first wife and their children still scared him.

'Eriador Day is our national day of mourning,' said Rory. 'We should never forget our loved ones. Even though even worse climatic conditions followed with the arrival of the Big Storm, our lives changed forever on Eriador

Day. It's hard to believe that nearly a thousand people lived peacefully, happily and contentedly in and around Malahide Castle before the Big Storm. Time is a great healer, as we of the older generation have discovered. Grieving needs time. Your grandmother and I now look to the present and the future, not the past. There are too many demons back there.'

'That's so sad, Grandad,' said Orla. 'It clearly hurts you to talk about it.'

Rory cleared his throat. 'Let me conclude tonight's dinner on a positive note. I wish good health and a peaceful existence to those assembled in this room.'

Water goblets clunked in unison.

Orla had the measure of her grandfather. While he may have a tough exterior, she believed he was the kindest and most considerate person in the community. She knew he had a soft spot for her, but she never abused the unspoken bond between them.

She really wanted to get to the bottom of what actually happened during and after the Big Storm. The adults never wanted to talk about it. Her poor grandfather was too tired to tell the story. He had a busy Eriador Day. She resolved to invite him for a walk in the morning to get him to talk. Isolation may have become a way of life, a comfort blanket, for some. Orla wanted off the island, but was not sure where to.

CHAPTER 4

Old Head of Kinsale

'This is the best view in the world, isn't it?' said Kate.

The sky was a clear azure blue as far as the eye could see. The slight breeze was barely noticeable. From their elevated position on the plateau of the Old Head of Kinsale, the low coastline of Cork Airport Island shimmered in the late afternoon light, far in the distance. The sun glistened off the sea that was not troubled with waves.

'It's certainly the best in our small world,' said Tony.

The siblings were taking a break from harvesting the season's new potatoes. The parallel drills with their distinctive green flowers ran the length of the field. At the far edge, the garden stopped abruptly. Beyond, with no guardrail, was a sheer drop of over a hundred metres down to the wild Atlantic below. Dozens of gannets and other sea birds flew on the wind and diving for fish, emerging moments later with full beaks. The noisy nests of hundreds of breeding gulls that speckled the cliffs were busy from morning to dusk. The disused Old Head of Kinsale lighthouse on the horizon provided a backdrop to the stunning scenery. Majestic in height to be sure, with a signature red and white top, it showed distinct signs of abandonment, not least its broken reflectors and peeling paint.

On the other side of the large and productive vegetable plots marked with broken wire fencing, the family house nestled snugly into the natural contours of the landscape. It offered significant protection from the gales that often, but less frequently of late, lashed the Old Head of Kinsale. The building, a former exclusive golf clubhouse, had been fully retrofitted to a high energy efficiency standard, giving the Henrys and their neighbours a lot of options in terms of setting up viable family dwelling units. The communal areas were generously spaced and designed, allowing the residents to enjoy each other's company while having separate living quarters. In addition, many of the old suites adjacent to the main building had been converted to winter food stores and housing for the animals. With much improved weather and another abundant harvest in prospect, the stores had been run down to a few weeks' worth of supplies. The animals seemed to enjoy being outdoors all year round for the first time. The communal housing complex atop the Old Head of Kinsale, fondly called the clubhouse by its residents, was a settlement that worked for the benefit of its thirty inhabitants.

'I was thinking,' said Kate.

'That's always dangerous,' said Tony. He had sensed his sibling had been a bit unsettled since the Eriador Day anniversary episode with their mother and her alleged Healing Hamper.

'We should start to explore our wider surroundings,' said Kate. 'And before you start telling me why mother wouldn't approve, could I say…'

'I agree,' said Tony interrupting his sister. 'I was thinking along the same lines. In fact, I have thought of little else for months. We've lived all our lives on this island, and with the weather improving, I think we should broaden our horizons, so to speak.'

'Why didn't you talk to me sooner? You never share your thoughts with me. We work together every day and barely make conversation. All we talk about are the vegetables, the chickens and the weather. You never share your innermost thoughts.'

'That's a bit unfair.'

'No it isn't. When was the last time we spoke about our dreams, our future, our lives as adults? You clearly have had enough of this place, and so have I.'

'I didn't think you would be at all interested to be honest.'

'Well, I am,' said Kate calming down a bit. 'What exactly did you have in mind?'

'We need a boat.'

'Smart boy.'

'We need a seaworthy boat,' said Tony. 'The small inshore rowing boat we've been using for fishing is not at all suitable for the open sea. I reckon we're at least thirty kilometres from Cork Airport Island. It will take us at least ten hours to get there, depending on the wind, tide and the currents.'

'Where are we going to get such a vessel?'

'I've something in mind. It's a long shot but it might work.'

'Tell me more, please. I'm open to any mode of transport that gets us off the Old Head.'

'Last week, I checked out the river cruiser that brought us here long ago,' said Tony.

'But it's a wreck. The hull and body are split open. It's an awful eyesore at the head of Garrylow Beach.'

'Indeed, it's shattered, and not a pretty sight but believe it or not, the emergency life raft module located to the aft appears to be intact and undamaged. And I believe we can salvage it despite its apparent decrepit condition.'

'Wow,' said Kate. 'Are you serious?'

'There's a set of instructions on a panel near the dashboard beside the steering wheel as to how to deploy the container unit. Basically, it was designed to be jettisoned from the back of the cruiser once the locking devices were disabled by two levers. On landing in the water, the raft should automatically open. It is fully enclosed and has the capacity for eight people, and should have two sets of fully extendable oars, a complete medical kit and other essential supplies stored in sealed bags inside.'

'Why are we waiting?' said Kate.

'I think we have enough new potatoes for the evening's dinner,' said Tony. 'Let's finish up and visit the cruiser in the morning. Not a word to anyone, OK?'

'Absolutely,' said Kate. 'We need to be totally discreet until we know whether this plan will work or not.'

They both slept fitfully, dreaming of far off lands and possible adventures.

Breakfast was taken as usual at the communal table. Tony and Kate did their best to avoid conversation lest they inadvertently revealed the true purpose of their day's work. They donned their smocks and said their habitual goodbyes. To all observing, it was just another routine meal before another routine day in and around the vegetable gardens.

'It's a thirty-minute hike to the abandoned cruiser,' said Tony once they were outside. 'I've put some basic tools that we may need in my rucksack. The levers will be rusty for certain, and the sea salt has corroded some of the strapping. Because the raft itself is encased in a PVC cover, we will be lucky if we manage to unlock the device.'

'Where there's a will, there's a way, brother,' said Kate.

They took in their surroundings as they walked past the gardens. It was another balmy morning, and at nine o'clock the sun was already generating the first heat of the day. In a few hours it would be quite warm – great for growing vegetables and fruit. The animals were also thriving in the better climate. The previous summers had improved slowly but surely. Now the sunshine was more intense and constant. In the absence of protective cream, they had started to wear wide-brimmed caps, and to cover their exposed skin with long-sleeved shirts.

The meadows, the former fairways of an eighteen-hole championship golf course, were full of thick grass and roots. The sheep and the goats took full advantage of the bounty. Most importantly, and for reasons nobody could understand, the seasons changed as they had long ago. No more Winter Day preparations. Winters could be bleak, but decades of endless tundra conditions were a distant memory. These moderate temperatures had melted the sea ice, except for a few coves that were protected by the cliff face on the east side of the Old Head. All had changed, utterly.

'Can you imagine what this place was like before Eriador Day?' said Kate. 'Nearly five decades have been lost.'

'And our task is to prepare ourselves for the next five,' said Tony.

They walked along the gravel track that had been built long ago for golf buggies. It descended gradually to a ledge above Garrylow Beach. Down below, at an elevation five metres above sea level, lay the remains of the river cruiser. It was spliced in two and lay astride sharp rocks that delineated the upper limit of the former ice line. Black seaweed entwined along the vessel's rails. Its black hull was riddled with barnacles.

'How long has it been there? asked Kate.

'The best part of twenty years,' said Tony. 'Mom told me about the day it was thrown on the rocks. The boatman miscalculated. He had set a course for the nearby Caher Beach assuming there would be a safe, sandy landing. But that was not to be. The wind changed direction at the last minute and propelled the cruiser onto stony Garrylow Beach below. As you can see, it settled on an outcrop of jagged rocks before the waves receded. They had minutes to get off safely.'

'Let's go,' said Kate.

'Yes, but be careful,' said Tony. 'I nearly lost my balance trying to climb down last week.'

'It's hard to believe the Old Head residents clambered up this goat track such a long time ago not knowing what their future held,' said Kate.

Tony held out his hand in support as they passed by a thicket that led to a small path. 'And I hope we can play a small part in shaping ours,' he said.

In short order, they descended to sea level. In reaching an outcrop beside the derelict cruiser they surveyed the huge hulk.

'I suggest we start with the lever mechanism located beside the steering wheel,' said Tony. 'If we can loosen the metal straps, we might be able to force or snap the trigger mechanism that is designed to open the container unit.

'Are you sure?' said Kate. 'Wouldn't it make more sense to try and manoeuvre the container unit off the brackets? If that works, we can manhandle the unit onto the beach below, and then try to open the raft. Otherwise we run the risk of having the raft torn on the rocks as it unfolds.'

'You're right,' said Tony.

Because the aft section was suspended on a rocky surface this made it difficult for Tony to access the container unit without running the risk of toppling it onto the rocks. With sheer grit they managed to pry off the cables that worked the levers used to release the unit. They pushed and shoved for nearly an hour. Decades of sea air and rust fought them. Sheer force and gutsy determination finally unlocked the levers.

'All we have to do now is to unscrew the brackets on the straps that hold the container in place on the aft deck,' said Tony.

After many repeated fruitless attempts at trying to apply his screwdriver to obstinate screws, Tony stopped.

'We need another pair of hands.'

'Don could help,' said Kate. 'After all, it's his boat.'

'Good idea in theory,' said Tony. 'But Don is over

seventy years old. He'd never make it down the track to the beach.'

'Tony, he knows this cruiser better than anyone else. Is there any harm in asking him?'

'I suppose not. I'll talk to him.'

'We'd better gather some vegetables before we return to the clubhouse. We need to show something from our long day in the fields.'

'I've gathered some sea mussels that will be popular as a starter,' said Tony.

'A good day's work by any reckoning,' said Kate.

The following morning Don stood at the top of the high cliff and looked down at what was once his pride and joy. He had stood at the very same spot on many previous occasions to view the cruiser, but never dared to venture down to the wreck since he had stripped it of all movable parts, including a full tool kit.

'I see you've removed the cabling connecting the raft container unit. That was risky. But at least that means the unit will not be propelled into the air when its supporting straps are cut. Unscrewing the brackets is not necessary. We need to cut the straps, but getting access to them is the problem.'

'That's what we thought, Don,' said Tony. 'Can you help?'

'I guess so, provided I don't break my neck getting down the track.'

Gingerly, the three salvagers supported each other as they descended the goat track.

They halted at the cruiser and stood in silence for a moment.

'What's the plan?' said Tony.

'It's good that I'm nearly half your weight, Tony,' said

Don. 'I suggest you and Kate sit on the mid-section to provide counter-balance and I will crawl out to the aft section to see what can be done. I brought a heavy duty saw that might work.'

'Where did you get that?' said Kate.

'I removed all the movable equipment off the cruiser back in the day. It took me months. The toolbox I assembled was put to good use at the farm and to adapt the clubhouse. This beauty, called a jack saw, has razor sharp edges.'

Tony and Kate did what they were told. The aft section rose slightly and was nearly horizontal as Don went on his hands and knees onto the deck. He used both hands to saw the nearest strapping, which split with a loud snap after a few minutes.

'Two more to go,' said Don. 'If I can undo the straps, gravity will take over. As the unit slides off the deck, expect the section to jolt backwards, so hold on tight to the guard rails.'

He slid around the back of the unit. It wobbled as predicted. Don looked down the five metre fall to the beach and swiftly returned his eyes to the job at hand. This was certainly not the time for a vertigo attack. He applied the jack saw with both hands into the thick leather strapping. It too had withered and did not resist the sharp cutting edge.

'This is the last one. Hang on. The raft container will spring off its bracket once the strap is cut.'

And that is what happened. The container unit toppled sideways off the rocky surface and fell like a lead weight onto the soft sand of the beach below.

Minutes later the three of them stood on the beach

looking at the intact module that contained the life raft. It was big – a metre high and at least three metres wide.

'I can easily undo the final clasps, but I suggest we wait,' said Don.

'Why wait?' said Kate.

'Three reasons,' said Don. 'First, you will need to have provisions ready before we launch. We'll need food and water for ten days. Second, you and Tony will need to tell your mother what you have in mind. She's the worrying kind, as you know well.'

'And the third?' asked Kate.

'I'm coming with you,' said Don. 'You'll need someone with seafaring skills, so don't argue.'

'That's agreed, then,' said Tony extending his hand without hesitation to Don who shook it firmly. 'Let's break the news at supper this evening.'

They walked back to the clubhouse in silence, each contemplating what lay ahead. The risks, threats, challenges and opportunities – hopefully.

On Kate's signal, a wink of her eye, Tony stood up after the main course.

'Can I have your attention please?' As it was unusual for anyone to stand up during dinner, let alone make a speech, the room fell silent. Some thirty pairs of inquisitive eyes stared at him. 'Kate and I are the youngest members of the community. We do most of the hard labour, without any complaints. Recently we have been talking about our future, and what is best for us.' Tony noticed he had the full attention of everyone. 'To cut a long story short, we've not only decided to leave the island, but will do so on the life raft that was once attached to the broken cruiser on

Garrylow Beach. We plan to row to Cork Airport Island. That will be our first port of call.'

As the siblings had expected, the reaction was predictable, swift, and furious.

'What?' said Hazel, her voice trembling with emotion. 'You can't possibly leave the island. It's far too dangerous.'

'Why? Tell us why.' said Kate. 'What sort of dangers are you concerned about?'

The siblings had agreed in advance that Kate would respond calmly to her mother's long list of expected anxieties.

'Don,' said Hazel. 'Tell them it's far too risky an endeavour to row to Cork Airport Island on the open sea.' She looked to her close friend for support.

'Actually, Hazel, I'm going with them,' said Don.

'Please, no. You can't do that, Don,' said Hazel. 'Why are you doing this to me, knowing I am totally opposed?'

'My motivation is simple, Hazel. I am at an age when spending more years being landlocked does not suit my temperament. I want to go back to sea again. The life raft is state of the art in terms of safety. We'll cross to Cork Airport Island when the conditions are right and should get across in less than half a day. It's the height of the summer now and its almost dead calm, so there's no better time to roll out the boat.'

'But you won't come back, I know it,' said Hazel as she burst into tears. 'Kate, Tony, I'll never see you again. Don't do this to me.'

'We promise we won't stay on Cork Airport Island any more than is necessary,' said Kate in a poor attempt to comfort her mother. 'What precisely is there to fear?'

she said pressing her case. She was determined, regardless of the upset it would cause her mother, that the voyage would start in the morning.

Hazel had first-hand experience of her daughter's stubbornness. While not surprised by her daughter's unwillingness to listen to her point of view, she knew no matter what she said, Kate would leave. She decided to try one more time. She calmed a bit down before she spoke.

'When we left Cork Airport Island on the only sea-worthy river cruiser, we left behind hundreds of citizens who were abandoned to their fate,' said Hazel.

'But our grandmother stayed behind,' interjected Kate. She was not interested in excuses that could result in a postponement in their trip.

'She did and that's the problem. She did not share her intelligence about the arrival of the Big Storm with the rest of the community until it was far too late. No preparations were made, and hundreds died as a consequence. Only the privileged, me, your father, and the trusted close neighbours at this table, not only got a timely tip off, but were also provided with a safe harbour.'

'What's that got to do with our proposal to revisit Cork Airport Island?' pressed Kate.

'There was bitter resentment among the few remaining survivors against your grandmother because of her inaction and apparent disinterest in protecting her community. If any of these survivors discover you are related to her, I would fear for your life. I can't be any clearer, can I?'

'That's a risk we'll have to take,' said Tony in support of his sister's arguments. 'It's almost two decades later and things have moved on. Getting off the Old Head of

Kinsale will give us an opportunity to connect with other Iceapelago communities, not just Cork Airport Island. Is that not something we should try to do? The alternative is that we stay put and in short order, given the community's age profile, we will all die without another generation to survive us. Who benefits from that approach, Mother?'

'It's clear that I'm to be left alone regardless of what I say.' Hazel stood up from the table without making eye contact with her children. She folded her napkin deliberately, placed it on the table and walked the short distance to her bedroom. She slammed the door shut.

Tony and Kate looked at each other, said nothing, and proceeded to clear the table as they did every evening. They went to bed early without speaking.

After breakfast, Tony and Kate assembled their provisions, clothes and tools for the trip. They made lots of noise but the door to their mother's bedroom remained shut. They wanted to say goodbye, but she remained in her room.

Later, on the beach, they stood looking at the raft container, which they had moved nearer to the water's edge.

'My pliers will sort out the clasps in no time,' said Don.

He knelt down and applied pressure on the first clip which snapped quickly.

'Just three more.'

The second and third were undone without too much effort.

'When the last one is cut, the raft will explode out of this casing, so stand behind me please.'

Unlocked, a bright red canopy jumped onto the beach and hissed as it filled. It was quite a sight. Within a minute, a two by four by three metres raft was fully inflated and ready for use, just as Tony had predicted.

'That's some trick,' said Don. 'Before we drag it into the water, I'll do a few checks inside.'

He walked to the flap that defined the entrance to the raft and pulled the zip. It moved without any difficulty. He stepped into the space. After a few moments, he stepped back onto the beach.

'Well?' said Kate.

'God bless German engineering. Inside there are life-jackets, several long-handle oars, flares, a small medical kit and water bottles. As far I could tell, the raft's floor is not punctured. I reckon we are ready for launch. Give me your gear and I'll put it inside.'

Once their possessions were stored onboard, it took them a few minutes to gently manoeuvre the raft into the shallow water.

'Kate, Tony, get in,' said Don, assuming the role of captain.

Once inside, they were surprised as to how relatively big the raft was. It was certified for eight people but could hold more at a push. Don stepped in through the main door flap.

'Open up the side window flaps. We'll be able to row through these apertures with the long-handle oars.'

Tony and Kate located the paddles and sat beside each other awaiting Don's instructions.

'It's an ebbing tide,' he said. 'I reckon a half an hour of solid rowing will get us around the headland, and once out of the secluded Garrylow Bay, the current and the tide will propel us in the general direction of our destination.'

'General direction?' said Tony.

'Yes,' replied Don. 'Once I get a sense as to how the currents are flowing, we will set a course for Cork Airport Island. It will be stiff rowing for a few hours, so don't over-exert yourselves. Save your energy.'

'OK by me,' said Tony.

He gripped his long-handle oar and placed it firmly in the rowlock, and when it clicked into position, he gently put it into the water. Kate did the same on the starboard side. Before starting to row, she looked out the flap towards the beach. High on the pathway she saw her mother in her distinctive bright yellow jacket. Kate waved vigorously and shouted as loud as she could, 'We'll be back.'

The din of the gulls and the rising wind muffled the message. Tony joined her at the opening. Their mother raised her hand to signal an acknowledgement. She then turned around and walked away. Kate vowed to herself privately that whenever the adventure was over, she would return. She owed it to her mother.

The scenery at close quarters was stunning. The immense, sheer and red sandstone cliff face of the Old Head of Kinsale dominated the view from the small life raft. The russet brown razor sharp rocks were peppered with hundreds of guillemot nests. At the base, vast caverns were carved deeply into the rock. Waves crashed with great whooshing sounds. The cliff panorama blocked off most of the horizon. Centuries ago, pirates plied their trade in and among these caverns and sea arches, far from the prying eyes of the militia men who knew that smuggling thrived at the base of the Old Head of Kinsale.

There was little time for sightseeing. What started as a bright sunny day changed when they were about five hundred metres offshore. Initial enthusiasm for the adventure soon gave way to an element of panic.

'Steady, steady,' urged Don. 'It's only a hairline crack by the looks of it.'

A splinter had punctured the base of the canvas, and this only became apparent after they had passed the headland and before they were in the mid-channel. Don was bailing out the water from the floor of the raft using a large water bottle. It was a slow process.

Tony and Kate rowed as fiercely as they could.

'How bad is it?' said Kate with growing anxiety.

She and Tony pulled even harder on the oars. Neither could swim. While wearing decade's old life jackets, they had limited confidence that they would work if put to the test.

'If it's not a wide tear, I think we'll manage,' said Don. 'We must have struck a sharp rock after we pulled the raft into the water. Give me a few minutes. There's a patch kit in the supply's box for this kind of problem. I'll do my best.'

Don was experienced in dealing with onboard mishaps and went about his task in a calm manner. The rubber repair patch was large enough to cover what emerged as a small but noticeable puncture. The issue was would the adhesive bind against a wet surface. Would it stick? He decided that a double patch would be a better option. He needed to get the first smaller patch into place quickly, and to overlay it with a second larger patch to completely seal the rip in the hard canvas. With the patches secure, and without too much effort, the three crew continued to bail out the raft. In twenty minutes, they managed to get most of the water out.

'Done,' Don said with pride. 'It's a sticking plaster solution of sorts but at least the flow of water has stopped. Let's continue according to plan. The current is getting stronger and should move us further into mid-channel without much effort. So ease off the rowing and let's go with the flow for now.'

Kate and Tony agreed readily. They were exhausted. The effort of rowing against the current while wearing a bulky life jacket was quite a challenge. While they were very fit, their arm muscles ached with the effort.

The raft drifted slowly with the current as Don had anticipated but as the hours passed, the wind speed increased quite noticeably, and so too did the size of the waves. This worried Don, and he could not disguise his concern. The raft was not designed for choppy sea conditions. It was meant to be used in the calm river channels that separated the islands of Iceapelago. He did not share his insights with his passengers for fear of their reaction. After all, this was their first time exposed to offshore sea conditions.

'What now, Captain?' said Tony. 'Sink or swim?'

'Neither, Tony,' said Don. 'I'm afraid we're being pushed quite strongly by the current and tide beyond the leeward side of the Old Head. If only the sea conditions abated.'

No sooner had he spoken than a large wave burst through the front door flap and flooded the already wet floor. Don got drenched. More water would have poured in but for the fact that he was sitting in the opening, which he tried to zip closed. But the ancient zip would not move.

'Bloody hell! Bail out as much as you can through the side flaps with the empty water bottles,' said Don.

As he issued his command, another huge wave crashed through the door flap followed moments later by another. The growing volume of water started to destabilise the raft. It began to tilt and with the extra weight of the water it soon became unresponsive to any attempt to steer it with the oars.

'Jesus, we're in trouble,' said Don without thinking how his fellow passengers would react to this honest opinion.

He looked at Tony and Kate, seeing fear in their eyes.

Another wave washed into the raft this time through the lateral flap that Kate was using. She too was drenched to the skin with cold sea water.

'Stay calm,' said Don, trying to regain control of the situation. 'Secure all the side flaps, and this will prevent any more water getting in.'

The side flaps were zipped closed. Tony held the main entrance cover with his hands as Don re-worked the zip that finally engaged. The raft was secure.

'These craft have great ballast capacity,' said Don trying to provide a level of assurance. 'Provided we keep the water level as low as it is, we will stay afloat. We may be wet, but we'll not sink.'

'That's reassuring,' said Tony with a note of sarcasm. 'Do we sit here with water up to our knees and drift out to the Atlantic?'

'Once the wind drops, and it usually does before dusk, we can reopen the flaps and continue bailing out,' said Don. 'That's in an hour's time. I expect we may need to spend the night on board. So break open the biscuits. I'm starving.'

Don's forecast was correct. In the dying light, the wind dropped. The water still swirling around the raft's floor was bailed out with great enthusiasm as a team effort. While some residual water covered the floor, the stability of the raft was fully restored.

'It'll be dark soon,' said Don. 'It'll be a clear moon-lit night, but cold. You should try and get some sleep as we are all exhausted. I will do the early night shift. Tony, I'll wake you after midnight, and Kate can do pre-dawn duty.'

'Is setting a watch really necessary?' said Kate who continued to shiver from her earlier soaking.

'Yes,' replied Don emphatically. 'I don't expect we'll meet too many other vessels on this sea channel. But we may get close to the shore and if that happens, we'll have to navigate to a safe landing place. Kate, by the way, you need to change clothes otherwise you'll die of the cold or hypothermia.'

'Luckily I have a change in my backpack,' said Kate.

'I thought we were heading to Cork Airport Island?' said Tony as he too put on dry clothes.

'We were, but the current has taken us much further along the coastline in an easterly direction. If the tidal speed does not change, I would expect we will travel some twenty kilometres during the night.'

With no light in the raft, the battery-powered torches failing to work, a gloom soon descended. It matched the mood of the passengers. Almost silently, with lapping waves barely discernible, the raft drifted along the current. Kate took advantage of the calm and dozed off peacefully using her backpack as a pillow.

Tony too slumped forward, exhausted emotionally and physically, and fell asleep.

After an eventless watch, Don woke Tony at midnight, who, in turn, woke Kate some hours later.

At dawn, all three were alert, but stiff having had to sleep on rough surfaces, and in the cold. They picnicked on more biscuits, not quite the last of their hard rations. The morning sun's intensity started to manifest itself, and so too did the rising winds.

Don looked out through the top of the main flap. The coastline was a few hundred metres away.

'We're near a landfall, but where I have no idea.'

'Can you find a beach or somewhere to land?' said Tony. His initial enthusiasm for the sea journey was waning. *Did I make the right decision?* he wondered.

'Landing safely is my immediate priority,' said Don. 'The tide is changing, and we are moving far too quickly to the rocky shoreline I'm afraid. We need to start rowing to counter the tide's movement.'

Tony and Kate did not need any persuasion. Their long-handle oars were soon in position on the rowlocks. They applied pressure.

'Together now,' said Tony calmly but with a hint of apprehension. After a few pulls they were rowing in unison. This combined team effort continued for five minutes or so.

'The tide is too powerful,' said Don. 'It's pushing us ashore and there's not much we can do about it. There's a shingle beach ahead. Row like hell in its direction, and if we get over the breakwater we'll be in calmer waters.'

Tony and Kate strained every sinew and muscle they could. Slowly but surely, they propelled the raft in the general direction of the beach.

'How are we doing?' said Tony. He was almost completely out of breath.

'I think we'll make it,' said Don.

An onshore gust did the rest. The raft eased its way over the breakwater.

'We're safe,' said Don. 'A few hard pulls on the oars should have us close to a landing spot.'

Tony and Kate did what they were told.

'Stay put,' said Don. 'I'll get out and secure the raft.' He jumped out over the back end of the raft into a metre of water almost waist deep.

'Oh my God, it's cold.'

He walked a few metres onto dry land and pulled the raft towards him with his strong arms.

'You can get out now.'

Tony and Kate did not need to be told a second time. They jumped onto the shingle sea shells that crackled under their feet, and helped Don pull the raft fully out of the water. They all sat down exhausted.

'Here, drink,' said Don. He handed Kate a bottle of fresh water.

They were so preoccupied with the effort of making a landing that they did not notice their surroundings. The beach rose gently to a hill crop dominated by a handful of abandoned houses. They looked like traditional thatched holiday cottages, without the thatch. The countryside was quite flat as far as the eye could see. There were no signs of any humans or animals. The outline of a road could be seen to the right of the settlement.

'We best find shelter in one of those houses,' said Kate. 'I wonder what island we're on?'

'Somewhere near a place called Youghal,' said Don. 'Look at the signpost over there.'

'That's some way from Cork Airport Island,' said Tony. 'We must have drifted at least thirty kilometres off course. It'll be impossible to get back to the Old Head?'

It then dawned on Tony that it was highly unlikely he would ever return to the Old Head of Kinsale where he had grown up. The reality hit him hard. He was not sad, but resigned.

Don did not respond and for good reason. While Tony and Kate were in a state of reflection while looking ashore for signs of life, he was observing seawards.

'Look behind you,' he shouted.

Tony and Kate turned around, and to their total astonishment, a twin-mast sailing ship was anchored not four hundred metres off the beach.

'What's that?' said Tony.

'It's a fully masted sailing ship, a brigantine,' said Don. 'About thirty-five metres in length, and it's crewed. Look, there are at least ten people on the deck. I've never seen its like before. It must be at least a hundred years old.'

Kate stirred back to life. Instinctively, she took off her life jacket and waved it vigorously hoping to catch the attention of the ship's crew. She did not have long to wait as several of the sailors waved back holding flags high.

'They're Portuguese flags, believe it or not,' said Don. 'I haven't seen one since I was a boy.'

'While we were beaching the raft they must have been observing our dilemma,' said Tony. 'Look, they're launching a rowboat. Are they coming to our rescue?'

'Looks like it,' said Kate.

She let out a big sigh of relief. Better to put one's fate in the hands of strangers than spend another night adrift in a dilapidated safety raft, or worst still, marooned on a deserted island.

The loud noise of the winches could be heard, and a longboat creaked down the side of the ship. Four crew stepped down into the boat and engaged their oars in an almost professional manner. A fifth person also descended swiftly and manned the tiller. He was clearly in command. The oarsmen were skilled. Within ten minutes they beached their boat beside the raft. A tall man with a white Panama hat dressed in full naval uniform with knee-length leather boots stepped into the shallow water and walked towards them. He was swarthy, fit, and had a wide smile.

Tony, Kate, and Don stood to greet him.

'*Olá*, my name is Vasco, Captain Vasco da Gama of the *La Santa Maria*.'

CHAPTER 5

La Santa Maria

It was a spacious room for a small ship, comfortably capable of seating ten on the rattan chairs despite the low ceiling and numerous supporting joists. The solid oak walls were covered in charts and old prints. A row of stained beer steins hung over the door. The large floor-to-ceiling painting framing the two portholes was the centre of attention. It was of a sea captain, rugged, dusky, and dressed for the part. The man was quite young for one in a position of command. His piercing eyes returned the stares of his admirers.

Tony and Kate visibly trembled with sheer excitement. Don was also awestruck. There were sets of silver-plated knives and forks on the long dark pine table that was defined by two silver branched candelabras. The table, with a red ruby runner was replete with food, full bowls of fruit and vegetables, the likes of which they had never seen before. A whole fish, a *Dorada* they were told, had been grilled and laid open on a large silver serving plate. And they had their first taste of wine, of any alcohol for that matter, from shiny goblets embossed with three castles, the coat of arms of some noble house. This was fine dining by any standard.

'It's a peach,' said Captain da Gama.

He smiled as he observed his guests tucking into the ship's best fare with gusto. Their cheeks were moist with the juice of the fruit.

'And that's a banana.'

Tony held the plantain not knowing what to do with it.

'You peel back the outer skin,' said Captain da Gama.

He lifted another banana from the large fruit bowl and unveiled the white fruit.

'My goodness,' said Kate. 'May I?'

'Yes, of course,' said the captain.

He handed Kate the ripe banana. She had seen photographs of a banana but had never held one, never mind eaten the soft fruit.

The siblings and Don were relaxed sitting at the captain's table. It was just an hour since they had been rescued from the now abandoned life raft. The rowers had returned them to the ship in silence with little obvious effort. Pulling at oars in unison came naturally to them. At the captain's prompting, the visitors clambered up the side of the ship using a rope ladder. Stepping onto the well-scrubbed deck a new vista awaited them. They had never been on a sailing ship before. They just stared, eyes wide open, capturing the scene looking aloft to the tops of the twin masts with layers of rigging. A few crewmen silently returned their stares. The captain ushered them below deck and in short order one of his crew, called the bosun, served up dinner.

They were too busy eating their fill to start a conversation. However, the wine soon loosened their tongues.

'So where are you from, Captain?' asked Tony. 'You're not from these parts, I gather?'

While he was determined to be polite to his host, his question was laced with raw curiosity. Despite the short time since they met on the beach, he had already formed the impression that the captain was a bit of an enigma. Very polite, but very measured. Too measured perhaps. Tony looked up and the painted captain's eyes met his. *If only he could tell his tales.*

Captain da Gama smiled at his young guest. 'I'm a proud citizen of Quinta do Lago in the Principality of Ria Formosa that is located in the south of Portugal. Well I was, before the La Palma tsunamis hit us hard. I then moved to a place called Loulé, which is inland but at a much higher elevation. I am a co-citizen of both towns – if that is a correct expression?'

'Portugal was hit by the tsunamis?' said Kate.

She had been taught basic geography by her mother and knew where Portugal was geographically.

'It was. Being close to La Palma, the first tsunami hit us within hours after the volcanic eruption at the Caldera de Taburiente. We are only fifteen hundred kilometres from the Canary Islands after all. The entire coastline suffered catastrophic damage from the flooding. No life, or animals I should add, under fifty metres above sea level survived. Buildings of every shape and size could not withstand the power of the water. Everything was flattened beyond recognition. It was as if an aquatic atomic bomb dropped. Ninety per cent of my homeland was no more. Millions died.'

'What about the aftermath?'

Kate did not press her question allowing the captain to gain his composure. She sensed, correctly, that their host had not talked about the trauma of the La Palma tsunamis for quite a while. It clearly triggered deep memories. Memories that had been and were still locked within his deep inner soul.

'The main difference was that we did not suffer from the harsher extremes of winter like all of Northern Europe.'

Captain da Gama moved towards one of the charts. He tapped a map with his index finger and pointed. 'Until quite recently, the winter sea ice stopped here, at the tip of the Iberian Peninsula close to Cape Finisterre. The Big Thaw allowed us sail further northwards as the sea ice thinned rapidly over the past years, and eventually disappeared. We are a proud seafaring nation. Sailing is in our blood, deep in our history, and that is why I travel these waters.'

'And how did you survive the La Palma tsunamis?' asked Kate.

'When the tsunamis struck, I was at sea on this very ship as a junior cadet sailor. We had left the port of Faro en route to the Azores and were about fifty kilometres offshore. A routine training voyage, we were told. And it was, until the skyline filled with water. Our captain, the man who is observing us from the safety of the painting, realised immediately what was happening. He took a high risk gamble and jibed the ship with a holler for those who could hear his order. The ship rode the first tsunami wave for ten minutes, and like a torpedo, it was catapulted forward towards the coast at great speed. The rigging was smashed to bits, and anything on deck, including the crew, were washed away, disappearing never to be seen again. We were then stranded before another even bigger mountain of water appeared over the horizon. The captain got lucky again, and successfully manoeuvred *La Santa Maria* abreast the front of the second cliff of water. All that I remember, bearing in mind I was below deck, was we ended up beached twenty kilometres inland from the coast. *La Santa Maria* ended up on its side at the bottom of what was the main pedestrian street of Loulé, our provincial capital. We, the captain, and I with the few remaining crew, walked off the ship bruised and battered but alive. Within hours of the last tsunami, the waters started to recede. Nobody along the seashore survived. But we did and, most importantly, so did *La Santa Maria*. The Noah's Ark of modern time.'

'What an adventure!' said Kate.

'And what happened here? I understand you call this place Iceapelago?' said Captain da Gama. By switching tack, he clearly did not wish to talk any more about the destruction of his homeland.

Being the senior member of the visiting crew, Don stepped in. He gave the captain a detailed account of the events since Eriador Day, the equivalent of their La Palma Day. Captain da Gama listened intently at first. He showed no emotion. When Don noticed his attention was waning, he wrapped up his short history lesson. He guessed the captain was not only well-informed about the tragedy that had befallen Iceapelago, but of more recent developments as well.

'And what brings you this far north?' said Don.

'Like my namesake, Vasco da Gama, Portugal's famous navigator, I am on a mission to explore these waters.'

'On whose behalf?' said Kate, a tad too quickly. 'Who's in charge in Portugal?'

Her line of questioning was a little unsubtle. This did not go unnoticed by her companions.

'Nobody, is the short answer.'

The captain's mood did not change. It was as if he expected a certain level of interrogation.

'Like all countries in the Northern Hemisphere, Portugal as a political and geographical entity does not exist anymore. We have dozens of independent mountain regions that try to keep to themselves. All are reasonably self-sufficient in food and essential supplies given the generally benign weather. Small ships travel between the islands. The sailing vessels that exist, such as *La Santa Maria*, are operated independently as a self-contained offshore community.'

'Who do you report to then?' said Kate.

'Myself! I best explain, Kate, as I see you have a curious manner.'

Kate was about to ask another question but paused.

'*La Santa Maria,* this ship you are on, was one of the few that was rebuilt and modernised after the La Palma tsunamis. It has been my home for the best part of forty years. When the captain passed away, he gave me possession of *La Santa Maria,* and the crew, all ten of them, like myself, knew living on-board was for the best. In fact, it was the only way to survive. Ashore, what remained of the population fought for remaining possessions, and food in barely habitable dwellings. Most of these communities are now extinct due to hunger and starvation. Yet we continue to thrive. We trade for food up and down the coast. We sell the fish we catch, and we get essential supplies in return. Some would call us pirates.'

Don listened carefully to the captain's tale of woe, and litany of disasters. The story did not quite add up. It seemed reasonable, but it was too obvious. Don realised he needed to be patient. The truth would out in good time.

'What sort of a ship is this?' said Kate.

'It's a square rigger, a double masted brigantine-type vessel modelled on *La Pinta*, one of the three Spanish ships used by Christopher Columbus in his voyage to the Caribbean back in 1492. It was restored at great expense as a training vessel for youngsters and launched a few years before the La Palma tsunamis. It weighs in at sixty tonnes so can withstand very rough seas. With a draught of a little over two metres we can get quite close to the coast. The biggest problem we have is that the ship with its five decks was designed to operate with a full crew of thirty. We have ten left, and as a result we rarely deploy full sails. Because we have fewer crew, the accommodation and storage is better than what you might expect. We have at least sixty days of fresh water in our barrels, enough fresh vegetables and fruit until we next reach landfall, and more than an adequate supply of wine. And the sea provides all the protein we need.'

'Was that the Christopher Columbus who discovered America?' said Kate.

'America was discovered by a monk called Saint Brendan, one of our own, and by the Vikings centuries before the Spanish arrived,' said Don. 'The big difference is that Saint

Brendan was smart. He told nobody about the new land he discovered when he came home. The Spanish on the other hand told the world about their discovery, with the consequences that followed.'

'Whoever discovered the not now United States of America is of academic interest at this stage, is it not?' said Captain da Gama. 'Nobody has been to or heard from America in decades.'

There was a natural pause in the conversation.

'Please treat the ship as your home for the time being.'

'Do we have another option?' said Kate.

'For the moment, no to be honest.'

'Were you ever attacked?' said Kate.

At this stage, Tony and Don sat back and were happy to let Kate continue her interrogation. They were highly amused at her line of questioning, and less than amused at some of the answers she was given.

'Many times. But we have the advantage of having some modern weapons and can easily fend off any mercenaries. The crew, all men you will have noticed, are not only fit but highly motivated as you will soon see. They all believe in survival, and that is why we are all still here decades later.'

'How come you travelled so far north?' said Kate.

'We are casting our nets a bit wider because we heard that Iceapelago was on the road to recovery. So we sailed north nearly two weeks ago across the Bay of Biscay to find our fortune.'

'You've come to wrong place,' said Kate. 'There's little left in Iceapelago of any value. Very few communities survived, and those that have, have very small populations.'

'What about Malahide Castle Island?' said the captain.

'Malahide?' asked Don. He sat upright, clearly astonished. How did Captain da Gama know about Malahide? His earlier and initial sense of suspicion was re-affirmed by this declaration.

'It has a fortified castle, does it not?' said the captain. 'And I am told that the land is fertile, and food is plentiful.'

'I couldn't honestly tell you,' said Don. 'I've never visited Malahide Castle Island. In fact, it has been years since anyone heard from them.'

'Is that so?' said the captain.

'What do you mean?' said Kate. 'How do you know so much about Malahide Castle Island?'

'They told us,' said the captain. 'They have a functioning radio as do we. I have spoken to their Six, I think that is the name of the leader, on many occasions. She is expecting us. In fact, I expect, we will arrive at Malahide Castle before dusk tomorrow evening.'

'You can't be serious,' said Kate. She was trying hard to absorb not only all that had happened in the past hours, but now the prospect of an imminent visit to an Iceapelago community.

'And what's your plan after you get to Malahide?' said Tony.

He had not only listened carefully to the exchanges, but watched Captain da Gama carefully as he explained himself. He was clearly a confident man, a natural leader, and a person who knew what he wanted. That said, Tony had an inkling that his outwardly bonhomie disposition hid another facet of his personality. He would have to dig deeper but not today. After all, the captain had not only rescued them, treated them like royalty, but was taking them to another Iceapelago island. Wasn't that what he and Kate wanted?

'Who knows honestly,' said the captain. 'We are explorers after all. We explore. We move on. We drift with the tide and take our chances.'

The captain's glib response was not lost on his visitors from the Old Head of Kinsale.

'You have had a long, tiring, and a rather stressful day,' said Captain da Gama. 'I will get my bosun to show you to your cabins. It is all very basic, but functional. We rise at dawn, which is a few hours away. So try and get some sleep.'

'Thank you, Captain,' said Kate.

'Call me Vasco. I am not one for formalities.'

They retired as suggested. The bosun escorted them to their modest cabins below the main deck. The other crewmen were not to be seen.

As the sun rose, Tony stood behind Captain da Gama who held the ship's vast wooden steering wheel in a gentle grip with his left hand. Atop the rear deck the view was panoramic. The forward and middle sails were full. The crew were busy with the trim of the rigging. *La Santa Maria* took advantage of the moderate southerly winds.

'Look to the far horizon ahead at eleven hours,' said the captain. 'See the grey shape amidst the forest.'

Tony strained his eyes. He could barely make out the shape.

'That is Malahide Castle,' said the captain.

'How do you know?' asked Tony.

'Look here,' said the captain.

He pointed to a folded marine chart that was secured on an adjacent table by two weights.

'The map is over a hundred years old, but I doubt if Malahide Castle has moved since this chart was prepared. The only difference between now and then are the water depths.'

'Good navigation skills, Captain,' said Tony.

Kate arrived after a while and stood close beside her brother.

'Kate, please follow me,' said Tony.

He held out his hand to which she held on tightly. He sensed she was a bit edgy.

'Let's walk to the bow of the ship for a better view, and a bit of privacy.'

As they made their way across the deck, Tony noticed all the crew who were high up on the rigging were staring down at Kate. Once he made eye contact with a crew member, they diverted their eyes. Kate did not notice the attention she was getting. Tony said nothing, but parked the episode for later reflection.

Tony and Kate stood close to the bow, both holding onto a spar. The forward sail was rigid against the prevailing wind. The shrill of close buffeting was constant against the folds of the vast canvases. The noise had the effect of preventing anyone hearing their conversation.

'What do you make of the captain?' said Tony.

'Outwardly a nice man, very polite, and he showed us great kindness, didn't he? He rescued us after all.'

'I'm waiting for the but.'

Tony knew his sister's thought process.

'But what makes me uneasy is his motivation for travelling so far north, and so far from his homeland. I don't believe all his talk about adventure and exploration.'

'Kate, you've a great way of reading people. What's your instinct telling you?'

'He's exploring Iceapelago, but for what purpose is very unclear. Is he alone? It would be unusual for a ship to sail solo, especially in these times. And that comes back to my question about his real motivation. Why would a Portuguese ship go to so much trouble to visit Iceapelago. Is *La Santa Maria* the head of, or part of an armada? Is the captain using his communication with the Malahide Six as a pretext for something else? Are they after our resources?'

'That's a very far-fetched proposition, isn't it?' said Tony.

'Is it? After all, take the Old Head of Kinsale as an example. We have a steady, self-contained, self-sufficient, stable, and safe community. Who would not envy us?' said Kate.

'Let's be alert to the captain's plans, whatever they might be,' said Tony.

They stared into the distance towards a rapidly emerging landscape. In short order, the outline of Malahide Castle Island was clearly discernible.

Don joined them.

'Will we get a chance to go ashore?' said Kate, barely hiding her excitement.

'He didn't say,' said Don.

With his visitors at a safe distance and out of earshot, Captain da Gama instructed a crewman to take over the steering wheel. He walked into the small cabin behind the steering wheel, closing and locking the door. The ship's most precious asset, a fully working radio set, was located on a small desk. It was powered by one of the ship's solar panels. The aerial was atop the crow's nest.

He turned on the radio set. The static was loud while he tuned into the frequency he had been given for Malahide Castle.

'*La Santa Maria* here, calling Emily.'

There was silence. The captain was in no hurry. When he radioed on previous occasions there was always a short delay before he got a reply. He expected a response within a few minutes.

'Emily here, *La Santa Maria*,' was the almost immediate response. 'I was expecting your call. I can see you are sailing due west of Lambay Island.'

'Nice to talk to you again, Emily. Yes, we are close by and on schedule.'

'Make your way to the large red buoy over to starboard,' said the Malahide Six. 'It's connected to the broken steeple of the Saint Sylvester's church. Then four hundred metres to port you will see a yellow buoy. It is quite shallow there. A perfect spot to anchor.'

'I can see it. Can we get any closer?

'Best not as the tide is about to turn, and the current along the old railway viaduct is very strong,' said the Malahide Six. 'You can launch your rowboat once you anchor. It's a good thirty minutes' hard rowing to the old marina that lies due east of the castle. I'll be there to greet you.'

'That is great, Emily. See you soon. Over and out.'

Captain da Gama turned off the radio set. He sat facing the transmitter and reflected. The ship's radio set had been out of action for years because there was no electrical connection. When *La Santa Maria* raided the small community at Cascais as part of their routine pirating up and down the Portuguese coastline, the crew stole several solar panels knowing the ship needed power for the radio and lighting. The panels were easy to install. One of the crew had been an apprentice electrician. The communication channel with Malahide Castle, a fluky chance connection made three months previously, had opened up new opportunities for the crew and the captain's associates.

He knew he had to be careful. His crew were fully armed and experienced in the use of firearms. They were sure the citizens living in Malahide Castle were also prepared for the worst. He had decided therefore to take a cautious approach.

'Away anchor,' shouted the captain at the recommended location.

The crew unclipped the heavy chains as they delivered the anchor to the seabed in a roar of iron. As the anchor took hold, *La Santa Maria* first shuddered, and then settled gently into a parking position with her bow facing in the direction of the castle's turrets in the distance.

'Lower the boat,' ordered the captain.

The crew needed no prompting. In short order and with great skill, the largest of the ship's rowboats descended from its davits and splashed as it hit the water. The captain moved towards the rope ladder, as did Kate.

'What about us?' said Kate. 'Will we be going ashore?'

'That depends, Kate,' said the captain, putting his foot on the first rung of the rope ladder.

'To be more precise, that depends on the decision of the Malahide Six.'

'What do you mean?' said Kate.

Don and Tony joined her.

'I have a long-standing personal invitation from the Six. I am afraid you do not,' said the captain.

'But we are citizens of Iceapelago,' said Tony. 'Be reasonable, Captain.'

'That may well be the case, but I cannot assume Malahide Castle hospitality extends that far. Be patient. I will tell the Six we picked up a few castaways, and if she wants to meet you, I will send a message back to the ship.'

'Alright,' said Tony.

He and his companions could do no more than watch the captain descend into the rowing boat. Once he was seated, and without any prompting, the four-person crew expertly put the oars into the rowlocks, and powered the boat to the shoreline, a distance of about five hundred metres.

'What's he up to?' said Kate.

'I really don't know,' said Tony. 'As I said earlier, I'm totally puzzled as to why a Portuguese ship would bother to sail all the way to Iceapelago, never mind to what appears to be an agreed rendezvous at Malahide Castle.'

'He's a pirate,' said Don.

'What does that mean?' said Kate.

'Pirates raid and plunder,' said Don. 'I suspect he is sussing out the lie of the land before he commits his crew to a particular course of action. I very much doubt if *La Santa Maria* is alone in this endeavour.'

As the three visitors continued to discuss the true motivation for his voyage north, Captain da Gama made his short trip to the shoreline. When he was about a hundred metres from the old marina deck, he spotted a person moving in the background. As daylight was fading he could not make out who it was. Whoever it was, they were alone. A bit strange, he thought. He was expecting a welcoming party. It would be rude not to greet an invited guest with some degree of fanfare. After all, in these times visitors were a scarce commodity. As he reached out for a rail to secure the rowing boat, he looked up to see an elderly woman standing above the decking. Not what he was expecting. She walked slowly towards him.

'I'm Emily, the Malahide Six. Captain, you are most welcome.'

She sensed his sense of disappointment. *I am not what he was expecting,* she surmised correctly.

The captain stepped onto the rickety deck and made his way to the solid ground above.

'Nice to meet you, Emily. Greetings from the Principality of Ria Formosa in Portugal.'

He was taken by surprise when she took hold of his hand with a firm grip. She stood squarely in front of him, a good head and a half shorter than he was.

'Send the boat back to *La Santa Maria*,' said Emily. 'They can collect you in the morning when we raise our pennant at the dock.'

'Off with you,' said the captain.

The crew did what they were told without a word of acknowledgement.

'This way,' said Emily.

She started to walk in the direction of the castle.

The captain was an observant person from both training and experience. In the short time it took him to get to the main entrance to the castle, he noticed there were no dwellings outside the main castle building. There were signs of derelict housing units, obviously long-abandoned, and a ruined church with an adjacent and full graveyard. The castle walls were not very tall but had been fortified, and despite the fading light, he could see that several observation posts peppered the old battlements. Importantly, it appeared there was only one functioning entrance, and the main door was made of solid oak.

Emily did not speak as they walked. She saw he was taking in his surroundings, and decided it was best that he was left undisturbed. There would be plenty of time for conversation later.

They stood astride the front door. The captain looked up at the double set of stained glass windows above. They looked as if they had been reinforced with iron bars.

'Ready?' said Emily.

'Of course,' said the captain.

Emily took a large copper key and inserted it into the lock. She deftly turned it twice, and when it clicked she put her hand on the handle and pushed the door open. They walked silently into the hallway. The captain again focused on his surroundings. Dusty portraits hung everywhere. He followed behind Emily as she made her way briskly to a door at the end of the corridor.

She turned to him and smiled in an impish manner.

'Don't be taken aback if the people you are going to meet are surprised.'

'What do you mean?' said the captain as the door was thrown open.

The dining room was full as dinner was about to be served. The Malahide Castle residents were taking their places at table when the creaking of the door to the hallway was accompanied by a shrill cry from Orla. Everyone turned to Orla who pointed her finger at the visitor as he walked into the room ahead of the Six.

'I have news for you,' said the Six.

That a was self-evident statement given the presence of the stranger who stood head and shoulders beside her.

'This is Captain Vasco da Gama. He is from Portugal. His ship, the *La Santa Maria*, is moored at the yellow buoy. Please welcome him. He has travelled to Malahide Castle at my invitation. Captain, you might introduce yourself.'

The captain knew immediately he was among a group of highly cautious people judging by their common expression of astonishment. They looked furtively at each other. One man picked up a knife from the table and stared at the visitor with a sense of trepidation. Nobody in the room was smiling, they all frowned. The seated diners stood up, and slowly formed a closed semicircle at the end of the table as far away as was possible from the entrance door. What was most noticeable was the silence. Nobody spoke.

It dawned immediately on the captain that the Six had not forewarned the residents of his scheduled appearance. Worse, the Six has deliberately left it to him to provide the required explanations. *What was her motivation?* he asked himself. She was an elderly woman after all and no threat to anyone.

'I gather my arrival has caught you by surprise,' said the captain.

Not unaware of the disturbance his presence was causing, he smiled but his attempt at humour was not reciprocated. Glum faces continued to stare at him.

'Best that I set the record straight. Your Six invited me to Malahide Castle. Rather than me give you an explanation, perhaps Emily might tell you why I am here.'

'Captain, can I suggest that you wait outside please?' said Rory who walked towards the new guest. He placed the knife back on the dining table. The captain could see he was the real leader, despite his age.

'The arrival of a stranger into our community has taken us by surprise. It is clear that you are also puzzled by our reaction. We haven't had a visitor for over a decade, and here you appear out of the blue. I would like to talk to the Six in private. Jon, could you kindly show this gentleman to the reading room upstairs? Captain, I'll call you as soon as I can.'

Jon hesitated but just for a second. The adults were displaying great concern in contrast to the younger siblings who saw the arrival of the handsome stranger as a sign of a potential adventure.

'This way please,' said Jon.

'Lead the way, young man,' said the captain.

He doffed his cap and bowed to the startled group, following his guide out of the room.

Rory stepped forward, closing the door with a bang.

'Emily, what have you done? We all deserve an explanation, do we not? Speak up.'

She may have been the oldest person in the room but the Six was also one of the wisest. Decades of intrigue, in-fighting, and the loss of close family members had left their mark on her. The arrival of the captain would be her greatest achievement. Or so she had assured herself.

'I invited him, yes. It was easy as his ship has a radio transmitter.'

The Six sat down in her usual place in the middle of the dining table. She paused, fiddling with the cutlery.

'In God's name, Emily, what possessed you?' said Rory. 'We've had a strict policy of no visitors since the abortive attack from our Dundrum neighbours many years ago. And not only did you invite a ship's captain but his crew as well?'

'Don't be so rude, Rory. I'm the Six remember? I've taken a solemn oath to do my best to protect Malahide Castle Island. And my private conversations with Captain da Gama, and there have been many, convinced me my decision is not only correct, but absolutely essential.'

'Essential?' said Veronica. 'You really do need to tell us what you've discussed with this man.'

'I will, if you stop interrupting me and show me some respect,' said Emily in a calm tone. She loved being the centre of attention.

'Firstly, it all happened quite by accident. I was carrying out routine maintenance on the radio transmitter. I've skills at my age I need remind you, and in flicking between radio frequencies the captain answered. I was as surprised as he was that contact was made. Neither of us had spoken to anyone outside our countries ever. We started to talk about our communities, and how they were faring. I didn't realise it at the beginning, but his radio was located on his ship, *La Santa Maria.*'

'Is he a pirate?' said Rory. 'I have met many unsavoury people in my day and can spot a malcontent by instinct.'

'Stop judging someone you don't know. Shame on you, Rory. I expect better from you,' said the Six. 'Let me continue please. Once the captain revealed that he and his crew of ten lived at sea practically all the time, I suggested he might sail to Malahide Castle, and make *La Santa Maria* available to us. He accepted the offer, and here he is.'

'What terms and conditions have you discussed with this stranger?' said Rory.

He sat opposite the Six as he sought to draw information out of her. The room's participants manoeuvred behind Rory leaving the Six isolated.

'I can't imagine he spent weeks sailing to Malahide Castle Island simply for the good of his health. Have you agreed to pay him anything?'

'No, I haven't. There were no T&Cs as you call them. I simply issued an invitation to visit, which was accepted with grace and dignity. Two traits that I now insist you display to the captain. I'm finished with explanations. Jon, please go ask the captain to join us for dinner.'

Except for special occasions, evening dinner at Malahide Castle was a predictable event. It was served at around seven o'clock. A seasonal salad was the standard starter followed by a fish or meat dish with garden vegetables. The residents who wished to eat in a communal manner just turned up. Everyone was on a rota to help out. The gardeners harvested the fresh vegetables, the shepherds butchered and presented the meat, the utility team provided the water, the cooks cooked, and all the diners helped set and clear the table and did the washing up. It was a classic communal and collaborative effort that ran like clockwork. Tonight was an exception, however.

In returning to the dining room, the captain expected that Emily had had the opportunity of setting the record straight, and that his offer to provide his ship to the service of the Malahide Castle Six, without pre-conditions, would have been welcomed. He soon discovered his optimistic outlook was misplaced.

'Please sit beside me, Captain,' said Emily. 'Orla, could you kindly sit the other side of the captain. The rest of you take your usual places.'

Rory sat opposite the captain as he wanted to get more meaningful answers than those provided by the Six.

'What is for dinner?' said the captain, trying to lighten the mood.

'Carrot and fennel salad for starters, and we have rabbit stew as the main course,' said Orla.

Only after she provided her explanation did she realise she had actually spoken to the first new person she had ever seen outside the island community since she was born. By the looks she got from her peers it was clear she had spoken out of turn. Unknown to Orla, this was the very cue the Six had been waiting for.

'My main motivation for inviting Captain da Gama to Malahide Castle Island is to give our youngest the opportunity to leave the community, and to join the captain and his crew, under their protection, as they visit the other communities around Iceapelago. We have to look to our future. Unless we mix and mingle with other islanders we will die out as a community.'

'You should've discussed this with us first, Emily,' said Veronica. 'The very idea of the my grandchildren leaving the island is abhorrent to me. Emily, is your memory failing? There's no love lost between us and our neighbours, have you forgotten? More importantly, we've no idea what has happened outside Malahide Castle Island since the Big Storm, nor the living conditions outside our self-made cocoon.'

'The alternative is that we stay put until the last person is left standing,' said the Six raising her voice, shrill with frustration. 'Is that what you all want? To die off one by one until we are all gone? Think of the children and their future. Do they want to grow old with nobody to look after them in their old age?'

'Emily, I have known you all my life,' said Rory. 'You've made some rash decisions in the past that we decided to brush over, not that we had any choice, but inviting a total stranger to our secure household is a step too far. We've no idea if this sea captain can be trusted, never mind trusted with our grandchildren.'

'Would it help if I was allowed to introduce myself properly?' said Captain da Gama.

'Could you please desist, at least until Six explains her motivation for inviting you to Malahide Castle,' said Rory. 'Captain, we respect the fact you are a guest, but the exact nature of this status has yet to be determined.'

'Rory, I beg your indulgence,' said the captain. He could see Rory was the person who was really in charge and was the person who needed to be convinced. The captain therefore decided to focus his attention on him. 'There is little point in the Six telling you why I am here only for me to repeat myself. May I continue?'

'OK, fair enough,' said Rory.

'Portugal was as badly affected by the La Palma and Eriador tsunamis as you were, if not worse,' said the captain. 'That is my starting point. We have struggled as a nation. I lost all my family. It was pure chance that I ended up as a cabin boy on *La Santa Maria*. I've spent most of my life on the ship.'

'But doing what exactly? said Rory.

'Helping the survivors, to be honest. Doing exactly what you all did in the aftermath of your Eriador Event. We transported food and medicines between our communities more or less in same way as your river cruisers did. We had coastal communities, not the interconnected islands which comprise Iceapelago. We worked incessantly around the clock as very few sea vessels survived the initial tsunami onslaught. You have nothing to fear from me, I can assure you.'

The Six knew Rory was about to continue his cross-examination and interjected turning to Orla. 'Stay or go?'

'Go.'

'Orla!' screamed her grandmother. 'You can't do that.'

'I'll be back,' said Orla.

'No, you won't,' said Veronica. 'If you leave the safety of Malahide Castle, never mind in the custody of someone we don't know, your life is at peril.'

'I want to go too,' said Jon.

The siblings' mother and Veronica burst out crying.

The captain paused while the sobbing lessened.

'I told Emily that *La Santa Maria* was available to your community to allow you to contact other Iceapelago communities. I understand your reluctance, believe me. After all, you have been isolated for so long and are, naturally, suspicious of strangers.'

'Do you blame us?' said Rory.

'To prove my bona fides, I have two young passengers from the Old Head of Kinsale Island aboard *La Santa*

Maria. Does that help re-assure you?' said the captain. 'They were marooned close to Cork Airport Island, and we saved them. Why would I do that if I had malign intentions?'

That was the first anyone from Malahide Castle had heard of the Old Head of Kinsale Island community since the Big Storm. They had assumed all had died.

The captain turned to face Rory.

'Rory, please come aboard my ship to meet them? You can act as chaperone for Orla and Jon if you want. Could we agree on an initial short voyage, for example to Dundrum Island, as a demonstration of my good intentions? We could be back within a week. I understand you know your way around Dundrum so we will not do anything that will put Orla or Jon at risk.'

'Grandad, please say yes,' said Orla.

Rory had the carpet pulled from under him. The captain's request seemed reasonable and rational. He was boxed into a position where he could not oppose the proposal.

'This is all happening too quickly,' said Rory.

Veronica nodded her agreement.

'Look at the situation from our point of view,' said Jon. 'As much as I love living here, I'm too young to have an opportunity to travel to a neighbouring Iceapelago community rejected outright. You have reared Orla and I as young adults, so kindly treat us accordingly.'

The Six saw the mood shifting in her favour.

'Can I suggest we all sleep on what we have been discussing and resume our conversation over breakfast?

Captain, I have a guest room ready if you were mindful to stay the night.'

'Glad to accept your kind invitation, Emily.'

CHAPTER 6

Captain Vasco da Gama

RORY SAT IN SILENCE on the rear seat as the team of four oarsmen effortlessly propelled the ship's launch down the viaduct from the Malahide Castle marina towards a sailing ship visible in the near distance. He was impressed by their skill.

Sitting in front of their grandfather, Orla and Jon were also silent, taking in the enormity of what was happening. For years, and in hushed tones, they had secretly discussed how to get off Malahide Castle Island. Now they were on the cusp of the adventure they had long wished for. Since they were young children, they had heard endless stories about Dundrum Island, mostly told by Rory. However, in the absence of a seaworthy vessel of any shape or description it had been impossible to visit another Iceapelago community. An impossibility until Captain Vasco da Gama's surprise visit.

The siblings knew that suggesting their grandfather travel with them was a smart move by the captain. As a consequence, Rory could not refuse the offer without losing face and, more importantly, upsetting his young grandchildren.

'Captain, how long will it take to get to Dundrum Island?' said Orla.

'Given there's an onshore breeze, which will help, I believe we could be there by nightfall tomorrow. Rory, you have travelled this route many times – what do you think?'

'It took a river cruiser around twelve hours depending on tidal conditions. I've never sailed to Dundrum, so I can't tell you. The last kilometre will require you to navigate through the width of a canal so it may not be possible to dock at the Dundrum marina. You will probably have to use this launch for the last part of the journey.'

'I had anticipated that, Rory,' said the captain. 'If needs be, we can row the final stretch. As you can see, this crew handles the boat with ease.'

Rory did not reply. He paused to think. He was surprised at the captain's ready knowledge of the navigational constraints at Dundrum. How did he know about the narrow entrance? This increased his unease about the captain. He seemed to be one step ahead all the time.

Orla, on the other hand, was full of chat. 'Tell me more about your passengers from Kinsale Head Island?'

'There is a boy and a girl. They are your age, and I guess they have the same sense of adventure. You will meet them soon enough.'

While Orla spoke to the captain, Rory focused on the oarsmen. They did not speak when they boarded and rowed in silence. It seemed the rhythm of their strokes did not require communication. He perceived they were all in their fifties. Considering their ages, they were fit and trim. Dressed in a common uniform of blue tops and shorts, he noticed a red floral cross design was embossed on their attire. Each had a small tattoo of a triple castle etched on the back of his neck. This suggested *La Santa Maria* was under the command of an organisation or a leader. He noticed that the captain also had the same tattoo on the nape of his neck. *What did this mean*? he mused. Rory decided to hold his counsel for the moment. Once aboard, he would try to find out more about the real owner of *La Santa Maria*.

The oarsmen manoeuvred the launch to the port side of the ship.

The Malahide Castle visitors looked up and saw two young people looking down at them from the deck above. The girl waved.

'OK, let us climb up the rope ladder,' said the captain. 'Rory, you go first, please.'

Rory did what he was told and ascended to the main deck in short order. His sore knee was long forgotten. Orla and Jon joined him moments later.

The captain's guests approached the new arrivals.

'Great to meet you, my name is Don.'

Introductions were exchanged politely. The four young adults smiled broadly as they eyed each other.

'How about lunch as we set sail?' said the captain. 'Follow me.'

As he turned towards the cabin door at the rear of the ship, he shouted an instruction in Portuguese, a language the visitors did not understand. The response was instantaneous. The ship's rigging was tightened by expert hands and as soon as the anchor was out of the water, *La Santa Maria* moved off her mooring at a steady pace.

Rory's concerns were heightened as he sat at the table. He could not be sure if the captain had set a course to Dundrum. And how come they were so familiar with the navigation channels offshore Malahide – especially the complex array of broken wind turbines that almost encircled Lambay Island? Being indoors and below deck, he was unable to see how the voyage was progressing.

His grandchildren had other priorities.

Seated at the laden dining table, the Malahide youngsters shared the same excitement experienced by the young Kinsale Head visitors the night before. They chatted endlessly, exchanging personal details and experiences. Their laughter filled the room. Rory could not but help notice how at ease the four were in each other's company. They were natural companions.

Don and Rory's conversation was of a more serious nature. They sat opposite each other at the end of the table.

'You were shipwrecked?' whispered Rory over the noise of the adjacent conversations.

'Yes, and it was a miracle that *La Santa Maria* came to our rescue. To be honest, we could have died but for the captain,' said Don. 'He has a powerful personality, but something lurks beneath.'

'I feel the same,' said Rory. 'My grandchildren see this as one big adventure, understandably so. I've a huge sense of foreboding. Did you notice the crew's tattoos, and the embossed motif?'

'Yes, look at your cutlery,' said Don. 'It's all engraved with what seems to be a coat of arms.'

'Have you discussed this with the captain?' said Rory.

'No, because I haven't had the opportunity. We were fed like royalty last night, and packed off to bed before I could have a serious conversation with him. And when I woke up, he had left for Malahide Castle.'

'Let's resolve to get to the bottom of that particular mystery as soon as we can.'

'By any chance are you Rory, the former Deputy Commander of Iceapelago?' said Don.

Rory was stunned. How did Don know about his role?

'Actually, I am, or I was to be more accurate. That was a long time ago. Did my reputation travel as far as the Old Head of Kinsale?'

'Oh, it surely did,' said Don. 'You should know that Kate and Tony are the grandchildren of Ruth Henry.'

'Oh my God,' said Rory. 'How's Ruth? I haven't spoken or seen her since the Big Storm exploded across Iceapelago.'

'She's dead, Rory, I'm sad to say. The Big Storm took her.'

Rory choked with emotion. He shuddered as he tried to absorb the news. He and Ruth were kindred spirits, true friends. Because she had saved his life, he had dedicated his career to supporting her role as Commander of Iceapelago.

'What happened to her? How come her grandchildren survived? Did Cork Airport Island survive the Big Storm?' Rory struggled to get his words out. He had so many questions to ask.

'All the people on Cork Airport Island died of hypothermia,' said Don. 'The Big Storm was followed by a rapid drop in temperature that lasted over three months. I found her actually. She was at home and at peace.'

Rory interrupted the emerging narrative. 'What's your position, Don?'

'I was the master of Ruth's river cruiser. Like you, I knew her well. You don't remember, but I met you on her cruiser years ago.'

'Yes. It was after we put a stop to the rising at Dundrum. She had just been elected as Commander and before she travelled back to Cork Airport Island she named me as Deputy Commander. So long ago.'

'She was one of the very best, Rory. She is never far from my thoughts.'

Rory reflected on his departed friend for a while, lost in a wave of memories. 'I think I'll take some air on deck,' he said.

He and Don left.

The young adults meanwhile were getting to know each other better.

'You nearly died, you poor things,' said Orla. 'We've lived the most boring existence compared to your adventures. Isn't that's so, Jon?'

'Speak for yourself, sister,' said her sibling. 'Aren't we all on an adventure now?'

'I hope so,' said Orla.

'What's life like at Malahide Castle?' said Kate. 'I hope we get to see it when we return.'

Kate had taken an instant liking to Orla. It was wonderful to be able to talk to another young woman her age. The pair chatted like talkative twins with their respective siblings being observers to their rapid exchanges.

'The community was almost a thousand strong a long time ago. The Big Storm had a dramatic impact. We were lucky that Rory was alerted by the Iceapelago Commander days before the storm hit.'

'That's Ruth Henry, our grandma,' said Kate.

'What a coincidence!' exclaimed Orla. 'She certainly saved a lot of lives. We were able to fortify the castle at short notice and moved most of our animals into our all-weather protected paddocks. The food stores were filled to the brim. Everyone on the island was moved to the safety of the castle. The Big Storm came and went. We stayed indoors for four months, oblivious to what was happening outside. Afterwards, as the temperature increased slowly but surely, the community went about the routine of planting and harvesting and husbanding our animals. We are totally self-reliant as we have a plentiful supply food and have freshwater springs.'

'Malahide Castle must be the safest place to live on Iceapelago,' said Kate.

'Probably,' said Jon. 'But our daily routines never changed, until yesterday. As the youngest and fittest of the community, Orla and I were given increased responsibilities. I am, or was, responsible for the animals' welfare, and Orla was in charge of food provisions. Long days are the norm. We're kept busy deliberately, I suspect. The community has become very reliant on us.'

'And that's why our parents, and Rory – who is our grandfather, by the way – were so upset when there was talk of us being able to leave the Island,' said Orla.

'We had almost the exact same conversation with our mother when we announced we wanted to leave Kinsale Head,' said Kate.

'So what's in store for us? said Orla.

'Who knows?' said Kate. 'Isn't that what an adventure is all about?'

'At least we'll get to see the much talked-about Dundrum Island,' said Jon. 'I've heard so many stories about that community since I was a toddler.'

'Mostly bad ones,' said Orla.

'Yes, but times change, and we need to change with the times.'

'What do you mean?'

'For instance, are the people Grandad fought against still living on Dundrum Island?' said Jon. 'Imagine if the community was populated with people of our age who cared more about the future than the past?'

'It's the same where we live,' said Kate. 'Everybody is transfixed about the past and can't see beyond tomorrow.'

They heard a commotion outside, which stopped their conversation. They walked out onto the main deck and approached the groups who were facing off. The siblings saw that Rory was clearly annoyed about something.

'This is not the route to Dundrum,' said Rory. 'Why did you tack towards Lambay Island?'

'It is a change of plan,' said Captain da Gama.

He turned the wheel vigorously. The main mast jibed and *La Santa Maria* shuddered as she sailed into the wind in a northerly direction. The crew high aloft the rigging shouted to each other. Those on the deck could not make out what they were saying.

'I agreed to come aboard with my children on your word that we were heading to Dundrum Island,' said Rory.

He was really annoyed. So much so that Jon put his hand on his shoulder to try and calm him.

'Grandad, what's happening?' said Jon.

'Ask your new best friend, Captain Vasco as he likes to be called.'

'Captain?'

'Jon, we are steering north to meet other ships of the fleet of the Principality of Ria Formosa off Skerries Rock.'

Without any beckoning, the crew descending from the rigging, and stood in a semicircle but at a distance behind the captain, awaiting orders from their leader.

'Best that you all go to your quarters for a while,' said the captain.

'This is outrageous,' said Rory.

He rushed towards the captain with his fists clenched. He barely made a second step in the direction of his adversary. A stone fired by a crew member from a catapult hit him in the centre of his forehead. He was stunned and fell like a sack of potatoes onto the deck. His grandchildren rushed to his aid.

'He will be fine,' said the captain. 'He will have a headache for a while. Jon, you and Tony take him to his cabin.'

Orla started crying. Kate scowled as she comforted her friend. The nature of their adventure had obviously taken a turn for the worst. With Orla sobbing loudly, they followed behind their brothers who were hauling their slumped human cargo to the cabin quarters on the lower deck.

La Santa Maria sailed under strong following winds for a little under an hour.

'Ahoy,' called a crewman from the crow's nest atop the main sail.

Captain da Gama acknowledged the signal with a wave of his hand. He opened the door to the cabin where the ship's radio was located, and once inside, closed it firmly. He made himself comfortable on the operator's wooden seat and switched the radio on. A green light lit up the basic equipment. He flicked the message dispatch button.

'Captain Vasco da Gama of *La Santa Maria* wishes to speak to Admiral Rodriguez.'

'I will get him, Captain,' was the instant response from the distant radio operator.

'Vasco, you old rogue. How are you, my friend?' said the admiral a few minutes later.

'In good spirits, Admiral,' said the captain.

'And the crew?'

'Everyone is fine. They know the end is near. They have been very patient over the past months at sea.'

'You are one of my best commanders, Vasco. Your crew know that. In fact, the entire fleet holds you in the highest regard.'

'Thank you, Admiral,' said the captain.

'The duke is captivated about your plans for Iceapelago,' said the admiral. 'You certainly have his full attention. We need to talk. When will you be alongside? I reckon you are three kilometres to starboard.'

'Maybe we can share a glass of Alvarinho within the hour?'

'Rest assured. I have a bottle in the chiller,' said the admiral. 'I will provide the refreshments. You provide the game plan.'

The captain turned off the radio. He sat alone in the small cabin contemplating the success of his voyage over the past months. With few resources and a lot of guile, he had visited many Iceapelago island communities, including Malahide Castle, Howth, Dundrum, and Cork Airport. But for the fact he had picked up the shipwrecked crew, he would have also tried to visit the Old Head of Kinsale. He had been tasked to find out about Iceapelago's defences and resources, and had done so diligently, in great detail and mostly in secret.

As they approached the fleet, the captain gestured towards the rowing boat, and without saying a word, two crew members started to unlock it from its davits. Two more crew positioned themselves at the stern and aft, and pushed the suspended boat over the side of the gunwale. One crew member jumped into the boat as it was slowly lowered into the water. Deftly he unlocked the hoist supports and held a line that kept the boat snug to *La Santa Maria*. A rope ladder was thrown over the side and landed in the boat with a thump. No sooner had it been cast than Captain da Gama descended in short order with a second crew member closely behind.

'*Obrigado*, that was a perfect launch,' said the captain.

He had barely time to sit on the rear seat before the crew had the oars in the rowlocks and dipped the long paddles into the choppy waves. The high sea conditions were not really suitable for rowing. That did not bother the crew or their cargo. It just took a little bit longer to get aside *La Santa Jorge*, the fleet's flagship.

'*Olá*,' said Captain da Gama saluting Admiral Rodriquez once he set foot on the main deck. He looked around in awe at the vastness of the *La Santa Jorge*. It was at least five times the size of his modest vessel. Sails and bedecked masts soared to the clouds. Dozens of chatting crew were busying themselves with all sorts of chores. The deck was gleaming from a recent scrubbing. The cannon brasses shone brightly. Even the cannon balls were aglow. All signs of a crew that had to be kept busy.

'My friend,' said the admiral.

He gave the captain a warm hug. A most unusual gesture for a military commander. The fact that he was the captain's uncle was also a factor in the display of friendship that did not go unnoticed.

'This is impressive,' said the captain as he took in the vista.

'She is a bit of a behemoth, I suppose,' said the admiral. 'But I am proud of this wooden battleship. She has a displacement of four hundred tonnes making her the largest vessel afloat, at least in this part of the world. There are two hundred crew although we have the capacity for nearly double that if we were in battle mode. We would need additional resources to man the cannons we have over three decks.'

'How many ships are now in the fleet?' said the captain.

'Excluding yours of course, I have eight with me, and fifty berthed in and around our home port of Quinta do Lago. All the once modern iron-clad battleships and coastal warships are totally redundant because we have long run out of fossil fuels. Most lie in a rusty pile near the Port of Sintra.

'You have built up a strong armada,' said the captain.

'I agree,' said the admiral. 'We have to be seen as strong in these challenging times. But less of the small talk. We have much business to discuss. Follow me.'

Walking behind him, the captain admired the manner in which the admiral carried himself. He had to be close to two metres tall. His feathered cap made him look like a giant peacock. His greatcoat, dominated by the red and green of the Portuguese national colours, had lines of silver braids on the edges of the fabric. A thick brown leather belt supported a scabbard that contained a long blade, the grip of which was decorated with the cross of their ultimate master, the Duke of the Principality of Ria Formosa. The weight of the uniform and its accoutrements could not have been borne by a man of lesser stature.

'Mind your head,' said the admiral.

He passed under a doorway that led to his personal quarters at the ship's stern. The captain continued to take in his surroundings. Several doors hung off the narrow hallway. The wooden walls had been treated with a thick brown lacquer paint. Between the doors hung sets of automatic rifles, no doubt primed for action.

'In here,' said the admiral.

He beckoned his visitor into the executive suite.

'Nice set up, Admiral,' said the captain.

The cabin was enormous, or at least much bigger than his own quarters. The ceiling was not high enough to allow the admiral to stand upright. He had to stoop before he sat down on a large ornate mahogany chair. A recent charcoal portrait of the Duke of Ria Formosa occupied pride of place between the floor-to-ceiling twin sash rear windows that allowed light stream into the cabin. The room was adorned with trophies, bric-a-brac and disorganised shelving full of dusty books, maps and ships' logs.

'This is my sanctuary,' said the admiral. 'I spend most of my time here. The officers report on the hour as and when required. I eat and sleep here as befits the highest officer of the Ria Formosa fleet. I have all conveniences nearby. My radio room is behind that door over there. An unusual feature is the spiral staircase that provides access to the top deck where an able lieutenant is, I hope, steering us safely. This is akin to a man cave of old.' His grey moustache twitched as he bared his teeth laughing loudly.

'How is the duke?' said the captain.

'Impatient, I think is the best way to describe his mood,' said the admiral. 'He has invested heavily in this venture and nothing short of a total success will please him. He attaches great store to your intelligence reports. I am sure his final decision about the exodus will be very much informed by your initial proposals and ideas.'

'No pressure then!' said the captain.

He did not dare share his sense of homesickness with the admiral. Being at sea in a small vessel, however well provisioned and with an agreeable crew, for almost a year was a tough station. But duty took precedence.

The admiral walked to a shelf and pulled out a large chart. He unfolded it and lay it flat on his desk, placing two silver candlestick at the edges to keep it in place.

'Iceapelago!' said the captain.

'Yes indeed, Iceapelago, including all the latest features and depth readings that we have discussed over the past months. Your navigation of this bleak territory would have done our fellow countryman Vasco da Gama proud.'

'Where should I begin?' said the captain.

'From what you have told me, we should start with the community at Malahide Castle. Have you not just re-visited the area?'

'My brief was to find a potential new home and base for the duke and our population. Malahide Castle is an almost perfect fit as a location. It comprises a suite of large rooms that would be most suitable for the duke's personal use. The estate is self-sufficient, has easy access to the sea, and the castle is by far the most secure building in all of Iceapelago.'

'And critically, how many could it accommodate?'

'From personal observation, the castle itself could easily manage five hundred. But what makes Malahide so special is there is scope to build houses in the immediate environs of the castle. The mature woods have enough timber for up to a hundred housing units.'

'Excellent. Tell me more.'

'The fields are fertile and support all year round crops of vegetables. If nothing else, the Malahide community are diligent farmers. The dry grain storage areas within the castle's walls are better than anything we have at home.'

'Great,' said the admiral. 'I am impressed with this attention to detail.'

'And believe it or not, they have hundreds of sheep and goats in the fields around the castle with basic indoor facilities when there are storms or cold snaps. And they have more chickens than I could count.'

'If we plan carefully, we could greatly increase the live-stock numbers quite quickly,' said the admiral.

'I agree. I reckon within a year there would be enough to feed at least two thousand.'

'The duke intends to bring our entire surviving population of five thousand to Iceapelago as soon as I give the all clear. A third could live quite comfortably at Malahide Castle. Your assessment will really please him.'

'Do I get to talk to him?' said the captain.

'Yes, once we have an agreed final plan of attack. By the way, how many people live at Malahide Castle?'

'The community comprises no more than twenty, and most of them are quite old.'

'So it will be easy to capture?' asked the admiral.

'Yes,' said the captain. 'With this in mind, I completed a full reconnoitre of the island two months ago and have identified a suitable landing site on the leeward side. There is a concealed beach close to the old graveyard that is no more than a kilometre from the castle. And the route to the castle is through a dense woodland area.'

'What about sea access?' asked the admiral.

'The marina deck is not only unusable, but quite inaccessible for our ships,' said the captain. 'We could repair it later to take ships the size of my own.'

'How many men will you need?'

'Six longboats, and twenty grenadiers should be enough, provided we land unnoticed. Our biggest challenge will be to access the castle's front door, which is usually bolted shut. However, there are times of the day, usually during harvesting time, when it is left open for hours on end.'

'And Dundrum?' said the admiral. He did not want to get into too much more detail at this stage. Within the hour, he would get his scheduled weekly call from the duke and above all else he had to able to deliver a positive progress report. The last time the duke had called, he got a terrible roasting about the absence of detailed attack and occupation plans.

The captain was going to mention that he had several guests from Malahide Castle and Kinsale Head aboard *La Santa Maria,* but did not get a chance as the admiral pressed him for reports about other potential locations.

'Dundrum is destroyed. Well, let me put it another way: it would not be my choice to live out the rest of my life.'

'But was it not the centre of the Iceapelago administration?' said the admiral.

'It was before the Big Storm,' said the captain.

'You had best explain,' said the admiral. 'My understanding was that there were many high-rise apartment blocks with lots of housing units.'

'There were,' said the captain. 'The windows of all the main buildings were blown apart during the Big Storm. Rain damage was left untreated for years. There is rust, refuse, flotsam and jetsam at every level apart from the basement area that is somewhat habitable by my reckoning. You must remember that most of the citizens of Dundrum scattered to other Iceapelago communities at the time.'

'You're well-informed, Captain. How did you get the information?'

'It was quite easy actually,' said the captain. 'Because the Dundrum marina is totally destroyed, my crew rowed me to a rocky outcrop about a kilometre from the main buildings. I just walked into the complex and sat down on a park bench close to the main entrance.'

'As simple as that?' said the admiral in awe.

'I should add I wore the same set of rags as everyone else, so I blended in. My beard shielded my skin colour. I could see what I assumed were guards, but nobody tried to stop or question me. There were many strangers in Dundrum so it would have taken a trained eye to spot me. As I said, I sat on a bench and in no time two vagabonds, for the want of a better word, sat beside me. They wanted water. I had none. Then they asked for food. Much to their amazement I gave them a banana, and after they had decided how to eat it, the conversation opened up.'

'Who were they?'

'A husband and wife who had worked for the Ears when Dundrum was in its prime.'

'Ears? What are you talking about?' said the admiral.

'Apparently, it was a secret organisation that spied on the Iceapelago communities before its dirty work was exposed. This pair had the lowdown on everyone and everything. I told them I had come in from one of the island communities and was looking for food and accommodation. In no uncertain terms, they told me to go back from where I came. The main reason was that law and order had broken down. Everyone lived hand-to-mouth, day-by-day. Stealing food was the norm. There were no medicines, and getting off the island was near impossible. The last time a cruiser landed, it was ransacked within minutes. Totally looted. The crew were thrown overboard and drowned. Five people made the cruiser their home.'

'Who is in charge?' said the admiral.

'There is a Six, that is what they call their leader, but nobody has seen her in years. We must assume this community of some four hundred is lawless, ruthless, hungry, and incapable of being subjugated.'

'Not a priority landing area then?' said the admiral.

'It could be, but there may be better locations for our population,' said the captain.

'Let us pause there, shall we, before we look at other options,' said the admiral. 'It is rude of me. I should have offered you something when you arrived. So go along to the galley and eat your fill. We might have a sherry nightcap, and you can then continue with your briefing.'

As the captain stood up to leave, he noticed Admiral Rodriguez was fidgeting with his bunch of keys.

When the captain left, the admiral unlocked the door to the radio room.

CHAPTER 7

La Santa Jorge

'I'll be fine.' said Rory.

He knew he was anything but fine. The headache that pierced the width of his head was not confined to where the stone had caught him in mid-temple. The legacy of the stone was a huge throbbing lump.

'Grandad, you really must sit down and rest,' said Jon.

This was the first time ever that they had seen their grandfather physically incapacitated.

'Stop fussing,' said Rory. 'I need a glass of water. My head is splitting.'

Rory started to raise himself from his chair to reach for a water decanter and glass. As he did so, his right knee gave way. He tumbled forward.

Jon knelt in front of his grandfather and pushed him back into a seating position.

'Please do what you're told,' said Orla.

'Alright, alright,' said Rory.

'Rushing the captain wasn't one of your brightest ideas, was it?' said Jon.

'But he misled us,' said Rory.

'That may be so, but there was no point in getting yourself killed in the process,' said Orla.

'Jon and I and our new friends from Kinsale Head all suspect Captain da Gama is not telling the truth,' said Orla. 'It's probably best to go with the flow and await developments.'

'Was killing your grandfather a development you had anticipated?' said Rory. 'I've met the likes of Captain da Gama in the past and wouldn't trust him under any circumstance. He's up to no good. And we shall soon find out what he has in mind.'

'Grandad, what do you think is happening?' said Jon.

'Before you were born and just before the Big Storm, a jealous nation planned to occupy Iceapelago and confiscate our food and medicines. While we saw off the mercenary invaders from Cymru, with little support from some neighbouring communities, I believed at some point in the future, greedy or desperate people would become aware of our success in surviving on Iceapelago and could see our land as a place where they could live.'

Rory would not admit it in front of the siblings, but his grandchildren had been brought up in a somewhat closeted and unique manner, unaware of worldly ways and potential threats from outside the community. This was not a deliberate choice. Living a spartan, isolated and physically demanding existence in Iceapelago had framed their developing personalities, and their limited view of the world, such as it was.

'I did my best to shield you and your brother from the turmoil of the past, the endless trials and tribulations of the decades before you were born,' said Rory. 'We've been lucky these past years, but I'm afraid our luck may have run out.'

'Don't scare me, Grandad. What are you talking about?' said Orla.

'You may not have noticed while out on deck, but a large sailing ship was on the horizon. The captain and his crew are not alone. When I saw this ship my temper got the worst of me.'

'What does this mean?' said Jon.

'There are only two reasons why ships might come to Iceapelago,' said Rory. 'To trade, which is unlikely as we have nothing of any value to trade to strangers. Or to conquer, which I suspect is the captain's real purpose.'

'Didn't he save us?' said Kate. 'He was under no obligation to help us.'

'He was also kind to us, don't forget,' said Tony.

Rory allowed the siblings to extol the captain's virtues among themselves for a few minutes. He then interjected forcibly. 'I'm afraid you are innocents. This man whom you seem to admire has a motive for being in Iceapelago that he has not fully explained to us,' said Rory. 'Maybe it's time for a reality check.'

Jon and Orla knew from his tone of voice that Rory was highly agitated.

'We're a community of just over twenty in Malahide,' said Rory. 'After the Eriador Event, the castle and surrounds housed nearly a thousand people. What happened over the past decades? People died from disease, malnutrition, accidents, and mostly from old age. And more people will die. The community will be no more quite soon as we have no children under twenty, and those we have – you two – want out.'

'That's a bit harsh, Grandad,' said Jon.

'Correct and harsh,' said Rory. 'Imagine what's been happening to other communities all over Europe since the dramatic climate events of the past decades. We've no idea to be honest. That's why the sudden and unexplained appearance of Portuguese ships should be seen for what it is – a direct threat to us.'

'But you've no evidence to support your suspicions,' said Kate. 'How can you be so sure?'

'Let's put things in perspective. We are a nation of islanders and have gotten used to that. We barely keep in contact with the other Iceapelago communities, never mind people from other nations. I had no contact with anyone from Cork Airport or the Old Kinsale for decades until Tony, Kate and Don appeared unannounced. Our collective *modus operandi*, in the absence of basic resources and raw materials, is self-sufficiency, and it has worked, at least so far. The Iceapelago communities feel safer and secure when they are left to their own devices.'

'Are we the last generation then?' said Orla.

'Orla, you are a member of the third generation of survivors, an Iceapelago 3 child. You have not experienced so many things that I took for granted before the Eriador Event. We had medical services, cars, planes and trains, electricity, clean water, a postal service, supermarkets, a plentiful supply of food, mobile phones, satellite access, television, radio, computers, the internet, social media and a thing called leisure time.'

'What's social media?' said Jon.

'That's a great question. It was a sort of electronic chatterbox that young people used to keep in contact. Like everything else, it is gone. No more holidays, no more music, no eating out as it was called, no theatre, no arts. In short, no more fun. Instead we eke out a basic existence and have done so for almost fifty years.'

'There's obviously a lot we don't know,' said Orla.

'And to answer the question you asked of me before my diatribe – yes, I am afraid you will be part of the last generation unless we, meaning you, do something about it. You will have children I hope, and they, in turn, will give you grandchildren. But as you can see from Malahide Castle, young people are a minority.'

'It's the same in Kinsale Head,' said Tony.

'Are there other communities we could link up with?' said Kate.

Rory was about to add further insights when a loud knock on the door interrupted his flow.

A crewman appeared, and gestured with his finger that they should follow him.

On deck, the first thing they saw was the huge mass of *La Santa Jorge* no more than a hundred metres on the starboard side.

'What in God's name is that?' said Rory.

Don pulled Rory's sleeve. 'Rory, a moment please,' said Don. 'Somewhere quiet. Over here.'

The two men walked to the prow of the ship. There was so much activity going on that they were barely noticed.

'What's up, Don?' said Rory.

'I've been observing a lot of activity since you went below deck,' said Don. 'I don't speak their language.'

'It's Portuguese,' said Rory. 'Nothing at all like English. More Roma than Roman.'

'Well, there's someone clearly in charge on *La Santa Jorge*. Captain da Gama rowed over just after you tried to strangle him. And what is more, several boats from other ships in the fleet made their way to the flagship. Judging by the colourful attire of the men and women that climbed aboard *La Santa Jorge*, I suspect they too are captains of the fleet.'

'It looks like a Council of War,' said Rory.

'I think you're right. They are hardly here for a holiday.'

'Did you see anything else?' said Rory.

'*La Santa Maria* has been fully re-stocked from *La Santa Jorge* with food and water. And not just that. At least thirty heavily armed soldiers were transported aboard. They have modern weapons, automatic machine guns and the like. They were taken to the aft quarters. *La Santa Maria* now has a full complement of crew.'

'Don, well done,' said Rory. 'What next?'

'My take is that *La Santa Jorge* has only recently arrived off the shore of Iceapelago. The mothership is supported by at least seven ships that are of similar size to *La Santa Maria*. This suggests to me that Captain da Gama was sent ahead for reconnaissance and when his work was done, he called in support.'

'That's more than plausible,' said Rory.

'*La Santa Maria* and the other ships have a very low draught. This would allow them get access to some Iceapelago communities in the same way as our cruisers did in the old days.'

'Are you suggesting the Portuguese have eyes on Iceapelago?'

'Yes,' said Don. 'And the man who seems to be calling the shots is on his way back to his ship.'

Don and Rory looked in wonderment as Captain da Gama, seated and strapped in a chair, was manoeuvred by a trip wire and pulley over the open ocean between the two ships.

Once unbuckled, he made a beeline straight for Rory.

'We need to speak. Mr Don, could you kindly leave us alone for a while?' Don did what he was told and went below deck. 'I am commanding a few ships of a fleet that will sail to Dundrum, and I would like you to join us,' said the captain.

'Do I have a choice?' said Rory.

'Yes, you do of course. I believe it best for your grandchildren that you cooperate.'

'Are you threatening me? It seems like that from where I stand.'

Rory's blood was beginning to boil. From past experience he knew he was tensing up. He started to breathe more slowly.

'The young adults will be safe. I promise you. Before we sail, they will be transferred to *La Santa Jorge* where conditions are much better.'

'I don't believe you.'

'You will have to take my word,' said the captain. 'You are known in Dundrum. I need you to be our contact with the community's leaders. That is not a threat. Only a request for a degree of cooperation.'

'I was known there decades ago. There's nobody alive in Dundrum that would recognise me,' said Rory.

'You would be surprised,' said the captain. 'Your reputation in Dundrum is still high. The Deputy Commander of Iceapelago is still talked about.'

'How do you know that?' said Rory. 'Aren't you sup- posedly a stranger to these shores?'

'I have my sources,' said the captain. 'Let us leave it at that.'

Rory was having none of it.

'Captain, my suspicions about you being in our waters are getting more profound. You turn up for dinner at my table by appointment, take our hospitality. You had us more or less locked up. And now it is all sweetness and light as I'm expected to be the lead for a visit to our old foe and unfriendly neighbour. What's the purpose of this visit, may I ask?'

'You may, but I am not at liberty to divulge this infor- mation. I am under orders.'

'So am I. I'm committed to keeping the peace across Iceapelago, and I'll not be part of any plan that seeks to threaten us.'

'Are you sure?'

'I've never been more certain of anything in my life.'

'So be it then,' said the captain. 'I have no option but to put you in chains.' He raised his hand.

Before Rory knew what was happening, two crewmen had him on the ground, shackling his hands and feet with a secure lock and chain.

'Curse on you, Captain,'

The captain turned his back on him and walked off. At the same time, the crew manhandled him roughly across the deck and through the door leading to the crew's quar- ters where the ship's prison cells were located.

All the while, the two pairs of siblings and Don were totally unaware of what was happening up on deck. They were having a leisurely lunch. The conversation, as before, turned to the past. There was so much to talk about. So much to understand.

'Don, tell us more about the inter-island cruisers,' said Orla. 'What exactly happened to them?'

Of all the young adults, it was becoming apparent to Don that she had the most heightened sense of curiosity and possibly the greatest sense of adventure.

'The Big Storm did all the damage,' said Don. 'I don't know about Iceapelago communities other than mine at Cork Airport Island, but our fleet of seven cruisers were flooded, sinking within hours of the first squalls hitting the coast. I suspect the cruisers in other communities met a similar fate.'

'Yes,' said Jon. 'The Malahide Castle cruisers were flung against the marina wall and were shattered to bits. One or two lie full of holes in shallow water to the east of the island. We salvaged as much as we could from the wreckage, including the on-board radio system and batteries as well as the solar panel used to power the unit.'

'And the cruiser that took my family and friends to the Old Head of Kinsale was beached and is in a state of disuse,' said Kate.

'In their heyday, the Iceapelago fleet comprised over a hundred cruisers,' said Don. 'These vessels were skilfully adapted and re-engineered from the tourist boats that used to cruise the River Shannon. Run on electric batteries powered by small solar panels, and with a very low draught, they could get to most locations with ease.'

'What was your job, Don?' said Orla.

'I was in charge of the Cork Airport Island cruiser fleet. Not only that but as we travelled to Dundrum most weeks, I got to know most of the other pilots as we were called.

Sadly, I have not met one of my former comrades since the Big Storm. They met the same fate as their beloved boats.'

'And with no transport, we had no option but to become self-sufficient island communities?' said Orla.

'Yes, and some Iceapelago communities managed better than others,' said Don. 'I guess only the most resourceful and those with solid housing structures survived. Don't forget the radio antennae we relied upon for inter-community communications were all blown down.'

'So there could be people on other islands?' said Kate.

'I suppose so,' said Don. 'But like us, they would be very wary of straying too far from their own island. As the seasons unfolded, we all became aware that life was going to get much harder, so I imagine, as we did in Kinsale Head, everyone knuckled down to grow crops, prepare meat and harvest water. All the basics, really.'

'What a disaster,' said Orla.

'I couldn't agree more,' said Kate.

They fell silent. The sound of bananas being chewed, tomatoes being digested and washed down with water filled the room.

Eventually, Orla spoke. 'Don, where's Grandad?'

'Not far. I left him on deck a while back talking to the captain.'

'I need to ask him a question. You continue the chat. I'll be back in a minute or two.'

Orla wanted to ask her grandfather what was going on. She had become very unsettled when the captain returned from *La Santa Jorge*. Instead of greeting his new guests as he usually did with a bow and a wave of his hat, he ignored them, striding towards the crew's quarters. She was good at detecting changes in peoples' moods. There were plenty of mood swings among the Malahide Castle community.

On deck, she was surprised to see only one crewman on duty, and he was repairing the jib sail that broke lose during the recent squall. There was another sailor at the tiller. Not knowing what to do, she walked to the door of the crew's quarters. She was about to open the door when it burst open. Captain da Gama appeared filling the entire door frame.

'Ah, Orla, I am glad we bumped into each other,' said the captain, stepping forward while closing the cabin door. Orla thought she heard muffled shouts before the door was shut tight.

'Plans have been made by the admiral. You, your brother and your friends from Kinsale will transfer first thing in the morning to the safety of *La Santa Jorge*. The flagship will remain in this vicinity while I sail with a few ships to Dundrum Island.'

'I left Malahide to sail to Dundrum Island,' said Orla. 'Being cooped up in *La Santa Jorge* may be more comfortable than here, but I would prefer if you could return me and my friends to the Malahide marina.'

'I am afraid my orders do not allow that,' said the captain.

'Orders? What orders? Whose orders?'

'The admiral is in charge of this fleet. We must do what he tells us.'

'I thought we were on a relaxed voyage to visit some of Iceapelago's communities under your charge. You agreed to chaperone us, did you not?'

'Things have changed, Orla,' said the captain. 'Now please retire to your quarters until the morning.'

'I want to talk to my grandfather,' said Orla.

'That is not possible,' said the captain.

'Why not? He came aboard as a free agent at your invitation.' Orla hesitated before continuing. She knew she might only have one opportunity to find her grandfather.

'He is still a free agent,' said the captain. 'In fact, he will join me and my ships as we sail to Dundrum.'

'He would never leave me and Jon without saying goodbye. What have you done to him?'

'Orla, please trust me,' said the captain.

'I couldn't possibly trust you. You're lying. You're concealing the true purpose of this fleet's presence close to our shores. And where is my grandfather? Tell me. Tell me now.' Orla rarely got angry. On this occasion she made an exception. She clasped her fist and swung it wide across the captain's face making contact with his nose.

The captain never saw the blow coming. The sharp pain as his nose broke stunned him. He dropped to his knees. As his vision re-adjusted, Orla was nowhere to be seen.

Having landed her blow, Orla ran as fast as she could to the dining room and burst unannounced into the room.

'What's wrong, Orla?' said Don. 'You look like you've seen a ghost.'

'Her hair is always like that,' said Jon.

Orla did not respond. Instead she started to push the table against the door.

'Help me. Help,' she roared. 'They've taken Grandad prisoner. We're next.'

'What?' said Jon. 'Is this one of your episodes, Orla?'

'Stop blabbering, for goodness sake. We need to reinforce the door before they come to take us.'

Rushed steps could be heard coming down the corridor.

'Now do you believe me? Push. Push.'

Five bodies heaved the solid oak table against the doorframe just as the persons outside tried to force it open.

'We need more weight,' said Orla, 'Drag the sideboard over here, will you?'

Willing hands had the solid wooden frame wedged atop the table in short order. With no other access to the room, they were safe – or so they thought.

With his personal quarters under siege and barricaded, and given Rory's unwillingness to cooperate, Captain da Gama decided to change his plan.

He met the captains of three other frigates of the fleet on the navigation deck.

'We cannot pander to the wishes of a few, so I have decided to proceed under sail to Dundrum straight away,' said the captain. 'It's about a ten-hour journey.' He pointed to a map location at a beach called Mount Anville. 'We land here. It is beside an old school complex. Two months ago, I personally did the reconnaissance of the track to Dundrum, which is no more than two kilometres away. We will arrive before dusk and should be at our target within an hour.

'What is the cover like?' said one of the captains.

'It is almost perfect,' said Captain da Gama. 'There is an old disused road between the beach and Dundrum Centre. It is covered by huge trees and lined by bushes. When I visited, there were no signs of recent activity on the route. We met nobody during the ten hours we spent checking out key locations.'

'Perfect.'

'Dundrum used to have a marina bustling with cruisers,' said the captain. 'I could find none during my short visit, not even wreckage. So finding a cruiser or two that could be repaired would be a bonus. They are much better suited at getting close to the shore than our ships.'

The sea captains continued to take notes.

'Time did not allow me to conduct a full search, but I suspect that Dundrum still has a working radio centre. The main building is over ten stories tall and has several antennae on the roof. I have no idea if they are active or not. The radio room should be taken intact if at all possible and kept secure.'

'What is the best outcome?' asked a captain.

'Dundrum was once the centre of the Iceapelago administration. That was then. Now it is almost deserted. We spotted very few people on the streets, and they were old and ragged. So securing its key buildings should not be too much trouble. The duke wants to be able to safely accommodate up to two thousands of our countrymen in Dundrum. Once Dundrum is secure, we will begin to occupy the neighbouring island communities starting with Malahide and Howth. When the final numbers are transferred from the Principality of Ria Formosa over five thousand of our citizens will be re-settled in the Dublin Bay region of Iceapelago.'

'Our poor countrymen cannot survive another season under oppressive heat and drought so rest assured, Captain, we will achieve our objectives,' said another captain.

'Between our ships, we have sixty well-armed grena-diers,' said Captain da Gama. 'Once we have dispatched any opposition, thirty will remain to secure the area, and begin repairs to house the first group of climate refugees that are due to land at Dundrum within two to three weeks.'

'What about the other ships?'

'We will then sail to either Malahide or Howth,' said the captain. 'I will decide when the time comes.'

'Prisoners?'

'There may be some loss of life if we are to capture Dundrum quickly, but I doubt if we will have any trouble given the high age profile of the community,' said the cap-tain. 'There is no need for senseless violence. If we meet armed opposition, we will deal with it. Move whoever opposes us to the basement area of the main building, which was once used as a gaol.'

'What about your troublemakers?'

'Rory will remain in chains below deck. He is useless to us and is more a distraction than an asset at this stage. The admiral can decide what to do with him when we have completed our mission.'

'And the others?'

'They are more a nuisance than anything else. Once we secure Dundrum, I will leave them there to stew. It will be their Van Diemen's Land. That is it for now. I will lead the fleet and will see you ashore at oh four hundred hours tomorrow.'

'Aye aye Captain.'

The ship's captains swiftly descended into awaiting rowing boats and were soon back aboard their own vessels shouting out instructions and orders.

Captain da Gama took charge of the tiller. He raised his hand. Within seconds, without a word being exchanged, the main sail and jib unfurled. Immediately *La Santa Maria* moved forward.

Rory sensed the movement and heard the lap of water against the side of the ship. He shuffled his chained torso into a more comfortable position in his cramped surroundings.

Those barricaded in the dining quarters also became aware that they were on the move. Where to, they had no idea. Tony was hungry and tired. He wondered if he and Kate had done the right thing in leaving Kinsale Head with such haste.

CHAPTER 8

Dundrum Island

'CAREFUL, CAREFUL,' SAID THE sergeant-at-arms.

His attention was focused on the tall reedy bank ahead. Metres from the shoreline, he leapt from the lead rowboat into waist-deep cold water. He held a rope tied to the aft hawser and pulled the boat closer to shore. Soon ten fully armed grenadiers stepped ankle deep onto the marshy landing point. They had been told it was a beach by way of a convenient explanation. But at this elevation there was no sand. As they pulled their boat ashore, five other craft followed in quick succession. The troops walked slowly to a gravel pavement a short distance from the landing point, and assembled in a line to await their orders. The quiet babble of low voices filled the dawn air.

'Sergeant,' said Captain da Gama. 'Your men are briefed, so proceed at pace.'

With a sharp salute, the sergeant signalled with his right hand, and jogged ahead of his troops. Within minutes, the early light of dawn slowly lit up their surroundings. Shadows disappeared. Tall wooden posts, what were once telegraph poles, framed the contours of the overgrown, weedy road that lay before them. There were no bird cries or animal noises. No dawn chorus.

A short time later, on cue, and from behind the cover of a building that was once the ticket deck for the cruiser terminal, the sergeant raised his left hand. His grenadiers instantly stopped and squatted.

'What do you see?' said the captain who joined the sergeant at the front of the column.

'Nothing for the moment, Captain,' said the sergeant. He scanned the horizon with his army binoculars. 'It appears the people of Dundrum do not take early walks. It is strange. No sounds either. At this hour, you would expect to at least see a few mongrels searching for scraps.'

The captain noticed it instantly. A smell, the rancid sickly odour of death.

'Sergeant, take a small detachment and proceed to that tall building ahead of us,' said the captain. 'It is the main entrance of the old shopping centre that is now used for accommodation. Let me know once you have secured the ground floor.'

Without a word, six grenadiers ran the three hundred metres up the overgrown steps to the entrance door breaking cover. It opened easily. The troops disappeared inside the building.

Captain da Gama turned to the other sergeants giving them orders to take the other buildings within the complex. They too broke cover and scattered in different directions.

Protected by a few remaining grenadiers, he again noticed the strong smell of early stages of putrefaction. It had dominated his hometown of Quinta do Lago after the Big Storm. Bodies remained where they had fallen for months. Nobody was prepared to bury the diseased and dismembered. They lay rotting until there was nothing left but raw carcasses. Over time, the process of the anaerobic splitting of proteins by bacteria and fungi ended. Only then did the air clear.

He was reflecting on this apocalyptic memory and did not immediately spot a sergeant beckoning to him from the entrance to the main building.

As there was nobody about, he had the confidence to walk across the concourse from the marina to the archway that delineated the entrance. The plastic sign above only contained the letters 'NDRUM.' The name sign of the building was broken as was much of the area around and inside the front door. Broken glass lay everywhere as did the detritus of uncaring users.

And the smell was much worse inside. Captain da Gama took out a handkerchief and put it over his nose.

'You will need that,' said the sergeant. 'It is intense on the lower floors. Follow me.'

The captain did what he was told. He had not entered any of the buildings when he did his earlier exploration and had no idea what to expect. He walked up the large spiral staircase. The concrete steps were chipped. The metal bannisters were greasy. He removed his hand from the railing, noticing a line of yellow slime on his fingers, which he rubbed off quickly on his trouser leg. *What was that?* he thought.

'Stop here, Captain,' said the sergeant. They were outside a door marked Medical Centre. 'You will soon find out why the place stinks.'

With his gloved hand the sergeant turned the handle and opened the door. A tsunami of hot, putrid air rushed out the opening. The captain hesitated as the waft of tepid air hit his nose like an express train.

'You will need to see this, sir,' said the sergeant. 'Come in.'

Captain da Gama walked two paces into what was the reception area for patients. All the plastic seats, some twenty, were occupied with rotting corpses. Their state of decomposition was well advanced. The skulls were mainly eye-less.

'What happened to these poor souls?' said the captain. 'It looks like they all died together, around the same time.'

'And there are no obvious wounds,' said the sergeant. 'Captain, do not go any nearer. I think the bodies may be contagious. See the yellow fluids on the floor.'

The captain gasped as on closer examination it was apparent that this coloured liquid had leaked from all the bodies.

'Get out of here. Lock the door and leave them. There is not much we can do at this stage.'

One of the grenadiers appeared by his side clearly out of breath.

'What did you find, Ramon?' said the sergeant.

'I did exactly what you told me. I went to the top floor, all ten stories high, and searched for the radio room. It wasn't too hard to find. I followed the smell and the bluebottles.'

'Did you find it, Ramon?'

'Yes, with two dead radio operators laying astride the equipment. I did not dare touch anything.'

'That was wise.'

'Let us go,' said the sergeant. 'Captain, are you OK for the climb?'

Before he could respond, the troops that had been dispatched to the other buildings arrived. They looked grey from fright as if they had seen a haunting of ghosts.

'Captain, there are bodies everywhere. Some look like...'

'Like they are infected,' said the captain, finishing his sentence.

'Yes, and the stink is over-powering. What should we do?'

'Get out in the open and stay there with your troops,' said the captain. 'We will join you as soon as possible.'

A sense of anxiety spread among the new arrivals about their presence at this infected site.

'Let us hope it is not as bad on the top floors. Sergeant, Ramon, you and I will scout the radio room.'

Five floors up, the odour was less pungent.

'Fewer people died here,' said the captain talking through his handkerchief.

'Seems likely,' said the sergeant. 'There are no accommodation units on the upper floors.'

They pressed on and soon reached the staircase to the upper level. A sign *Executive Suites* was prominently displayed opposite the unused lift shaft that was open with its steel cables visible.

'I imagine this place was a hub of activity once,' said the captain.

'This way,' said Ramon.

He opened the swing doors that revealed a long corridor. The captain opened the first door. This time with his gloved hand. He walked into the room.

'Look here.'

Atop the Dundrum Centre the vista was stunning. All the floor-to-ceiling windows in what had once been a large meeting room that occupied two sides of the building were broken. A stiff breeze diluted the dominance of the smell.

'There is our ship,' said the captain.

La Santa Maria was anchored offshore about two kilometres to the east. An ocean of blue water covered what was once the City of Dublin. The vastness of an enlarged Dublin Bay lay before them. Two red and white columns defined the near distance.

'According to the charts,' said the captain, 'They are the tops of a long disused power station. And way far in the distance is the Hill of Howth. Over there is the tip of Killiney Hill. It is uninhabited. So too are the high hills of the Dublin mountains.'

'This is very much like Quinta do Lago,' said the sergeant. 'Only the lowest points remain habitable.'

'The La Palma Event may have happened long ago, but we still live with its consequences,' said the captain. 'No time for sightseeing. Ramon, where is the radio room?'

'Four doors down on the left, sir.'

They walked further along the corridor.

'Be careful, Captain,' said the sergeant. He pushed the door open. 'Do not touch anything whatever you do.'

The smell was less intense. They could see why. The two bodies that lay prone across the radio set were not long dead, but dead they were judging by the yellow snot oozing from their noses.

'What are we to do?' said the sergeant.

'The plan was to report to the admiral on the outcome of our sortie. Depending on what we found, he would give us fresh orders.'

'The set is live,' said Ramon. 'See the green response button.'

Sure enough, under the arms of one of the corpses, a light flickered. The captain noticed that the body held a microphone in her hand. He could also see that the person had some stature judging by the quality of her uniform.

'Sergeant, lift them away from the equipment.'

Despite the risks, the sergeant and Ramon pulled the bodies away, and dragged them out of the radio room into the corridor.

Being trained in using radio equipment, the captain examined what lay in front of him and on other desks in the room. He pressed the live button.

The sergeant and Ramon returned.

'This is the largest radio unit I have ever seen,' said the captain. 'In addition to this main set, which is live by the way, some seven operators would have worked here. This must have been the Dundrum communication hub. Amazing. I have never seen anything like it before.'

'Is that you, Six?' said a voice coming from the speaker. 'I've been trying to contact you for days now.'

'Who is speaking?' said the captain.

He took the microphone in his gloved hand.

The radio voice detected a strange accent.

'Where's the Dundrum Six? What's going on there?'

'Who am I speaking to please?' said the captain.

'The Howth Six,' came the reply.

'Nice to talk to you. My name is Captain Vasco da Gama. I was invited to Dundrum as a guest of the Dundrum Six,' lied the captain. 'I have bad news, I am afraid.'

Once he explained the gruesome circumstances of the deaths pervading Dundrum, the captain spoke to the Howth Six for nearly an hour. He was friendly in tone, and as a result, the Howth Six opened up about his friendship with the deceased Dundrum Six. More importantly, he spoke about his own community. He confirmed much of what the captain had gleaned from his covert visit. Slowly but surely, the captain built a level of trust with the Howth Six.

'Where will you go now?' asked the Six.

'Could we visit Howth for a night or two while we take stock of our situation?' said the captain. 'Rest assured, we are all healthy and virus-free. We kept well away from all infected people.'

'I suppose so,' said the Six. 'I would have doubts if you were carrying the virus.' While still grieving for his friend, the Six did not have time to think through the implications of the invite.

'How many are you?'

'My ship's compliment is ten,' said the captain.

'We'll manage that number. See you in a few days then. I best sign off.' With that the line went dead.

'So Howth Head is next?' said the sergeant.

'Obviously,' said the captain. 'This time, though, I will bring Rory along. He and the Howth Six seem to be good friends of sorts. Let us get out of this godforsaken place.'

'And leave the dead to the crows,' said the sergeant.

CHAPTER 9

Escape Plan

'IT'S BEEN NEARLY TWENTY-FOUR hours since we returned from the short sailing trip to Dundrum,' said Orla.

'And three days since we had any food,' said Jon. 'Can we not get out of here? What's the point in barricading ourselves without access to food and water?'

'They'll move us to the *La Santa Jorge*,' said Don. 'Can it be any worse than this place?'

'I suppose not,' said Kate. 'We've nothing to lose at this stage.'

The lack of sanitary arrangements and communal claustrophobia, while not mentioned expressly, were the backdrop to a noticeable change in mood among the self-incarcerated.

'Let's remove the furniture from the door and take our chances with this admiral guy,' said Don. He sensed the young adults needed a bit of leadership. Left to their own devices they would dither and delay. Years of living an agrarian and routine existence had knocked a sense of daring and risk-taking out of them. *So much for the younger generation,* he mused.

With little effort, but with much noise, the door's blockages were removed.

Don opened the door and followed by the four siblings walked down the narrow short corridor and up the stairs to the main deck.

Four sailors met them. It was as if they were expected. Gesticulating furiously with their tanned fists, they pointed to the zip line tripod that connected *La Santa Maria* to the flagship at anchor some one hundred metres to starboard.

'I think they want to transfer us to *La Santa Jorge* straight away,' said Don.

'There's no way I'm getting on that contraption,' said Jon. He saw the cabling was being tightened for use by one of the crew. 'I can't swim, you know.'

'The sea is calm,' said Orla.

'I don't care whether it's a gale or not. I'm not getting on that rig.'

'We've no option, Jon,' said Orla. 'Please be reasonable for once.'

'You're not listening to me. I hate heights more than I fear the sea. Give me some slack please.'

'I know. This is not easy for any of us,' said Orla.

They could see activity aboard *La Santa Jorge* as a counterpart crew readied the zip line at their end.

A sailor moved forward with his sword drawn. He grunted at Jon, jabbing him in the stomach with the point of the sword. The cut tore his shirt but did not penetrate his skin. The angry, impatient gesture was enough to persuade Jon to change his mind.

'You're first, it seems,' said Orla. 'Let me help you get into the bucket seat.'

She pulled the bucket seat towards her and held the main cable with her right hand.

Two crew members gently removed her grip. With expert hands, they strapped a pliable Jon into the seat, placed a leather safety harness across his chest, and secured it in place. He watched in stunned silence as the seat was then attached to two cables. It jolted as it was raised into position about a metre over the deck.

'Oh bloody hell,' said Jon, closing his eyes.

The crew roared at their opposite numbers on the *La Santa Jorge* and made signals with their hands. The cables tightened. The bucket seat rose sharply in the air and was over the side of the ship in an instant. It zipped across the water before Jon could cry out.

Jon imagined the transfer took several minutes. In fact, he was unloaded onto the main deck of *La Santa Jorge* in under twenty seconds. The crew grunted at him as they removed the safety harness in a hurry. He moved aside as the bucket seat was raised off the ground and flew back over the side of the ship with the cables tightening under the control of the crew.

He looked across and down at *La Santa Maria*. She was much smaller than the flagship. He reckoned the main deck was at least five metres higher. The width of the ship was also impressive, and as for the towering masts that held a vast acreage of sails ready for use. His observations ended abruptly as his sister, securely strapped in the bucket seat, flew over his head. The crew carefully lowered their human cargo and held her hand as she stepped out.

'Well, that was some experience,' said Orla. 'I've never enjoyed myself as much. What an adrenaline rush. Do you think they would let me do it again?'

'You're incorrigible, sister,' said Jon, hugging her. 'I'm just glad you're safe.'

In short order, Don, Tony, and Kate were also transported aboard.

'That was some thrill,' said Kate.

They heard a huge steely clattering noise that blocked out their conversation.

'They're raising the anchor,' said Don. 'We'll be under sail in a moment.'

The main sail and jib were released from the masts by unseen hands. The ship shuddered as the wind caught the sails. It moved at speed in short order. The group were mesmerised by the manoeuvre. When they turned around, they discovered they were face-to-face with the admiral and a small armed entourage.

'Where's my grandfather?' said Orla.

'Safe and secure,' said the admiral in a heavily accented tone and a much deeper voice than Captain da Gama.

'He is on *La Santa Maria* that will be soon setting sail to Howth Head.'

'We left him behind,' said Orla. 'I didn't know he was still on the ship. We were told he was part of the visiting party to Dundrum and would be staying there.'

'His dogged obstinance forced me to change my plan,' said the admiral.

'You have no right to keep him locked up.'

'I see obstinacy runs in the family,' said the admiral, smiling to reveal a set of broken, crooked teeth. 'You and your friends are going nowhere anytime soon. I will lay anchor off Lambay Island and await the outcome of our meeting with the Howth Six. *La Santa Jorge* is at your disposal, so make the best use of it. You will have a large cabin with bunk beds that will not be under lock and key. You are free to walk about unaccompanied. The only exception are the crew's quarters on decks three and four. What's your name?'

'Don.'

'See that these young people behave themselves, Signor Don,' said the admiral. 'My crew are under orders to use force if they cause any trouble.'

'I'm not their parent,' said Don.

'Their parents will not thank you if you do not keep a close watch on them. Remember you are all here under the grace and favour of Captain da Gama. Why he ever took you under his charge is beyond me.' He turned to the siblings. 'Am I clear?'

They nodded. While the captain was stern, his boss was certainly not one to cross. They walked slowly to their cabin, which was compact and warm.

'I'm bored,' said Orla hours later.

'I'm not,' said Jon.

'But we've been sitting about doing nothing,' said his sibling. 'What's the point being on this behemoth of a ship if we're not able to go where we please? We left Malahide Castle on the premise that Captain da Gama would sail us to other Iceapelago communities.'

'Plans changed as you know, sister. There's not much we can do about it is there?'

'We might try to escape,' said Orla.

'Be realistic, Orla. Even if we got off *La Santa Jorge* where would we go?' said Don. 'There are at least six ships in the fleet around us.'

'And over two hundred armed sailors,' said Tony.

'But we're just six kilometres as the gull flies to the marina at Malahide Castle,' said Orla.

'It might just as well be a hundred kilometres,' said Jon. 'Think it through, Orla. If we tried to get off the ship our absence would be noticed almost immediately. What then? We'll be tracked down for certain. The admiral would punish us. I don't think we want to be on the wrong side of an argument with him.'

'Remember what the admiral said,' said Don. 'I'll not be responsible for jeopardising anyone of you. Besides the Malahide community is not aware that this fleet is anchored so close to the castle. Cleverly, the admiral has his ships out of the direct line of sight of Malahide Castle behind the offshore wind arrays.'

'What's in store for our family and friends?' said Orla.

'I dare not speculate,' said Jon.

'By the way, is there a cruiser anywhere on Malahide Castle Island?' said Don.

Jon looked at Orla who blurted out 'Yes, but it's not seaworthy.'

'Where is it?' said Don.

'As far away as possible from the castle,' said Jon. 'After the Big Storm, we managed to float it after it sank at the marina.'

'So it is in working order?' said Don.

'Actually no,' said Jon. 'The basic idea was to get the cruiser away from the marina that had been destroyed to a safer location on the opposite side of the island near a cove beside the old graveyard. We intended to repair the cruiser over time as it was our only means of transport off the island. However, when we were under way it became apparent that the tear to the hull was unrepairable. The cruiser started to sink. We managed to beach it before we got to the cove. I saw it a few weeks ago. The top deck is visible at low tide.'

'Were its solar panels working before you abandoned ship?'

'Yes.'

'Hmm,' said Don. 'I like a challenge.'

'What do you mean?' said Kate.

'Well, didn't I get you off the Old Head of Kinsale?'

'But that was on an inflatable?'

'All Iceapelago cruisers have inflatables. Does your wreck have one?'

'I don't honestly know,' said Jon.

'Can I speak?' said Tony.

'Sure,' said Don.

'Forget about salvaging the cruiser for a moment. Let's do a reality check. Why are we locked up?'

'You tell me,' said Kate.

'I suspect the admiral is awaiting a report from Captain da Gama when he returns from whereover he is at the moment. That will determine what he does next.'

'Meaning?' said Kate.

'Watching the sailors, I'm in no doubt that they came to Iceapelago to occupy some of our communities.'

'Get real, Tony,' said Orla.

'Real means that if conditions in Portugal are as bad or worse than here, the admiral has plans to ship his citizens to the safest and most sustainable islands of Iceapelago.'

'Bless your imagination,' said Jon.

'I think Tony is right,' said Don. 'It's not the first time that invaders for the want of a better word tried to steal our homes and supplies. Would I be correct to say that Malahide Castle and its environs could easily house a thousand climate refugees if food production was stepped up?'

'But we are a small community of barely twenty people,' said Orla.

'Yes, but not that long ago, and after the Eriador Event, the castle lands hosted over two thousand people. The castle itself could easily accommodate five hundred.'

'At a push,' said Orla.

'If you were facing drought, starvation, and potential destruction, you wouldn't care if your new living conditions were a bit crowded.'

'The point being?'

'Desperate people will do desperate things if they have no alternative.'

'That sounds credible, but can we get back to my proposition? How do we get off this ship?' said Orla.

'Don, have you any ideas?' said Tony. He knew Don had more experience of the world than all the siblings combined.

'I've been on all the decks, and they have one thing in common,' said Don.

'What are you talking about?' said Orla.

'*La Santa Jorge* is a converted sailing ship that was originally built nearly two centuries ago. It is big, at four hundred tonnes with a three metre displacement, and capacity for five hundred crew. Though it has much less than that at the moment. For marine safety reasons, it is fully equipped with inflatables located at the stern of each deck. We'll launch one into the sea and sail off into the sunset. That's our exit strategy.'

'Brilliant,' said Tony. 'I never doubted you.'

'Early this morning, I managed to spend half an hour unseen at the stern of deck level three.'

'Isn't that beside the admiral's quarters?' said Tony.

'It is but believe it or not, because of the cold, he keeps the window portals firmly shut. Even if he was in his cabin, he couldn't hear us. I got onto a two metre wide ledge that is accessible from the main storage area aft. It's a blind spot, that's for sure. The inflatable is more or less the same size as the one we salvaged from the cruiser in the Old Head of Kinsale. I was able to loosen the safety fasteners. I reckon with little effort we could cast it into the sea.'

'What then?' said Tony.

'Here's the rub,' said Don, 'when it hits the water, it will automatically inflate to full size. That means we have to wait for that to happen before we jump in the sea.'

'Jump in the sea? I can't swim, need I remind you!' said Jon.

'I've taken that into account. I'll jump first to secure the inflatable. It's only a drop of five metres. There will be life jackets inside. I'll put these in the water, and you can then jump. When you surface hold onto the nearest jacket. Tony and Kate are good swimmers, and they will go first. Then you Jon, followed by Orla.'

'That seems far too easy,' said Orla. 'Can we assume the crew will silently watch on? There are armed guards posted all over the ship 24/7?'

'Last night I did a walkabout to meet these guards. There are six, three on each side. They are armed, yes. At two o'clock in the morning, all but one was asleep at their posts. The guards change at midnight. The new guards had the benefit of a long dinner with plenty of wine. It's no surprise they were asleep on duty. Also they are positioned on the main deck. We'll be in a blind spot at the stern just above the rudder. If we make noise, there is a risk we could be found. If we're careful, my plan might work.'

'Anything to get off this dreadful ship,' said Orla.

'When do we go?' said Tony.

'I've also been busy checking the tides,' said Don. 'I guess we're on the leeside of Lambay Island. This area is very tidal, and it looks like there is a strong rip current at low tide.'

'What does that mean?' said Tony.

'Low tide was at three o'clock last night. We need to be positioned about five hundred metres off the starboard bow for the current to take us towards the channel at Malahide. That means we should plan to leave in about six hours' time. If we catch the current, we will drift almost silently past the fleet. With two of you at the oars it should take us no more than three hours to get to the Malahide marina.'

'Great,' said Orla. 'That simple!'

'At least it's a plan that can be abandoned at any stage prior to us jumping into the sea. I suggest we save our strength over the coming hours and get some rest.'

Tony approached Don when the others had dozed off. He beckoned him to move out of the cabin with him.

'What's up?'

'I have a confession to make,' said Tony.

'Go on,' said Don.

'My laptop, well my grandmother's laptop, contains details of an armoury that is concealed on Cork Airport Island somewhere at the rear of the airport.'

'Armoury? What are you talking about? Cork Airport Island was destroyed long ago. It's totally abandoned to the best of my knowledge.'

'I know, but the last time I could access this computer I saw photographs of all sorts of heavy equipment.'

'What has this to do with our escape plan?'

'If we get the Malahide cruiser afloat and it is seaworthy, I suggest we go to Cork Airport Island to locate and test the equipment. The admiral's ships have primitive defences compared to the best of what the Canadian Army rangers left behind them.'

'Tony, I am really puzzled. Are you suggesting that we could attack these ships?'

'Not only that but we could sink a few. I have seen a video of a drone, a hoverbike it is called, that is mounted with a machine gun pod and small rockets.'

'Who is going to fly the drone?'

'Details, Don, details. I am telling you this in confidence. Kate does not even know about the cache of arms. And if she knew I had grandmother's computer, I'd be scalped.'

'Very well then. The prospect of travelling to Cork Airport Island will surely motivate you and I to ensure that we get off this ship tonight.'

CHAPTER 10

The Howth Six

Rory was unshackled before he was told to disembark. The crew fed him well during the short voyage. He awaited news about the reason *La Santa Maria* had sailed to Howth Head. He suspected that it was something to do with the sortie to Dundrum that had happened in his absence.

He was engulfed with emotions as he stepped onto the decking of the Howth Head marina. His eyes welled with tears. His whole body shuddered as distant, sad, and frightening memories flooded in.

Before the Big Storm he had travelled every year to Howth Head to take part in the annual Eriador anniversary event commemoration hosted by the then Commander of Iceapelago. It was his time to pray for his first wife and young boys who like so many others were drowned when the Atlantic and La Palma tsunamis hit what was then Ireland. It was hard to believe that was over forty years ago. And he had not visited Howth Head since the Big Storm. He wondered if anything had changed.

With the crew of *La Santa Maria* and a second vessel secured at the quayside, Rory looked around to try and find familiar buildings.

The first thing that struck him immediately was the absence of anyone. There were no other vessels tied up at the marina. Years ago, hundreds of people would be milling around the harbour area, especially ahead of the commemoration with endless speeches from the great and the good. Traders, travellers, and troubadours mixed and mingled. Not so today.

He observed that most of the buildings had survived the Big Storm. They were solid, mostly built from granite blocks. He recognised what was once the harbourmaster's office, or at least what was left of her office. The storm surge had burst through the windows that were open to the elements. He wondered if the buildings higher up Howth Head were in better shape.

He sat on a cement bollard just off the quayside as his thoughts overwhelmed him. He was almost dizzy with anxiety. After Malahide Castle, Howth Head Island was one of the most prosperous communities in Iceapelago. *Now look at it. Everything has changed utterly in a few short years.*

Thinking about his dead wife and family, something he had not done in years, Rory became maudlin. He sat for ages processing his recollections of a wonderful woman and his two darling boys who were among the first victims of the Eriador tsunamis. With a deep sigh he snapped out of his dark mood. He was in Howth Head for a purpose. Best to concentrate on what might lie ahead.

He saw a movement out of the side of his eye, or at least he thought he did. He stood up and walked slowly towards the body of a rusty derelict truck. Its tyres had been removed. The tailboard proclaimed it was *Wrights of Howth – Fishmongers*. He recalled vividly the mackerel fish suppers from Wrights. A summer treat of oily fish that was devoured by his family as they sat on a bench at one of the many restaurants that traded opposite where the trawlers were moored. That was then. Happy days long gone.

He discerned another flash of movement this time under the truck. He stepped back a few paces and looked under the chassis. A pair of soulful eyes met his. He recognised the ragged, bony frame of an Arctic fox. She sat still as if communicating that she too was suffering. Her circumstances also changed for the worst after the Eriador Event. The fox pawed the ground and turning on its heels, sped off in the direction of the nearest building. Rory guessed that this fox or one of her family, had chased his dog Alfie when they last came to Howth. He was glad to see the Arctic foxes had survived, as indeed had the humans they sought to avoid.

'Over here, Rory,' said the captain.

This command brought Rory back to reality with a bang. His nightmares would have to wait.

Three lines of armed grenadiers stood to attention on the quayside awaiting orders.

'Where does the Howth Six reside?' said the captain.

'The Howth Six? I haven't seen him since the Big Storm. Glad to know Brendan is still alive. He and I were good friends.'

'Friend or not, where does he live?' said the captain.

'He is a resident of the Abbey Tavern. This famous hospitality venue was adapted after the Eriador Event to house the Six, his family and their retainers.'

'Where is this Abbey Tavern place?' said the captain.

'Is he expecting you?' said Rory. 'Never mind. It's a five minute walk up the street. Follow me.'

The captain signalled the bulk of the grenadiers to follow, leaving a handful to guard the two ships that had been secured at the berth.

Rory knew the Abbey Tavern well. It was from its raised deck that he had observed the speeches at the Eriador Event anniversary from a discreet distance. Built in the sixteenth century, the Abbey Tavern was a renowned hospitality venue, and was the main reason to visit Howth for many. This iconic venue, with its original stone floors, blazing turf fires and memorabilia on every wall, was once a constant draw for thirsty and hungry clients.

But Rory's trek up the main street of Howth to the Abbey Tavern had a different purpose. Of that, he was sure. He walked slowly without the support of his cane.

On turning the corner at Main Street, Rory was surprised to see the Howth Six and other senior members of the community standing on the elevated porch in front of the main door of the Abbey Tavern.

'Rory, is that you?' said the Howth Six. 'You've aged well, it seems. What are you doing here?'

'Brendan, it's great to see you,' said Rory, moving forward to give his old friend a manly hug.

'Can we go inside?' said Captain da Gama. 'We can do our introductions better from the comfort of inside the building.'

Rory and the Howth Six exchanged eye contact. They moved inside to the vast dining area. The captain ignored the display of wall decorations advertising the many famous musicians that had played the venue over the generations. Obviously completely disinterested in the building's history, he took a stance at the centre of the table and beckoned the Howth residents to take a seat.

'Captain, we have arranged some refreshments for you and your companions in the lounge area,' said the Howth Six.

'That can wait. I am here on business, not as a tourist.'

Rory sat down beside the Howth Six and his colleagues directly opposite the captain who sat alone at the table.

The formal introductions took a short while.

'It's been decades since any foreign visitor has visited Howth,' said the Howth Six. 'When we spoke on the radio, Captain, you said you would like to stay for a day or two. I'm glad to offer Howth hospitality, but I can't but help notice that you have brought heavily armed soldiers with you.'

Captain da Gama stood up suddenly, pushing back his chair. It clattered to the floor. After this dramatic gesture, he looked down on the leaders of the Howth community sitting peacefully in front of him across the narrow oblong inlaid mahogany table.

'I told you, Six, when we spoke on the radio that I had important business to discuss,' said the captain. He put his two hands on the table and made direct eye contact with his host. 'And thank you for agreeing to meet with me. My message is simple. I have an order from Admiral Rodriquez to requisition Howth Head Island and all its properties and peoples on behalf of the Duke and the Principality of Ria Formosa.'

'What?' said the Howth Six. He jumped out of his seat to face the captain who towered over him.

'You heard me. Please sit down. I am here to sort out the practicalities. What I am saying, and let me be clear, is that I am authorised to occupy Howth Head Island and to acquire all its properties and supplies.'

'You'll do no such thing,' said the Howth Six. 'We've lived here for generations under the protection of the Commander of Iceapelago. We'll not allow strangers to take what we possess and rightfully own.'

'Yes, you will, Six,' said the captain.

In a split second, Captain da Gama, stretched across the table, swiftly withdrawing his gilded side knife from its scabbard. With the minimum of movement, he plunged it upwards into the Howth Six's neck under his jawbone. He twisted the dagger before removing the weapon. He stepped back as a fountain of blood burst from the wound covering anyone who was seated beside the Six.

The Howth Six remained suspended briefly, trying to gurgle a response before he collapsed like a bag of bones to the floor. His blood covered his lifeless body.

'And do not try anything stupid,' said the captain turning to Rory. 'You are in charge here now.'

'I'll have nothing to do with your murdering intent,' said Rory who was covered in his friend's blood.

'Oh, but you will,' said the captain. 'Let me put it this way – for the sake of your grandchildren.'

'You wouldn't dare,' said Rory.

'All that I have to do is to radio the admiral and they will be past tense. If you calm down, nobody else will get hurt.'

Rory had long suspected that the mariner was a chameleon. All was sweetness and apple pie when he wanted to persuade people to his way of doing things. And now the captain's true character had finally emerged. He was totally ruthless, totally uncompromising if he was crossed. He was on a mission and would not be stopped. The corpse of the Howth Six at his feet confirmed his worst fears.

'For the sake of his wife and the other women, can we remove his body?' said Rory.

'Whatever you need to do, do it. I will be back here in ten minutes. Then we will discuss how my orders will be obeyed.' The captain gestured to his sailors who snapped to attention and marched out of the room.

The worst of the bloody mess had been cleared up before the captain returned. The Six's widow was being comforted by family members who were all in a state of shock.

'This is a one-to-one meeting, so everybody else must leave the room,' said the captain.

'Do what he says,' said Rory. 'Nobody wants any more bloodshed.'

Silently the room emptied.

'I want guarantees about my grandchildren's safety before we go any further,' said Rory.

'You are in no position to negotiate, Rory,' said the captain.

'And you're in no position to secure the collaboration of this Iceapelago community unless I make it happen. So here is what you're going to do. I'll listen to what you have in mind. But before I do anything, I want to speak to my grandchildren on the radio. You've a working set on *La Santa Maria,* and the Howth Head radio is similar to what we've at the castle.'

'I will sort that out, Rory, I promise.'

'I don't trust you or any of your promises, am I clear? You broke your word to provide safe passage to my grandchildren and their new friends from Kinsale Head, don't forget.'

'Things changed with the arrival of the admiral,' said the captain.

'Get on with it then,' said Rory.

He noticed that the captain was starting to perspire, and his hand trembled slightly. The room was cold so he thought it might be the beginnings of a fever.

'Our population in the Principality of Ria Formosa cannot survive because of climate change, and the myriad of natural disasters that have befallen us,' said the captain. 'Admiral Rodriguez asked me months ago to scout options for a new frontier as a place to settle our clans. And I found Iceapelago. Not ideal in some respects, but the surviving communities in the Dublin Bay region have the capacity, food and basic medical supplies to cope with our planned exodus. Your temperate climate, despite the rain, makes Iceapelago one of the most attractive destinations in the Northern Hemisphere for climate refugees. We intend to colonise Iceapelago before another population gets the same idea.'

'I can't believe what I am hearing,' said Rory. 'You're breaking the law in forcing us to share our resources with a strange people we've never met.'

'Rory, there are no laws. Or at least nobody willing or able to enforce them. You are making an incorrect assumption that we want to share your resources. As soon as I have an inventory of what is available on Howth Head Island, everyone here will be shipped to Dundrum Island. There will be no sharing of anything.'

'But I was told Dundrum is a wasteland,' said Rory.

'It may well be,' said the captain. 'But that is where these people, everyone at Malahide Castle and adjacent communities will be moved to, probably within a week.'

'Malahide?' said Rory.

'Can I be any clearer? I need to make space for our people.'

Rory's shock was clearly evident to an increasing sweaty captain.

'In a few days, troops from *La Santa Jorge* will occupy Malahide Castle,' said the captain. 'I gave the admiral a precise battle plan informed by what I observed during my recent dinner when enjoying your hospitality, and indeed when I visited two months ago in secret.'

'You're a thug and there's no other way to describe you,' said Rory.

'Thank you for the compliment,' said the captain. 'I am not expecting any trouble because you'll be there to explain what we want.'

'Why me?'

'Why not?' said the captain. 'My sources tell me you are the most respected man on this side of Iceapelago. Who better to smooth over any difficulties?'

'You're naïve. This will not work. There will be resistance.'

'I understand there are less than thirty survivors living in Malahide Castle and about the same here. You have some small firearms, excluding your hunting rifles, of course.'

'Dundrum will come to support us.'

'I very much doubt it judging by the state of the place.'

The captain was mindful not to mention the mysterious disease that was spreading. He was becoming more aware that his shivering and mild sweats suggested that he may have been exposed to the virus.

'Back to Howth Head,' said the captain. 'I need to have a full inventory of all supplies, food, energy, animals, accommodation, anything that we might need to sustain a population of up to a thousand. And I want it by sunset tomorrow. When you deliver the inventory, you will get to speak to your grandchildren. Get on with it. I'll be taking the rooms upstairs until our business is finished here.'

Rory was left in the room on his own. Flies were buzzing around where the Six had fallen. *Brendan was an old man of nearly eighty years old and had lived a good life,* he thought. But what a way to go. And in front of his wife and family.

He knew he had an impossible task ahead. The Howth Head community had survived so well and for so long because the housing units were relatively undamaged being at a high elevation. And some three hundred sheep and goats roamed the fertile flanks of Howth Head. For the most part, this Iceapelago community was self-sufficient. As the population aged, there were the inevitable deaths. However, unlike in Malahide Castle, there were many families with young children. And also unlike his community, Howth Head had a doctor. He estimated there were nearly a hundred people on the island, and not thirty as the captain had guessed.

What are they going to say, indeed what are they going to do, when I tell them what is in store?

'Sheila?' called out Rory.

The slain Six's widow came into the room and approached him in a trance.

'Could you kindly assemble the elders? I've news.'

CHAPTER 11

River Cruisers

While his charges rested, Don walked the deck and checked their escape route one final time. His presence did not draw any attention as the guards were used to his strolls at all hours of the night and day.

It was time to make a move.

'The same guards as last night are on duty,' said Don on his return to the cabin. 'They're all cosy and dozing off. The Alentejo Reserva must have been good tonight. Take off your shoes and tie them to your belts. We need to be as quiet as mice. Remember what we agreed. Walk slowly behind me. We will descend one floor to the storage area that is directly beneath us. The entrance door is not locked. We will exit through a rear door that leads to a narrow walkway. It's a twenty-metre walk to where the inflatable raft is located. Thankfully, the sea is calm so there will be very little movement as we walk along the outside ledge. I unloosened more ties this evening. I am confident once I undo the security straps and with one good tug, we will have the raft in the water in short order.

Plan B is that we can, and should, abort our departure if the unforeseen happens. If we are spotted by the guards, we stop. Is that clear?'

Four heads nodded.

'Let's go then.'

Getting to the raft went according to plan. The group was lined up on the walkway with their backs to the wall as Don busied himself unlocking the safety straps. He had only two to go.

Suddenly, the night air was disturbed by the crackling sound of a radio set. What Don had not realised that the ship's radio room was just metres away on the same deck level. When the crackling started, someone opened the window to let air into the stuffy room.

The group stood frozen in fear.

'Get the admiral immediately,' said a voice.

'Aye Captain, but he is probably asleep.'

'Just do what you are told.'

The voice of Captain da Gama could be heard over the radio. He was clearly agitated.

Don put his index finger to his mouth indicating that everyone should sit down and stay quiet. The siblings did not need any prompting.

They heard a blend of noises and grunts as a half-dressed, half-asleep admiral entered the radio room. They could not see inside. All they could do was to listen.

'Captain, to what do I owe this pleasure at three o'clock in the morning?'

'There have been important developments that are time sensitive. I decided to call you now as it may be too late by morning.'

'Please explain.'

'We need to change our plans and do so quickly. Dundrum Island is infected with some sort of contagious disease. As a result, we cannot use it as a base. The few people we met had advanced symptoms of a fever with yellow fluid oozing from their sores. We cannot risk moving the Ria Formosa population to Dundrum.'

'That is a change alright. There is enough accommodation in Dundrum for more than half our people. Not being able to use it presents a major problem. What are you proposing?'

'We accelerate the occupation of Malahide Castle and move our plans for attack forward to tomorrow or the day after at the latest.'

The Malahide residents on the ledge outside the radio room did their very best not to choke on hearing what was being discussed.

'Can that be done in such a short time period?'

'My business in Howth Head is finished. I will sail direct to Malahide and should be there by nightfall.'

'Is Howth Head secure?'

'Yes, thanks to Rory's good relationship with the local leaders. I put one of my trusted captains in charge of thirty grenadiers who will start preparations for the planned exodus from Ria Formosa over the coming days.'

Orla and Jon exchanged glances on finding out their father was safe. Not in Dundrum, but safe, nonetheless.

'Do you expect any trouble?'

'No. Rory is known to the local leaders who trust him for some reason.'

The captain decided it was best not to reveal that he had killed the Howth Six in case he incurred the admiral's wrath.

'Did Rory cooperate willingly?'

'Let me put it this way. The fact that you are holding his grandchildren hostage did influence him.'

'That is good to know. Have I understood correctly, Captain? We will relocate five hundred of our peoples to Howth and two thousand in and around Malahide Castle.'

'Yes, that is what I have in mind. We need to surprise the Malahide defenders, so whatever you do, *La Santa Jorge* should remain hidden on the leeside of Lambay and astern the array of wind farms. Depending on what happens, I may need your cannon firepower. And before you ask, I will travel to Cork Airport and Kinsale Head Islands once we have Malahide Castle subdued. We should be easily able to settle the balance of our people at these locations.'

'OK Captain, let us proceed as you suggested,' said the admiral.

The admiral was too sleepy to notice that he was not giving but getting orders from a junior officer.

The crackling sound stopped as the line went dead. The open window was shut soon after. The radio operator had had enough excitement for one night.

Don knew he had to stay calm given they were all dumbfounded by what they had heard. The listeners were privy to a plan of action that would see several Iceapelago communities becoming subservient to the Duke of the Principality of Ria Formosa. The very existence of their family and friends was under threat.

'Let's discuss all we've heard when we are safely on the raft. Agreed?'

He did not wait for a reply. With a tug of his right hand he dislodged the final security clasp. He and Tony pushed the raft over the edge of the ship into the water five metres below. Don jumped without waiting for the raft to inflate fully. The siblings looked at each other and did likewise. Orla took Jon's hand as they entered the water silently.

While they were getting over the shock of the cold water, Don was already on-board the fully inflated life raft. One by one, he pulled the siblings out of the water. Jon was inside the raft before he could think about the fact that he could not swim. Without being told what to do, Tony and Kate opened the side flaps, and inserted the short paddles into the rowlocks. Their experience with the Kinsale life raft ensured they were ready to get underway in no time.

'Hold,' Don whispered.

He wanted to make sure they had not been heard. The sound of silence with distant snoring dominated the night air.

'Put your back into it. We need to be as far away from *La Santa Jorge* as we can manage, and as quickly as possible.'

The Kinsale siblings pushed the paddles deep into the water. They were soon rowing in unison.

Don observed their progress from the front flap of the life raft. As its height was no more than a metre and a half over sea level, and given its dark colour, it would be hard to spot the raft in the dark at a distance. It was also fortunate that there was good cloud cover.

After thirty minutes, the rowers were quite exhausted, and it showed. Some strokes were missed, and the raft started to move left and right. Don was not at all concerned. As expected, the rip current south of Lambay Island came into play. At first a slight motion was discernible. Within minutes the raft was being propelled at a pace much faster than the rowers could achieve.

'Take a rest,' said Don. 'If my calculation is correct, the rip current will take us to an area called the Short Deep to the east of the sunken village of Malahide. It's no more than two kilometres from there to the Malahide Castle marina, and the last stretch is up a sheltered channel.'

This brief interlude gave them time to consider the ramifications of the radio message.

'I knew that Vasco fellow was a total rascal,' said Orla. 'The Malahide Six was duped for sure.'

'Weren't we all?' said Don.

'Let's turn what we know to our advantage,' said Jon. 'We've the best part of a day to secure the defence of Malahide Castle. We'll be in position, armed when these raiders attempt to gain access.'

'Don, Kate, and I need to make haste to Cork Airport Island,' said Tony.

'What are you talking about?' said Kate. 'We're going to Malahide, aren't we?'

'Let me explain,' said Don. He knew he had to move quickly to prevent a row starting between the Kinsale siblings. 'Many years ago, some heavy weapons brought to Cork Airport by the Canadian Rangers were left behind and stored secretly near one of the hangers. We need to find out if we can get these weapons operational to support the defence of Malahide Castle.'

'I'm confused, forgive me,' said Kate. 'Are you really suggesting that we can mount an attack on the Ria Formosa forces? That's totally daft.'

'Two military drones are in storage,' said Tony. 'We can use one or the other.'

'Who will fly them, for goodness sake?' said Kate.

'I'll do it, Kate,' said Tony. 'It's not as complicated as it might appear. When we're on our way to Cork I'll explain.'

'But it will be dangerous,' said Kate.

'I know,' said Tony. 'Can we leave it at that for the moment? We need to start rowing.'

'You better have a proper explanation,' said Kate. 'And a very good reason why we shouldn't stay in Malahide to support Orla and Jon.'

Don was glad that the brief exchange ended in a draw.

At first light, and with the dawn chorus at full song, the life raft glided up to what remained of the marina. Don jumped onto the shattered wooden deck and secured the raft to a bollard with a tie line.

'Back home at last,' said Orla.

She took in the vista of the vastness of the castle, and its many outbuildings in the background.

'It's hard to believe we only left here a little more than a week ago.'

'We couldn't have imagined what has happened in such a short period,' said Jon. He too was glad to be home. As the youngest and fittest of the community he anticipated that he would be kept busy preparing the defences. The prospect of distant travels would have to wait for another occasion.

'It's time for us to say our farewells,' said Don. 'I'll go with Tony and Kate to the sunken cruiser on the other side of the island.'

Although they had known each other for a very short time, the two sets of siblings had formed a really strong bond. Having been in almost constant close proximity for over a week, early feelings of attraction had been ignited. They hugged each other warmly, and back-slapped each other in the knowledge that they all faced an uncertain few days.

Kate gave Jon an extra hug and kissed his cheek. 'I'll miss you,' she whispered into his ear.

Jon smiled at her. 'Me too.'

'You look after yourself Tony with that drone contraption,' said Orla. 'I'll be watching out for you.'

'I'll drop in for a cup of tea in a few days,' said Tony blowing her a kiss.

'One final thing,' said Don. 'Jon, when you get time, deflate the life raft and move it somewhere secluded. You may need it again.'

'Will do.'

Jon and Orla walked up the track to the castle. They did not look back.

'We've an hour's walk ahead of us, so let's get going,' said Don. 'We'll pass in front of the castle before taking the dirt track to the eastern side of the island. At this early hour, I don't expect we'll meet anyone.'

Tony and Kate walked in line behind Don. They were so preoccupied with their thoughts that they barely noticed the grandeur of the castle and its towering buttresses. The flag of Iceapelago, with blue and white crosses representing thirty island communities, flew in the wind atop the main entrance. Protocol demanded that the flag of Iceapelago would never be taken down. It was dropped to half-mast all too frequently as residents passed away, but it had never been removed.

After a while, Kate spoke out loud. An observation not addressed to anyone in particular.

'What will become of us? I don't want to become a slave to some foreign regime.'

'We must never give up,' said Tony. 'Our families survived the worst traumas imaginable over the past decades. We must not allow Iceapelago to become a vassal state. Mark my word, I'll destroy the admiral and his warmongering mariners.'

Don did not react. A response was not necessary. These young adults were well aware they were the last of their generation. He did not need to motivate them.

'It's around the corner, beyond that treeline,' said Tony. 'Jon's map is very accurate.'

Don pushed his way through the bushes and trees. He could hear the lapping of the water. And precisely where Jon had estimated the location to be, they came across the part-sunken cruiser. They stared at the boat for ages.

'I had expected worse,' said Don. 'The top structure above the main deck hasn't been flooded. All the damage is below deck. Critically, the solar panels look like there're intact. The tide is ebbing fast, and this may allow me to locate the fractures in the hull.'

Tony and Kate watched on as Don stripped to his underpants.

'What are you doing?' said Kate.

'I'll have to find where the hull is punctured. See you in a while.'

The siblings felt useless. Yet they knew if anybody could re-float and repair the cruiser it was Don. He had handled every incident imaginable with the Iceapelago cruisers as an experienced pilot and technician.

His soaked bald head emerged. 'Nothing obvious along the starboard or port sides. I will try the front cabin section next.' He gave a thumbs up, took a deep breathe, and dived again below the waterline.

He was under water for much longer the second time before he emerged with a smile on his face. 'There are two tears on either side of the bow section, just below the waterline. One is quite small and will require a patch up job. The other will be more difficult to repair.'

'How can I help?' said Tony.

'Bend down and you will see a lever under the canopy of the bow deck.'

'Yes, I can feel it,' said Tony.

'Give it a good tug,' said Don.

A cover popped open revealing a cavity containing several metal boxes.

'When we designed these cruisers, we deliberately posi-tioned the spare parts and repair equipment as high as possible to keep them dry. This is an Aladdin's cave. Let me show you.'

Don, still dripping wet, pulled out a sealed oblong blue metal container.

'Watch,' he said. With experienced fingers he snapped the seal. The lid of the container opened to reveal tools of every shape and kind. 'I'm looking for sealant and a spatula. They are here somewhere.' After further rummaging he extracted a large red tin from the container.

'How will the sealant help? said Kate.

'If I manage to seal the cabin door that is the entrance to the bow section this will isolate the flood water to the front of the cruiser. We can then try to get the water out of the rest of the cruiser using bilge pumps and buckets. There should be spare pumps in a container somewhere.'

Further rummaging revealed two pumps.

'What do we do now?' said Kate.

'Nothing until I seal the bow section cabin door. Once we get off the Island, and are en route to Cork, I will pull in and try and fix the holes from the outside. The weight of the water in the bow section will not allow us to travel at full speed. What is most important is to get this craft afloat and out of here pronto.'

Don grabbed the sealant, and shoulder high in water started to apply the thick glue with the spatula to the section of the cabin door that was above the water line. 'And now for my next trick.' He fused a sealant gun, and squeezed out a thick layer of polymer along the line of the door ducking under water as he completed the task over the space of an hour.

He surfaced for the last time. 'Job done. Let's use the bilges. They work using foot pressure. It's like cycling a bike. When you press downwards the water pressure will force the flood water out. This is going to take a lot of time and energy. We should work in relays with two of us doing shifts until one or other tires.'

'How long will this take?' said Kate.

'We've a huge volume of water to move. I guess it will

take us probably five hours to get enough water out to allow the cruiser to re-float. Once we have buoyancy, I will start the engines assuming the solar panels give us a charge. We will continue to pump the water out while we sail towards a place called Straffan.'

'And how long will it take us to get to Cork Airport Island?' said Kate.

'In the olden days, we would travel along the coast and get there, depending on tides, in two days. With an enemy fleet offshore Malahide, we'll go inland. Sea vessels cannot navigate inland so at least we'll be safe. The first section will take us along the line of an old canal system. It's about one hundred and forty kilometres to the Athlone station. We will then sail southwards on the Shannon River Basin to arrive via Mallow at Cork Airport Island, a total journey of about two hundred and sixty kilometres. I have managed to do twenty kilometres an hour on these cruisers in calm waters with no cargo. Our cargo is the equivalent of a couple of tonnes of water, so the sooner we get rid of this ballast, the quicker our journey will be.'

'Let's start bilging,' said Tony.

Tony, Kate and Don set about foot-pumping water out of the hull. The tubes connected to the bilge pumps spewed dank water out over the side of the cruiser. The three of them worked solidly under cloudy skies.

'The water level has barely gone down,' said Tony taking a well-earned rest.

'I didn't say this was going to be easy. Be patient, young man,' said Don.

They soon got into a routine. Before the sun set, the water level had dropped noticeably.

'The cruiser is widest on top deck. The volume of water we need to remove from the lower deck will not be as great. Another hour or two and we'll be on our way.'

'What's for supper?' said Kate.

'Let me see,' said Don. He returned to the storage area in the bow section. He picked up a small black box. 'There should be enough emergency rations here for four days. Dried biscuits and crackers it is for the next while.'

They were truly exhausted. Their day had started at two o'clock in the morning aboard *La Santa Jorge* as they started their escape. Twenty hours later, it was time for a good rest. They sat munching their dried rations.

'Don, do you know…'

Tony did not get to finish his sentence.

A loud rat-a-tat-tat sound could be heard in the distance. It was followed soon after by muffled explosions.

'The captain has arrived, it seems,' said Don.

'I hope Orla and Jon are safe,' said Kate.

'To be honest, we need to be more concerned about our own safety, Kate,' said Don.

He was about to caution her further when they heard noises from up the coastline. The intensity of the sound rose gradually, suggesting someone was approaching.

Don, Kate and Tony fell silent and ducked below the deck line.

Three hundred metres further along the seashore at a bend, they could make out the sounds of rowing boats that were clearly trying to find a landing spot as light was fading rapidly. Shouts and curses suggested boats were landing ashore. The officers in charge did not waste time. As soon as they strapped on their equipment, several groups of grenadiers were marched off in the general direction of Malahide Castle.

'That was a close escape,' whispered Don. 'We need to find out if they left a sentry behind to mind the boats. The bilge pumps are noisy. Unless we are absolutely certain the coast is clear, we'll have to stop pumping water. That will inevitably delay our departure.'

'I'll go,' said Tony.

'Be careful,' said Kate.

She knew Tony was well able to manage himself. He was young, fit and muscular, but had never harmed anyone before.

'Take this,' said Don.

He handed him a long-bladed knife. He did not need to explain its purpose.

Tony leapt off the cruiser onto dry land. He had two options. To go along the water's edge, or to potentially expose himself in the wide glade that defined the landing area in the distance. He decided it was better to walk slowly along the seashore while trying desperately not to splash and make noise. It was dark and his eyes were already adjusted to the gloom. He stopped short of the where the first rowboat was pulled up onto a grassy verge. He used its cover to explore his surroundings. He had expected that he would find nobody, but that was not to be. Fifty metres away, and facing out to the open sea, sat a burly grenadier in front of a small open fire. His equipment lay spread-eagled on the grass. Tony delayed approaching. He had to be sure a second sentry was not nearby. The grenadier did not budge or talk to anyone during Tony's visual search for a possible colleague. Tony concluded that the sentry was on his own.

Tony manoeuvred himself into a position behind the seated grenadier who was completely focused on eating his rations. The crackle of the fire deadened the sound of his steps. He was a few metres behind his target. Tony did not flinch. He thrust the knife deep into the base of the grenadier's head. He fell headlong into the fire, dead before he hit the embers.

The deed done, Tony cleaned the blade in the man's coloured tunic, and strode back to the cruiser purposefully.

He had killed a man, and he knew it would not be his last. Neither was he at all surprised that the taking of a human life did not bother him. He had just cause after all. It was clear that the climate invaders would show no mercy as they sought to take over what were peaceful and almost defenceless Iceapelago communities. So why should he not defend Iceapelago's interests by force if required?

Don nodded to him as he returned to the cruiser. Kate put her hand on his shoulder. Neither said anything.

'Let's get working on the bilges,' said Don. 'Another hour should do it.'

CHAPTER 12

Uncle Paul

Malahide Castle was protected on all sides by three-foot-thick stone walls covered by layers of cement. The exterior walls were steep, some were four metres tall in places. The windows with steel protection lattices were located high up on the second and third floors. The castle's solid mahogany front door was a foot thick and secured by double steel rods. The castle had weak spots. The principal one being the rear entrance door to the main kitchen at the inner courtyard. But to get to that door, attackers would have to climb over a three-metre wall at the rear battlements of the castle.

Jon and Orla's arrival with news of an imminent attack gave the residents, once they got over the shock, the best part of a day to prepare. All ladders were moved indoors. The outward facing windows were shuttered. The few arms they had were distributed, cleaned and primed. The food stores were full, so the animals were released to roam freely in the vicinity of the castle.

Because *La Santa Maria* could not navigate all the way up the channel to the marina dock, it anchored at the entrance of the old railway culvert close to what was once the town's award-winning railway station. Three rowboats with armed grenadiers were launched and set off for the marina about a kilometre away. They were spotted in good time.

Jon's plan of action was put into play. He had worked out that the ship would have to offload its attackers by rowboat, and more importantly, given the distance to the walls, the ship would not be able to use its cannons on the castle.

Jon and his uncle lay hidden behind outbuildings close to the channel awaiting the assailants in the first rowboat that was no more than fifty metres away on the open water. On cue, they both fired two old shotguns.

The pellets blasted into the grenadiers. The sound of the blast stunned the sailors. Riddled with hot pellets some stood up with the searing pain. Their heavy body armour prevented mortal wounds. However, one fell backwards awkwardly, and toppled out of the boat pulling an oarsman with him. His colleagues tried to save him just as another blast from the shotguns arrived. With several grenadiers newly wounded, standing and cowering, the boat became unstable, and it began to take water. It sank. As all the grenadiers aboard were carrying full equipment, they had no chance. It all happened so quickly that the cries of the dying did not last long.

Those on the packed second rowboat watched in disbelief as their comrades drowned in front of them. They, and the crew of the third rowboat hesitated, and turned back to *La Santa Maria*.

Jon and his uncle retreated immediately to the safety of the castle before they could see the outcome of their ambush.

'The attacking group comprised three rowboats with ten grenadiers on each,' said Jon to the assembled defenders on the rear battlement. 'I think Uncle Paul and I dispatched the lead boat.'

'You sure did,' said Orla. 'Good shooting. The other boats retreated, but I expect they'll be ordered to turn around.'

'What surprised me was the grenadiers only had small arms and some automatic weapons,' said Jon.

'Maybe,' said Orla. 'But this is just the start. We should not be in any way complacent.'

The loss of his troops infuriated Captain da Gama. He seethed with anger as the two rowboats approached *La Santa Maria*.

'Get back to the marina,' roared the captain. 'You need some backbone.' He turned to the bosun. 'Launch another boat that I will lead and load it up with more automatic weapons.'

Within the hour, the captain had landed at the marina. He marshalled his troops in a semicircle in front of the castle.

'Group One, fire on my command at the second floor window, and Group Two concentrate on the front door.' The attack started in earnest. The machine gun fire bombarding the front wall and the shutters of the bay window above the entrance was deafening, but did no harm or damage other than chipping blockwork dating from the sixteenth century. A grenade thrown against the front door bounced off the portal and blew up at the bottom of the steps, causing no damage.

'Cease fire, you louts,' screamed the captain.

He had wasted a lot of scarce ammunition to no avail. A different approach was needed.

When the shooting stopped, Orla looked out from a small slit atop the bay window. In the distant past, this narrow aperture would have been used to fire arrows at attackers. The first person she spotted under the tall oak tree opposite the main entrance was Captain da Gama. He had a large group of grenadiers with him.

A sergeant was remonstrating with him. 'They knew we were coming, Captain,' said the sergeant. 'We have lost the element of surprise, never mind ten of our best men.'

'Stop pestering me,' said the captain. 'Let me think.'

He knew the interior lay out of the castle from his recent visit. His plan was to secure the front door. Once that was done, the castle would fall. He knew the residents had some arms but nothing like the automatic weapons his grenadiers carried. He was really puzzled about losing the element of surprise. How could anyone know the castle was to be attacked? Worse still, it was clear the residents had had time to fortify the castle.

'There is not much we can do with this small company,' said the captain. 'We will await the grenadiers who landed on the east side of the island. They have dynamite. One controlled blast against the front door should get us in.'

Orla could not hear the conversation between the captain and his men. She suspected they had worked out by now that the castle residents had the advantage as the element of surprise was gone.

For the past two years, Orla had been the castle's designated ranger and hunter. She owned a heavy calibre rifle handed down to her by her father. It was a clumsy weapon when it came to killing deer, but it worked with a degree of accuracy within a hundred metres. Orla reckoned the captain was beyond her normal range, but what the heck. She loaded the single bore rifle with a bullet. She raised it to her shoulder and through the viewfinder could see the captain's upper torso in her sights.

Pull slowly, her father had taught her. And that is what she did.

The captain heard the crack of a rifle shot. Almost instantaneously he felt the effect of a red hot poker going through his right arm just below his shoulder. It was a clean shot. The captain fell to his knees in agony.

'I have been shot,' he wailed.

His sergeant stooped down to help him.

Orla's second shot was more accurate. It hit the sergeant in the nose, blowing his head off just as he was crouching above the captain. The captain, pinned to the ground by the lifeless sergeant, a heavy man, was covered in thick globules of blood and brain matter.

'Get him off me,' the captain roared over his pain.

The sergeant was abandoned as the grenadiers retreated with the captain to the far side of the oak tree, out of range of the castle shooter.

'Did you hit a target?' said Jon. Unknown to his sister, he was in the room behind her as she focused on her shots.

'I think I winged the captain. He will need medical treatment, otherwise he will bleed out. That may have the effect of slowing down their attack.'

'Well done, Orla,' said Jon. 'What are they doing now?'

'Let me see,' said Orla.

She looked through the spy hole.

'There's a group of grenadiers approaching from the west. They must have landed near the glade close to the graveyard.'

'How many?'

'Hard to make out, but a lot, at least twenty. Wait, there's a second group arriving, and they're carrying heavy backpacks.'

'Trouble ahead then.'

'Is Uncle Paul briefed?'

'You bet.'

'Let's see what they are up to.'

The captain knew he needed to be evacuated to his ship in short order so that his wound could be tended to. He was bleeding but not heavily. The rough bandage that was applied to the wound stemmed the flow of blood somewhat. The wounded arm was numb and lifeless. He placed the wrist of the hand into the centre of his tunic for support, Napoleon-like. Based on his experience of previous gunshot wounds, he knew he had about an hour before he lost consciousness.

'Gather round me,' he ordered the new arrivals. 'The easiest way to get access to the castle is through the front door. Do you have the explosives?'

'Yes, Captain. I can prime the package now,' said a grenadier. 'Ten kilos should be enough.'

'I will take your word for it. Listen up. There's a shooter, and the only way we can be seen is from the apertures beside the window above the main entrance. On my command, shoot up the area above the doorway. That will provide cover for – what is your name?'

'Magnus.'

'Then you can approach the door with less risk. If there is no return fire, we will charge the door just after the blast. Am I clear?'

The grenadiers nodded.

'Jon, they're up to something,' said Orla.

'What do you see?'

'They're raising their machine guns and… Get out of here now,' she roared just as bullets whipped and ricocheted across the ceiling.

In the relative safety of the hallway outside the library, Jon shouted, 'Uncle Paul, be ready.'

As ordered, Magnus sprinted the hundred metres to the front door holding his package of explosives. He placed it carefully in position. Magnus had practiced this task many times before. All he had to do was flip the hand-held switch and run like hell away. The timer would detonate ten seconds later.

When they saw him bend down to place his dynamite in front of the door, the grenadiers, not detecting any contra firing, ran in the general direction of the castle.

'Stop! Wait,' said the captain.

He was too late. His orders were to advance after the door was blown open.

'Fools, all of them. Too eager for their own good.'

What the assailants had not reckoned with was Uncle Paul, fresh from his successful shotgun shoot. The castle's eighty-year-old engineer held a detonator. The side of the door frame contained an almost invisible narrow arrow slit that gave a limited view of anyone approaching. Once Uncle Paul saw someone lowering a package onto the granite steps, he pressed the button.

He and Jon had earlier hidden dynamite in the two large planters that were positioned on the steps that led to the front door. They reckoned that the blast would be sufficiently far away as to not to destroy the door. They had their calculations right.

Magnus did not even know he was dead before his body was torn to shreds. Uncle Paul's charge also detonated Magnus's package, so the two almost simultaneous explosions tore through the rows of grenadiers who were in position close behind Magnus. Body parts fell like confetti.

The heavy oak door rattled with the force of the explosions but did not crack, and stayed on its steel hinges.

'Well done, Uncle Paul,' said Jon. His ears tingled as a result of the blasts.

'It's been a good morning's hunting,' said Uncle Paul. 'Good practice as the game season is still months away.'

Inside the castle there were loud cheers. They had seen off the attackers with a severe loss of life and limb. The expected siege was underway.

At the far side of the oak tree, and at a safe distance, Captain da Gama winced in pain and frustration. A thick pall of grey smoke flecked with red blood blocked the view to the castle door.

'Get me out of here,' he pleaded to his much depleted force.

He could walk, just about. Going the long way around, he made it eventually to the marina.

Back aboard *La Santa Maria* a medic patched up the wound and gave the captain a sedative. As the ship did not have medical equipment to stabilise the broken arm, he had no option but to take a rowboat to *La Santa Jorge* where he would get better treatment. Above all else, he did not want to have his arm amputated. Attacking the castle could wait.

As *La Santa Maria* set sail towards Lambay Island, the captain radioed ahead.

The admiral was less than pleased and during their initial exchanges he made it clear he had no interest in the captain's injury.

'You cannot give up, Vasco. Go, do the job we agreed.'

'You do not understand, Admiral…'

'Do not give me any of that you do not understand nonsense. Time is not on our side, have you forgotten? I cannot give the order for the exodus from Quinta do Lago until we have secured Malahide Castle. Not having use of Dundrum is bad enough, but now Malahide Castle remains beyond our grasp. I need action, Captain, not excuses.'

The captain was weakening from his blood loss. He made one final attempt to convince the admiral.

'What we need to do is to sail *La Santa Jorge* as close as possible to the castle and use your heavy guns to bombard the lower rear walls. I will then attack with a ground force.'

'That is the first sensible thing you have said in ages,' said the admiral. 'OK, we'll get you medical support first, and then we will put an end to this futile resistance.'

At the same time in Malahide Castle, Orla was on the radio to her grandfather in Howth Head.

'My Lord, I wasn't expecting to hear from you,' said Rory. 'We'll have to be quick. There are guards everywhere. How did you know I was here by the way.'

Orla explained the early morning conversation she had heard between the captain and the admiral.

'How's your grandmother?' asked Rory.

'She is cooking and fussing. The usual. Like everyone, she can't get over what's happened in such a short space of time.'

'You're safe in Malahide?'

'If you consider we successfully repelled the first onslaught, yes. But when the captain returns, I don't think he will make the same mistakes. If he brings heavy weapons to bear, we'll be in trouble.'

'Make sure the safety tunnel is ready for use. You and I have used it many times to get to the north coast of the island.'

'Will do, Grandad. What's happening in Howth Head?'

'I was forced to assist the captain because I thought you and Jon were held captive. Now that's changed…'

'What are you doing?' said a voice with a strange accent. 'Is that radio live? Who are you talking to?'

Orla listened in shock as it was clear one of the guards was in the radio room.

'You were warned,' said the guard.

There was a commotion and a lot of muffled shouting. The radio line went dead.

CHAPTER 13

Straffan

'That doesn't sound too good,' said Kate.

She stopped pumping the bilges as the sound of twin explosions roared through the air.

'Keep pumping,' said Don. 'We're making great progress. I've told you we cannot do anything to help. We must save our own skins.'

'Don's right, Kate,' said Tony. He left it at that and resumed his work at the bilges.

'The good news is that the tide is rising fast,' said Don. 'We'll know soon enough if we have emptied enough water out to float the cruiser. I have checked the solar panels. I had to repair a few, but we are good to go.'

They had spent the best part of half a day at the bilges and were physically exhausted. Smaller volumes of water were being sucked out of the hull with greater effort.

All of a sudden, the cruiser shuddered, not by much but there was movement.

'It's the tide,' said Don. 'It needs to rise by less than half a metre before we can try to reverse out of here.'

Over the next hour, they smiled as the shuddering was replaced by the lapping of water under the hull. As Don had predicted, even with a good amount of water still in the bottom of the hull, the cruiser's buoyancy was improving. Tony and Kate continued on the pumps as Don prepared the engine.

'Where did you find the ignition key?' said Kate.

'It was standard practice to keep a spare key above the steering wheel in the stern cabin, and that's where I got it.'

'The wonders of the Iceapelago cruiser fleet,' said Tony.

'They were built to withstand all conditions,' said Don. 'And we'll soon find out if outdated marine engineering will work for us.'

He turned the ignition key.

Silence.

He tried again.

Nothing.

'I forgot,' said Don. 'It's been a while since I drove one of these. I should have engaged the electricity current powered by the solar panels before I turned on the ignition.'

He pulled down a lever above the steering wheel. The hum of electricity was instant. He then tried the ignition again. The dashboard lit up.

'We're in business,' he shouted.

Tony and Kate joined him in the small aft cabin where the controls were located.

Don gently moved the gear stick towards him. 'This is the reverse thrust.'

The cruiser responded. By inches, it slowly moved away from the shoreline. The loose gravel under the hull eventually lost its grip and the scrapping sounds lessened.

Don applied more pressure. The cruiser was in mid-channel. He then pushed the forward thruster and the cruiser responded immediately.

'We'll soon see if we have sufficient buoyancy,' said Don.

As expected, the water level in the front section forced the bow section down, but well above the waterline.

'We've done it,' said Kate. She hugged her brother.

'Do I get one too? said Don.

'Sorry, of course,' said Kate.

This was the first positive experience they had in quite a while.

'There are six hours of daylight left,' said Don. 'That should be enough to get us far away from this place. The solar panels usually charge the reserve batteries. Because they haven't be used in ages, we may have limited power once it gets dark.'

'Remind me, how fast can we go? said Kate.

'It depends on the weight of the water still below the hull,' said Don. 'I'll need to be careful until I get the measure of the boat. When fully laden with twenty passengers and full cargo, the Iceapelago cruisers could achieve speeds of over twenty kilometres an hour on flat calm waters. We might do close to that, if we're lucky.'

'At least we're underway,' said Tony. 'Back to the pumps.'

He and Kate resumed their chore with a heightened sense of purpose.

Tony and Kate took in their surroundings as Don, with sure confidence, motored the cruiser. He was in his element. Leaving Malahide Castle Island, they headed west and soon passed Castleknock Island. There was no sign of life. Tall trees and huge bushes grew everywhere.

They sailed over several housing estates that remained below water. When Don went close to shore they could see rusty cars, buses and trucks scattered here and there.

The Dublin Bay region, being low lying, had suffered terribly as the sea water rose, a result of the Greenland icecap melting completely. Water submerged huge swathes of urban life. From time to time, they could see antennae sticking out of the water, or an isolated chimney. The top floors of large apartment buildings were everywhere. They had one thing in common. The windows and facades were shattered from the force of the storms.

As they continued their journey, there was a sameness to the scenery. Nothing lived. No birds. No animals, and certainly no humans. The buildings were derelict. Thick vegetation grew everywhere. There was total silence, apart from the soft lapping of water around and under the cruiser's hull.

Don knew the route towards the midlands canal and onwards. He drove the cruiser at a steady pace, and she responded. His priority was to find a safe spot before nightfall. He had a favourite from the old days. The lock house at the old Straffan Estate above what was once the River Liffey. The building, originally a golf clubhouse, was renovated to accommodate the dozens of cruisers that passed by its front door every day of the year.

'Look ahead,' said Don. 'We'll dock here for a break and a rest.'

'Where are we?' said Kate.

'About a mile from what once was the happiest spot on Iceapelago. I will tell you more when we are alongside.' With his local knowledge, Don manoeuvred the cruiser effortlessly, and tied up adjacent to a red brick building over two storeys tall. 'Welcome to the K Club,' he said.

As they walked towards the building, they could see its windows had been blown in. Fallen trees, branches and leaves lay everywhere. It really did not look inviting.

'This way,' said Don. 'There's a basement entrance close to what was the tenth golf tee. This is where the goods were delivered when this was a functioning operation years ago.'

The lee side of the building was less damaged. Don approached the door with its *Deliveries Only* sign. He turned the knob on the door. It opened easily.

'Come in, we'll be safe here.'

'I get the impression you've been here before, Don,' said Kate.

'Most weeks back then. This was the centre of the universe for cruiser pilots. Straffan was the gateway to the west and the southwest, and by far the busiest overnight destination. It had basic lodgings and simple food, all that was really necessary for us travellers. Many a great night was had here. The singing and conversations would go on until the early hours. Now look at it. Sad, sad indeed. Never mind my moroseness. Let's find a place to put our heads down for a few hours. There should be a few sofas in the foyer.'

And sure enough there were.

Tired bodies fell asleep in safe surroundings.

Tony and Kate woke before dawn fully refreshed. They went looking for Don. They found him chest high in the water at the bow of the cruiser.

'What on earth are you up to?' said Kate.

'While you two sleepyheads were snoring away, I busied myself trying to affix temporary patches to the torn sections on the front hull. I managed to cover the smaller higher one with a polymer coat, but the bigger crack lower down in the hull is beyond my skill set. We would need to have the cruiser in a dry dock to fix it. The good news is that with little effort we should be able to remove some more water from the forward cabin, and if that works, it will help our buoyancy.'

'And allow you to motor at a faster speed,' said Tony.

'Yes,' said Don.

He pulled himself onto the deck and went to the lower passenger cabin. He emerged a short while later with a biscuit tin.

'Hard tack for breakfast anyone?'

'What I wouldn't do for a hamburger and fries,' said Tony.

'Or even a mixed omelette,' said Kate.

The hungry siblings laughed.

Once he dried and dressed himself, Don was back at the steering wheel.

As they proceeded with their journey, Tony and Kate pumped out the front section. The water flowed out of the cruiser's bow, allowing it rise slowly but surely. As it did, Don pushed the cruiser to its limits along flat calm waters.

Their manual work over, the siblings then spent most of the day sitting astern as they took in the surrounding scenery. They passed a village called Kinnegad.

'Where's everyone?' said Kate.

'Gone to their makers,' said Tony. 'I hadn't realised that there were so few remaining Iceapelago communities. We're lucky with what we have on the Old Head.'

'We certainly are,' said Kate.

By noon, they had made good progress by reaching south of Athlone Island and its long-abandoned cruiser repair yard.

'This place gives me the creeps,' said Don. 'Some of my best friends died here during the Big Storm. If you want to rest, go below and use the blankets we found at Straffan. More biscuits, Kate?'

'Coming up, Captain, but not that captain, I should add.'

Their collective good humour improved the further they travelled from the area of conflict in the Dublin Bay region.

'I can now appreciate why you made your career as a cruiser pilot,' said Tony. 'What a carefree life out in the open, making full use of your skills as an engineer, and meeting people all the time.'

'The camaraderie was the best,' said Don. 'We were a band of brothers in the true sense of the word. They were wonderful times alright.' He took a deep breath as he welled up inside. 'I think I'm the only cruiser pilot still alive.'

'You may be the sole survivor, but you're the best, that's for sure,' said Kate.

The siblings were so grateful to Don. Less than two weeks had passed from the time he brought them down the cliff at Garrylow Beach at the start of their adventure. When they started to talk about leaving Kinsale Head, he was not part of the picture. Given what transpired in the meantime, they could not see themselves doing anything without his guidance and support. Don had become their hero and close friend. It had taken some time, but their respect for Don had grown. Back in the Old Head of Kinsale, he was in the background, almost taken for granted. He was not part of the family's inner circle. In observing a man at close quarters who still had pride in his long career and personal achievements, the siblings changed their point of view. Kate attached huge importance to people she believed to be reliable, and by extension trustworthy, and hard working. And Don sure ticked those boxes.

Don knew his relationship with Kate and Tony had changed much for the better since they left the Old Head. Although it was unspoken, he had become their protector and guardian. They relied on him, and he knew it.

When they were farming the land, often from dawn until dusk, doing their myriad of chores as the youngest in the community, Tony saw Kate not as a sibling, but more as a fellow worker. The family tie was pushed back to a state of near non-observance. The toil of the day had long since replaced the space where young children, and they had just passed that threshold, had time for each other. Family life in Iceapelago was not one of mutual caring, but one of indifferent personal survival where graft unfortunately replaced love. Eking out an existence was a much more important task than spending time developing personal relationships. Days ended in exhaustion. Sleep came easy. There was no Sabbath as farming and cultivating did not recognise a religion. The only break the siblings ever got was after lunch on Saturdays. And even with that, they were always on call to assist the older members of the community.

Obviously, the last weeks had changed their routine quite profoundly. Tony had spoken to his sister more often and with a higher degree of sensitivity and feeling than he had in all the years gone by. And they talked with such ease. It had taken them to the end of their teenage years to realise they were real friends. The Henry brother and sister had bonded. It may have taken them their lifetime until now, but they had become a unit of mutual solidarity. They did not pine for lost time. That was discounted. Their shared future was the priority, and it was a future full of hope, or so they thought in their innocence.

They both agreed that there was no doubt but the children of Iceapelago were the greatest sufferers of the environment in which they found themselves. They were survivors, the Iceapelago 3 generation.

Don could see so much of Ruth Henry, his idol, in Tony and Kate. But he feared for them. They had never had sexual partners and were total innocents when it came to such matters. They would never have had children had they stayed behind in the Old Head. And now liberated, the situation had not improved. The age profile in Malahide Castle was the same. Their erstwhile partners in crime, Orla and Jon, faced the same desolate, barren future. That said, he had observed a subtle but quasi-physical mutual attraction developing between the siblings and their new friends. Although she did not know it, Don reckoned that Jon was smitten with Kate. Orla had also fallen for Tony. He vowed to himself that he would do his best to link up the fledgling love birds as soon as it was practical to do so.

The stark reality was that Iceapelago was on its last legs in more ways than one. Something had to be done. Ageing small communities living separate spartan existences was a recipe for certain extinction. Don did not agree with the admiral's methods, nobody did. They were clearly those of a desperate man; but he was beginning to realise his motive was arguably just. It was certainly well-intended. Faced with a comparable dilemma, securing the future of his friends and community, Don would do the same. But was there a different way, a common ground where nobody got hurt?

'Hold your counsel until I get you safely back to Kinsale,' said Don.

'Via Cork Airport please,' said Tony.

'Agreed,' said Don. 'And via many other places as we head south via the old course of the River Shannon. What was Lough Derg is now more than double in size but very navigable. After the floods, we installed new marker buoys all the way to Cork Airport Island.'

The journey continued with the passage through the Mallow Gap a highlight. It might have been boring in parts, but who cared.

Tony and Kate took it in turns and shared the motoring under Don's watchful eye.

At the end of the second day since leaving Malahide Castle, the radar tower dome at Cork Airport shone bright as the descending sun caught its contours before dusk. At the helm, Tony spotted the landmark first. He was pleased his final destination was less than an hour away. Don took over the steering wheel as they approached the dock. He glided the cruiser into position as he had done hundreds of times in the past. Tony and Kate secured it to two posts.

Tony had a sense of trepidation about his plan to fly the hoverbike, but could not afford the time to dwell on what lay ahead.

Tony reflected as he took in the scene. This was where Ruth Henry, his famous grandmother, had lived and ruled as Commander of Iceapelago. The dilapidated terminal building in the foreground was once was a hub of airline activity before the Eriador Event and was used for quite different purposes thereafter. The large hangers to the right of the runway were open to the elements. The engineering buildings were showing signs of long abandonment, as were the residential quarters on the perimeter of the complex.

They approached the entrance to the airport terminal.

'I need to find a source of electricity and a socket,' said Tony.

'What do you mean?' said Kate.

She noticed Don was not at all surprised by her brother's demand.

'There are several arrays of solar panels on the complex, it's just a matter of finding one that works,' said Don.

'Will somebody answer my question please?' said Kate. She did not know who she should best put the question to.

'I'll explain all when I get a charge for the laptop,' said Tony.

'What's with that silly computer you carry in your backpack morning, noon and night?' said Kate.

'It's not silly, Kate, believe me. Our grandmother left messages on the laptop that you need to see, hear and read.'

'I'm lost,' said Kate. 'We escape with our lives from Malahide and grandmother's computer is now the centre of attention?'

Don knew Kate liked to be in control, and as she was out of the decision-making loop that clearly annoyed her.

'Tony, are you telling me you have searched the laptop before now, and never confided in me as to what you found? I thought the computer was stored in mother's Healing Hamper. Why did you steal it? When did you steal it?'

'I…'

Tony could not start his sentence by way of reply.

'And for how long have you been accessing the computer? We used to play silly games with Mother and the contents of her Healing Hamper. All that time you concealed something from me. How dare you?'

Weeks of tiredness and general fatigue had not helped Kate's otherwise calm demeanour.

Don did not want to take sides, but he concluded she had a point.

'Spill the beans, Tony, or I will,' said Don.

'Grandma left some important messages on her computer that will help us save Iceapelago from the likes of Admiral Rodriguez and Captain da Gama,' said Tony.

'Be specific,' said Kate. 'Stop waffling.'

'You may remember the old stories we were told as kids about Grandma's exploits. Her father, our great-grandfather by the way, landed in Cork Airport with a company of Canadian rangers and it was those rangers that saw off the insurrection led by General Gove and his Welsh mercenaries. The rangers returned to Canada soon after.'

'How is this relevant to anything?' said Kate. 'Spare me the history lesson.'

'Please stop interrupting me,' said Tony. 'As I was beginning to explain, when the rangers left, and importantly for us, they left a cache of weapons behind. This was Iceapelago's insurance policy.' Kate began slowly to grasp the importance of Tony's backfill story. 'Before the Big Storm arrived, Grandma decided to hide and secure the weapons. She left clear instructions on her computer not only where to find them but how to use them.'

'What exactly are we talking about?' said Don.

'Heavy machine guns, automatic pistols, rocket fired grenade launchers, and a few anti-tank weapons. Everything one might need to supress a rebellion, I should add. But that is not why we are here. We do not have enough people to use these weapons obviously. The *pièce de resistance* are two military drones with long-range capacity.'

'Drones?' said Kate. 'What are you talking about, Tony? I never heard of such a thing.'

'Drones are remotely-flown aircraft that were once used to deliver commercial packages across great distances. Armies used them to drop bombs and for aerial surveillance. These drones were at the time the very latest in military technology.'

'And what are we going to do with them?' said Kate.

'It's all set out clearly on Grandma's computer, including the operating and flying instructions that I have been studying for months. Can we find a charger that will help us reveal the contents of our Pandora's Box?'

CHAPTER 14

Admiral Rodriquez

'YOU NEED TO REST, Captain,' said the medical orderly. 'While you lost blood, you were somewhat lucky. The shot went clean through the bone of your upper arm. It did not hit an artery. I have you bandaged well. The biggest risk is an infection. You best stay here for a day or two so I can observe you.'

The captain surveyed his surroundings as he lay on a gurney below deck on *La Santa Jorge*. By the smell of it, he knew he was in the ship's infirmary. The orderly had administered chloroform to his patient as he cleaned out the wound. The smell of the gas lingered in the confines of the small cabin. He was post-op groggy. His whole arm throbbed and not just at the point of the bullet entry.

The captain tried to raise himself up with his good arm but did not have the strength to do so. He slumped back in the bed mumbling profanities.

'Be careful,' said the orderly. 'If you cause further damage to your arm, you could lose it.'

The captain had no intention of listening to any such advice at a time when he was most needed. 'Does the admiral know I am here?'

'Yes, he met you when you returned on board, and accompanied you to the infirmary.'

'I do not remember that.'

'I am not surprised,' said the orderly. 'When you got here, severe shock had set in. You were barely conscious. To be honest if your treatment had been delayed, you would be dead by now. You are strong and fit, so you will be back on your feet soon. As I said, please be sensible for a day or two.'

'Do I have a fever?' said the captain, expecting the worst.

'No, why?'

'It does not matter,' said the captain. At least he had dodged the Dundrum yellow virus bullet.

Captain da Gama knew he had no option but to rest for a while. He had received several superficial wounds in the past, but nothing as potentially compromising as this. What was gnawing at him was the identity of the person who shot him. From what he saw when he had dinner with the Malahide community the vast majority in the room were elderly. With Rory in Howth Head, he reckoned one of the siblings he had sought to befriend had shot him. He determined that he would exact his revenge when the castle was taken.

The orderly was correct in one respect. The captain was indeed exhausted. Once he fell into a deep sleep, the orderly left him be. He had other work to do. Bodies needed to be prepared for burial.

While the captain slumbered below deck, the admiral called his other ship captains and senior officers of his fleet to his quarters.

'What a mess. A total shambles!' he roared at the captains, not acknowledging his part in the recent fiasco. He glared fiercely at the group from the comfort of his ornate chair.

Fifteen men and women stood in a circle around the periphery of the room around the admiral's banqueting table. They were all identifiable by their uniforms and badges. Dedicated sailors, and soldiers of the Principality of Ria Formosa all. Dedicated perhaps but running scared of a furious admiral whose short temper was in overdrive.

'Not only were the residents of Malahide Castle warned in good time about our plans, but the hostages escaped. How did this happen on your watch?'

The ship's captain who was responsible for the prisoners knew the question was addressed to him.

'They escaped in the early hours of the morning on one of the ship's inflatable life rafts,' said the captain.

'I already know that, stupid,' said the admiral. 'The life raft they used was the one on the third deck astern, yes?'

'Yes, Admiral,' was the meek reply.

'The one outside the radio room?'

'Yes, Admiral.'

'And when precisely did the escape happen?'

'I reckon about three in the morning.'

The admiral guessed correctly that the escape must have coincided with his long and animated early morning radio call with Captain da Gama. He had not told his captains about the call and would not now. The escapees were not only forewarned about the plans for Malahide Castle, but more worryingly, they were fully aware of the steps to facilitate the proposed imminent arrival of the climate refugees from Ria Formosa.

After reflecting a moment on his shared culpability, the admiral's anger abated. There was no time to waste arresting and executing those responsible for letting the prisoners escape. He had to focus on marshalling his forces to secure a safe and secure environment for his people. If he did not, the duke would have his head.

'OK, let us recap,' he said.

Sensing a change in tone, his captains visibly relaxed. On previous form, they really believed the admiral would find a scapegoat and have one of them killed. Not today thankfully.

'Is Howth Head secure?'

'I left twenty of my grenadiers behind on two ships when I sailed with Captain da Gama to Malahide Castle,' said one of the sea captains.

'What is your name?'

'Reus.'

'Well Reus, I want you to return immediately to Howth Head with an additional complement of grenadiers. You are to dispose of the Commander of Iceapelago, the man they call Rory. When that is done, radio me. I will then order the first ten ships at the Quinta do Lago marina to set sail later today for Howth Head. Your job is to welcome them on my behalf, and to get them settled. Tell them I will visit in a week or two.'

The captain, who was quite junior and inexperienced, was taken aback. He had never been given such a responsibility before. He did not respond immediately to the admiral's orders.

The admiral glared at him.

'Are you still here? Get going. I expect your call before nightfall. I will have you shot if you do not dispose of the Iceapelago Commander.'

Reus did not need to be told twice. He bolted out of the room.

'We will talk about the Malahide Castle situation shortly,' said the admiral. 'But first, who will volunteer to take a ship to capture Cork Airport Island for the Principality of Ria Formosa?'

The sea captains looked at each other. They knew rank had to be respected so the most senior officer spoke.

'I can set sail within the hour. What is the mission?'

'Are you stupid or what?' said the admiral. He rose slowly, and deliberately from his chair and walked to the sea captain. 'Where have you been for the past weeks? Why are we here at all? Have I not made it clear? Has the information not penetrated through your thick skulls? To save your families' lives. Full stop. Time is not on our side.'

'Understood, Admiral,' stuttered the captain.

'I better re-explain the sense of urgency. We have had to change plans because Dundrum Island is unusable. A contagious infection has killed the population, and it cannot be inhabited by our people as planned. I have been forced to look elsewhere. The large hangars at Cork Airport can be used as temporary shelter until permanent accommodation is erected. Captain da Gama confirmed the structures are safe, but shoddy. Another factor is that there is a large radio centre on top of the airport control tower, which must be secured as a priority once you land. My captain will give you the sea charts of the area around Cork Airport and the Old Head of Kinsale Islands that were recently, and helpfully, updated by Captain da Gama during his recent voyage along the southern coastline of Iceapelago.'

'Understood, Admiral.'

'And one final thing,' said the admiral. 'I am assuming you can land and secure what I am told is a vacant island with a small troop of grenadiers? The population of Cork Airport Island did not survive the Big Storm so there is nobody there to oppose you, at least that is what Captain da Gama told me.'

'I will obey your orders, Admiral,' said the captain.

'Oh, I am sure you will,' said the admiral. 'It will take you no more two days to sail to Cork Airport Island. Once this meeting is over, I will send a signal to the duke at Quinta do Lago to have a part of the fleet that is lying in waiting, probably twenty fully laden ships with two thousand people, to sail immediately to Cork. They should arrive two or three days after you take Cork Airport Island. Off with you.'

With the captains of two ships of the fleet dispatched with orders, the admiral turned his attention to his biggest problem – the resistance at Malahide Castle. Despite his bluster, he knew he could not allow the full exodus from Quinta do Lago unless and until the castle was taken.

'Captain da Gama is recovering from a wound. I will take direct command of the attack. Who has the latest intelligence?'

'If I may, Admiral?' said one ship's captain.

'Go on.'

'I spoke to some of the grenadiers who were part of the initial attack.'

'The failed attack,' said the admiral.

The captain knew better than to take the bait. He set about delivering what he believed to be a correct status report.

'We need heavy explosives to gain access. The front door is the obvious target. However, there are perhaps other parts of the battlements that we could target. For example, the rear of the castle faces down the sea channel, and unlike the front door, it is in a direct line of fire from one of our ships.'

'Are you suggesting we bombard the castle?' said the admiral.

'There is no other way.'

'Go on.'

'If *La Santa Jorge* could be navigated as near as possible to the channel leading up to the castle, you would have a firing range of about five hundred metres. The cannons' range is I believe a thousand metres.'

The admiral had instructed that old cannons be loaded onto *La Santa Jorge* before he set sail from Quinta do Lago. He had ammunition but had no idea as to the weapon's range or accuracy.

'Firing from the ship is not an option,' said the admiral. 'A cannon will need to be dis-assembled and transported ashore.'

'That is going to difficult as we only have row boats.'

'Difficult yes, but doable. The crew of *La Santa Jorge* have trained on the weapon. They can take it apart and re-assemble it in in short order. Make sure they travel with you after you have found the best location for the weapon.'

'We would need to land several troops of grenadiers before the attack,' said a captain. 'Once the walls are breached, we should be able to climb into the inner court-yards. Once inside, we will secure the castle.'

'What about the defenders?' said another captain.

'Captain da Gama had dinner with the community two weeks ago,' said the admiral. 'While they are mostly elderly or infirm, two of the younger adults are preventing our ships leaving Quinta do Lago. If the duke knew that, he would skin us all alive. We will go with my plan. Start making the preparations please. It has been decided.'

'What about Captain da Gama?' asked the senior captain.

'He is recovering from his gunshot wound and will not be of much use to us over the coming days. Get on with it. Whatever you do, make sure the weapon is fully calibrated before we aim it at the castle.'

With instructions to hand, the captains left. The admiral had one more task – to call the duke. He walked to the radio room at deck three, ordered the operator out of the room, locked the door, and inserted the code for the duke. He pressed the engage button and it lit up.

'Admiral calling…' He did not get a chance to finish his call signal.

'And about time too,' was the instant reply. 'When do we set sail?'

'I need to talk to you about that,' said the admiral.

'I am not interested in talk – we have had enough of waffle these past months. When do I set sail? Can you not answer a simple question?'

'There has been a change in plan, I am afraid.' While a strong character in front of his men, the admiral quaked when speaking to his superior who instilled fear in him.

'Be up front and honest with me, Admiral. As you know I do not suffer fools gladly. What has happened?'

'I will start with the good news. We have taken Howth Head Island and have two ships, and a company of grenadiers in place.'

'But Howth Head was never the primary target,' said the duke. 'It is far too small for our needs.'

'I had to change the plans. When we landed at Dundrum, we discovered the island was riddled with a plague of sorts. Something to do with an highly contagious animal virus that had spread to humans. Dundrum is off limits, I am sorry to say.'

'But we planned to base ourselves there! Captain da Gama gave the place a glowing reference two months ago.'

'He may well have, I admit. But in the intervening weeks, the virus has killed most of the population. It is off limits for the foreseeable future.'

'That leaves Malahide Castle,' said the duke who was extremely familiar with the geography of the east cost of Iceapelago. 'Have you taken the castle and its twenty elderly inhabitants?'

'Ah, that is what I want to talk to you about.'

'What is there to talk about? You were present, were you not, when the captain spelled out how easy it would be to secure the castle?'

'It might have seemed easy at face value. The captain is in the infirmary with a bullet wound because he made the wrong assumption. The castle is well defended.

Though it appears the defenders were forewarned when we attacked.' The admiral wisely chose not to reveal the overheard conversation. 'As we speak, all my ships are sailing to support the assault on the castle. Our cannon should be in position facing the weaker rear battlements before the end of the day.'

'What does this mean, Admiral?'

'You need to stay at Quinta do Lago until I send you word that Malahide Castle has been secured.'

'I have fifty ships packed with my citizens at the quayside. When do you expect an outcome?'

'By midday the day after tomorrow at the latest.'

'And the ships that are scheduled to set sail for Howth Head?'

'I have ordered them to proceed at full sail. They will arrive in four days, or thereabouts. And as part of our new plan, I have another part of the fleet about to set a course for Cork Airport Island.'

'Why Cork? It was never mentioned by Captain da Gama.'

'There were circumstances out of my control.'

'Admiral, I have known you and your family for decades. You are my appointed Commander-In-Chief of the combined forces of the Principality of Ria Formosa.'

'I know, sir. It is a great responsibility and honour.'

'Honour it may be. If my departure is further delayed beyond midday tomorrow, I will personally pick the nearest yardarm, and hang you myself. I will leave your carcass to the seagulls.'

'No pressure then,' muttered the admiral as the radio line went dead.

CHAPTER 15

La Santa Fabio

RORY WON THE BRIEF fight in the confines of the small radio room. Actually, it was no more than a spirited scuffle.

While he might be over seventy years old and had a dodgy knee, he was fit for his age and, unlike his foe, had practical, though not recent, experience of hand-to-hand combat.

The grenadier was knocked out with a single punch to the side of his head. He collapsed like a sack of potatoes. Rory then gagged and secured him with rope. Once he was trussed up, Rory locked the door of the radio room as he left and took the key.

Armed with a lot of new information, Rory had little time to think though the pros and cons of his next move. His overwhelming instinct was that he needed to support his family and friends at Malahide. He could not leave his wife and children to the mercy of the climate hoodlums. He needed a plan. His thought process began to crystallise as he worked through some ideas in his head.

He sought out Sheila, the widow of the murdered Six. She was the key to what he had in mind. He found her in the library on her own. She was sitting on a sofa, staring vacantly at the wall, clearly trying to absorb the impact of the murder of her husband of fifty years. He expected that the early grieving stage was about to overwhelm her.

There were guards in the building, but they had not been ordered to keep anyone prisoner, so everyone had the liberty to walk about as they pleased. As far as the admiral was concerned, Howth Head was secure. It was his and some essential preparations had to be carried out before the peoples of Ria Formosa arrived. The sole dynamic was timing. The admiral believed the current residents of Howth Head were not a risk to his master plan.

'Sheila, can I have a word?' said Rory, closing the door.

'Oh Rory, I can't comprehend that my Six is gone. Poor Brendan. We bury him this afternoon. Can you believe it? He's hardly dead a day. I haven't had time to think, never mind make the necessary preparations.'

'Sheila, I've known Brendan for nearly as long as you have. We've always had a good relationship, despite all our challenges and the occasional healthy disagreement.'

'I know. He always spoke well of you, despite your very public differences. Believe it or not, he held you in high regard. He trusted you. And if he trusted you, so do I.'

'I need your help, Sheila,' said Rory. He was keen to put his cards on the table while being as sensitive to the widow's feelings as was possible. That said, he had not fully thought through what he wanted to say. Accordingly, and out of character, he made up his pitch as he went along. 'We're all in trouble with these climate refugees. It's hard to believe after all we have been through that Iceapelago now appears to be a more sustainable place to live than most other parts of the Northern Hemisphere. I fear the planned exodus of the Ria Formosa population is but the first we will experience. Many other communities have been displaced. We are lucky that our traditional temperate climate has returned, with some extremes admittedly. But to the south and west of Europe, desert conditions are the norm. In a way, I can understand peoples' instinct to survive. Would we do anything different if the tables were turned?'

'What has this to do with me and my community?' said Sheila.

'Everything. Let me explain.'

'Please do.'

'There are over a hundred people living on Howth Head Island, and you all eke out a good life in the current circumstances. There is plenty to eat, you have family supports, and your buildings are sturdy. Hard to believe perhaps, but Howth Head Island is about a fifth the size of Malahide Castle Island and has five times the population.

'I don't disagree,' said Sheila.

'In Malahide, we are just twenty. Once Malahide Castle Island sustained over a thousand.'

'Before the Big Storm,' said Sheila.

'Yes, but my point is that why do we have two Iceapelago communities almost adjacent to each other, yet so far apart. Could we not share resources for our mutual benefit despite our historical differences?'

'Rory, what are you saying?'

'I would like to invite you, and your community to move to Malahide Castle as fellow citizens, and permanent residents. We've more than enough resources to sustain both our communities.'

'And abandon Howth Head?'

'Yes, to the people from Ria Formosa. They are going to take over one way or the other, and let you be in no doubt about that. Under my proposed arrangement, you take all of your personal possessions to Malahide. We have more than enough space within the castle's walls to offer generously spaced accommodation to your families. This transition can be done in stages if you wish. And you will have the safeguard of calling a halt if perceived difficulties present.'

As soon as the Howth Six's widow heard the word 'difficulties,' she backtracked. 'Who will be the Six? We would need to have somebody in charge.'

'I will support you for the position,' said Rory. 'I'll ask Emily to step down. Believe me, I have reflected on this. Our community is so small that we'll literally die out over the next decade unless we get fresh blood, so to speak. Please consider my proposition carefully and discuss it with your elders.'

'Rory, rest assured I will. Frankly, this is quite a lot to absorb. It's not as if I had nothing else to consider. When do you need a decision?'

'That depends on the timeline.'

'What do you mean? I am confused,' said Sheila.

'I'm aware that the admiral's plan to relocate the majority of his climate refugees from Quinta do Lago to Dundrum has been thwarted. It seems the so-called yellow virus that destroyed the Arctic fox population has spread to humans. Dundrum is off limits for the foreseeable future. As an alternative, Admiral Rodriguez is now turning his attention to my community. If he succeeds, the planned integration of our two communities will not happen.'

'Why not? Surely your community could transfer here?' said Sheila. 'Is that not an unreasonable question?'

'The saying goes possession is nine tenths of the law,' said Rory. 'The Principality of Ria Formosa has taken Howth Head, and there's no going back on that. Malahide Castle on the other hand is still free. I need to be blunt, Sheila, and please forgive my straight talking. Time is not on our side. For our plan to work, I need your best men and women to come with me to Malahide Castle to support our defences, and hopefully repel the admiral's forces. The alternative, as has been made very clear by Captain da Gama, is that the Howth Head residents will be moved to Dundrum and be exposed to its pestilence.'

'We wouldn't last a week in Dundrum. We've had a few cases of that dreadful yellow virus.'

'I know.'

'But it's a big ask,' said Sheila. 'I'm beginning to understand the importance of this proposition.'

'A big ask yes, but a reasonable ask.'

'Explain to me exactly what you have in mind?'

'You have thirty people in the age cohort between late teenager and forty?'

'That is correct.'

'And you have some small arms that are still concealed?'

'Yes, I dare to admit.'

'I'll bring this armed group to Malahide Castle on one of the admiral's ships. I'll only do it with volunteers.'

'You must be mad.'

'Not for the first time in my life, I'll have to take a risk,' said Rory. 'To make my plan work, we need a diversion. The basics of the most covert manoeuvres. I don't want to be disrespectful, but could we use Brendan's funeral procession as a way to catch the grenadiers off-guard?'

'Rory, you're stretching my tolerance to the limit.'

'Bear with me, Sheila. Say you start the funeral procession from here and instead of travelling down to the harbour area as is tradition, you walk in the direction of the old summit area. You might let it be known to the senior grenadier that his presence and indeed those of his troops would be appreciated given the circumstances of the Six's death. As you approach the summit, I will lead your volunteers to the harbour area. We'll take the larger of the two ships that are at the dock and sail it to Malahide Castle.'

'Alright, I'll do it. That's what Brendan would have wanted. But what you have in mind will not be that easy. Both ships are heavily guarded, are they not?'

'I walked the area this morning and could see no more than four guards.'

'That's a lot, and they're armed, I assume?'

'Yes, they all have light machine pistols. I am hoping that one, and preferably two, get distracted with the music of the funeral march. If they do, they may leave their posts. I have a pistol and will deal with the remaining guards if they resist.'

'What's the downside? Severe retribution for those of us who remain?'

'The sea captain who was left here is junior, and he will not do anything without orders.'

'He will surely radio the admiral?'

'He'll try. But not only have I locked the door to the radio room. I also disabled the radio set. Here's the key, by the way.'

'More genius. It's no wonder Ruth Henry relied on you so much, God rest her.'

'Are we agreed?'

'That is a lot to take in, but yes. I'll spread the word. Let's meet back here at three o'clock. I'll schedule the funeral procession for four. When we meet, I should know how many volunteers you'll have, and how they will be armed.'

'Thank you,' said Rory. 'I'll not let you down.'

After Sheila left the library, Rory sat down to reflect on his conversation. While there were risks and there might be some fatalities, what other option was there? He had two hours to kill. Putting his head on the sofa's cushions, he soon dozed off.

Rory woke with a start. He checked his watch. It was five to three. Minutes later the door opened. Sheila and the Howth elders entered the room. Seeing Sheila with her elders, Rory assumed the worst. He sat upright, still slightly dazed from his rare nap.

'Don't look so worried, Rory. You already know my elders, so we can dispense with the introductions and get straight down to business.'

'Fair enough,' said Rory. 'What's your response?'

'We agree to your plan with two conditions. To minimise the loss of life we looked for twenty, and not thirty volunteers.'

'And what was the response?'

'Actually forty-five residents wanted to help. So we

have reduced the numbers, and not allowed more than two from the same family to join you. They are all skilled at small firearms.'

'And the second condition?'

'I will not be the new Six of the joint Malahide/Howth community. We want you to lead us.'

Rory gasped audibly. This was not what he expected. The decades' old rivalry between the two communities had been put aside in the interest of the common good.

'I'd be honoured, Sheila. Thank you,' said Rory. He shook Sheila's hand firmly and gave her a light hug. The elders clapped in appreciation.

'Well, that's that,' said Sheila. 'We've a funeral to attend. You've a job to do. The meeting point is the old harbour-master's office, half a block back from the quays.'

'I know where that is. Thank you. Thank you all.'

Sheila and the elders left to attend to the funeral of her beloved Six, her husband.

Rory made his way to the rendezvous point.

Over the next hour his volunteers arrived in small groups, and very discreetly. They assembled in the main office that dominated the lower harbour. Introductions were made. Rory reckoned the average age was late twenties. All looked fit and able. From the short conversations he had with the early arrivals, it was clear the task ahead and its challenges had been explained to them.

'OK, here's what we are going to do,' said Rory. 'I checked out the harbour area just now, and as I expected, two guards heard the funeral music and have walked up Howth Hill to check out the procession. This gives us a window of opportunity of about twenty minutes. Mary, is it?' said Rory pointing to one of the new arrivals.

'Yes, that's me.'

'I would like to take your hand as we go for a walk in the direction of the closest ship. It's called *La Santa Fabio* and it's no more than two hundred metres from here. The guard will spot us as there is not much else happening on the quayside. You wave to him to catch his attention when we are abreast the ship's gangplank. When he responds, I'll charge at him. If he resists, I'll shoot him with my hand pistol. If he has any sense, he will jump overboard when I challenge him. And when the ship is secure, the rest of you should follow. I'll cover you in case the second guard gets trigger happy. Is that clear?'

The volunteers nodded.

The plan worked. The sentry on *La Santa Fabio* took an instant shine to Mary who gave him her very best smile. He dropped his gun and put his hands up as soon as he was challenged by Rory. Once given the opportunity, he ran down the gangplank at speed. His friend guarding the second ship did the same, while throwing his gun into the harbour. The volunteers then ran forward to board the *La Santa Fabio*.

'Have any of you sailed before?' said Rory.

'We're from Howth Head, remember,' said Mary. 'We've all been on the water since we were children, but never on something as big as this.'

'Let's improvise then. I'll admit I too am a bit of a novice.'

He did not have to say anything further. The volunteers split into groups, and without any prompting went about their tasks. *La Santa Fabio's* ties to the harbour bollards were quickly loosened and released. She drifted away from the marina deck. Four sets of hands untied the sheets and released the mainsail and foresail. Mary took charge of the tiller. They glanced off the second ship when reversing out of the harbour, and slowly and surely turned into the wind. *La Santa Fabio* sailed silently into the choppy waters of Dublin Bay over the peak of what was once Ireland's Eye.

CHAPTER 16

CorkHurling3*

'It seems so complicated,' said Kate.

'You'll get used to it,' said Tony.

The siblings sat beside each other at a desk in the office complex at the airport terminal with Ruth Henry's fifty-year-old computer between them. Thanks to Don, the solar panels on the rooftop were reconnected to provide electricity. Tony's backpack contained a power cable that linked to the computer. Once powered up, the screen displayed a dialogue box that requested a password.

Before he entered the password, Tony turned to his sister. 'Do you know, Grandma could have sat at this very desk.'

'She did,' said Don. 'This was the office used by the Iceapelago Commander and her staff. This place brings back vivid memories, and not all of them are positive. This was Ruth's control centre. She effectively lived here. Given the myriad of problems affecting Iceapelago at the time, she more often than not was the first in, and the last out. I call that dedication.'

'We've gone full circle, haven't we?' said Tony. 'For all she did, and don't get me wrong, we're no better off decades later. Arguably, we are on our collective knees.'

'Let's not dwell on the past, otherwise we'll be here all day,' said Don. 'Can we get back to the task at hand?'

'Right so. You have the password, Tony?' said Kate.

'Sure do.'

'Another treasure from the Healing Hamper?'

'Correct in one,' said Tony. 'The password is *CorkHurling3**. Let's hope it hasn't changed.'

Tony tapped in the characters and pressed the return button. The screen lit up with ten blue folders occupying the centre of the screen.

Kate gawked in amazement. While she had seen the computer before, she had never seen it working. The pure astonishment of it. Computers were an historical footnote as far as she was concerned. They did not put food on the table, nor collect eggs.

'What are we looking for?' she asked.

'The folders are all labelled, see? Grandma was an organised person. The first thing we need to find is where she hid the drones, and one of these folders will help us.'

'Try the one called *Arms*,' said Kate.

Tony clicked the folder open and several more folders appeared, each with a distinctive label.

'There,' said Kate pointing. 'It says *Drone*s.'

The opened file also contained many more folders.

'It's like a Christmas tree structure, isn't it?' said Kate. 'I'll try the folder called *Storage*, shall I?'

'Go for it.'

Clear images appeared of six large wooden box crates, each with unreadable letters embossed on the front. Three sets of eyes viewed these images that were taken such a long time ago.

'I recognise the backdrop,' said Don. 'That's an area at the back of the engineering works building, which is located behind one of the smaller hangars. There's a storage room there, or at least there was when I went looking for spares for the Cork cruisers.'

'That's a good start,' said Tony. 'Let's close the computer and go see.'

Ten minutes later they walked into the vast open door of Hangar 3. The huge space that once contained aircraft and helicopters was empty. Decades of rubbish had blown into the corners of the building and lay strewn in dirty mounds everywhere.

'What we're looking for is over there,' said Don.

He walked diagonally to the far end of the hangar, and without hesitation, he opened the door under the sign *Engineering*. They went into a much smaller space. Tony expected to see the crates sitting on the floor. He was disappointed to see all sorts of scattered equipment and detritus, but no crates.

'Where are they?' said Tony.

'Remember that when your grandma took these photos, she knew Cork Airport was in the eye of the Big Storm. It is possible the crates were concealed or protected. They could also have been moved after the photos were taken.'

'Let's search a bit harder,' said Tony.

He did not have to wait long. In another building at the back of the engineering building, they came across a sunken works area that was used to repair the underside of cars or trucks. There was a canopy covering something. That something when they removed the cover was the crates they were looking for.

The unreadable letters were legible with each crate declaring *Property of the Canadian Air Force.*

'Shall we start opening the cargo?' said Tony.

'Let's get going,' said Don. 'There should be jemmies on the shelves. We'll need them to break open the containers.'

It took several hours of hard work to move the equipment out of the sunken works area to the centre of the hangar. Don's agility with a small pulley and a lot of collective physical shoving and pulling ensured they finally had the crate's contents laid out on the floor for inspection.

'What exactly have we got here, Don?' said Kate. 'You said these things fly, didn't you?'

'I sure did,' said Don. 'I was in the control room when they were used to destroy the Cymru ships that were sailing into Dublin Bay with the aim of capturing Dundrum Island and, by extension, controlling Iceapelago. There are two quite different types of drones. The smallest – I think it's what came out of the first two crates – is a remote drone capable of firing rockets and rocket-propelled grenades over a distant of two kilometres. What should interest us more is the second machine. Once assembled, it can be flown by an onboard pilot. And what's more, it has the capacity to hold a second person who can be strapped to the rear compartment. This is a very versatile drone by any reckoning. It's called a hoverbike.'

Kate listened in awe to Don's explanations.

Tony had seen images of drones from books, but had never seen one at close quarters before, or at least the components of what would be a drone once fully assembled.

'Your grandmother didn't want this equipment to fall into the wrong hands. That's why she went to so much trouble to conceal it. She was paranoid about security for good reason.'

'How do we assemble them?' said Kate. 'Is there an instructions book?'

'Not here anyhow,' said Don. 'Ruth presumably took the sensible precaution of separating the operating and assembly instructions from the actual equipment.'

'She did just that,' said Tony. 'Our Cork Hurling protected friend holds the secret. Let's find a level surface and I'll open the laptop.'

Ruth Henry must have anticipated that her precious drones would be used after she died. Instead of providing a tome with instructions, she had several videos recorded and stored on her laptop.

'Look, there's a folder called *Hoverbike Assembly*,' said Kate. 'Open it.'

With a click the video presented itself.

'Shall I play it?' said Tony.

'Of course,' said Kate.

He had played this particular video several times when nobody was watching. It had a huge impact on him when he first listened to it.

'I should warn you that Grandma does the introductions before she hands over to a Canadian Air Force engineer.' Tony clicked the play button and stepped back allowing all three of them to view the small screen.

'Hello, my name is Ruth Henry. If you are watching this video, I'm assuming Iceapelago is in trouble again. I'm also assuming my computer is in good hands. This video message is about your insurance policy. My good friends from Canada generously left some military equipment before they returned to their base. These drones are powerful weapons when used correctly. So whoever is watching me should bear that in mind.'

'Oh my goodness,' said Kate. 'That's my grandma speaking. I never heard her voice before. What a beautiful Cork accent. She looks so pretty, doesn't she, Tony?'

Tony had the good sense to press the pause button once Kate spoke. He looked at Don who was sobbing, overcome with emotion.

'Don't mind me,' said Don. 'This brings back so many vivid memories of a woman we all admired and loved so much. Hearing her voice just triggered long-forgotten feelings deep within me. Sorry. Sorry, I'll be alright.'

Tony let Don recover his composure and once he had, he pressed the play button.

After the Iceapelago Commander's brief introduction, she left the remainder of the twenty-minute presentation to the handsome Canadian engineer. He was very clear. In storing the drone component parts, every effort had been made to ensure they could be reassembled quickly with the right tools. The core fuselage of the remote drone required six units to be bolted using plates secured by standard nuts. From the video this appeared to be quite straightforward apart from the issue of connecting the electronic cabling. The large drone, the hoverbike, demanded a somewhat similar assembly method. The main difference was that the hoverbike had additional features to be added, including a rocket launcher to be attached under the fuselage.

'It's a bit like a jigsaw, isn't it?' said Kate.

'A three thousand piece jigsaw perhaps,' said Tony. 'What do think, Don? How long will it take the three of us to have this kit up and running?'

'A day at most,' said Tony. 'If we only assemble the hoverbike, we could have a viable weapon much sooner.'

'Let's do that then,' said Tony.

'But we still have a major problem,' said Don.

'What's that?' asked Kate.

'These things can't fly to their full potential without access to satellite-based communications using what was once called the internet.'

'What are you talking about?' asked Tony. 'I understood they had solar panels and a support battery.'

'They do for propulsion purposes,' said Don. 'But we need satellite access to lock and fire the rocket systems. While the hoverbike is fully controlled and navigated by its pilot once the course is plotted, its precision weapons system needs to be pre-programmed. To do that we need internet access.'

'I read about this internet thing,' said Kate. 'Wasn't it the way electronic things worked, or something like that?'

'The Internet of Things it was called when our mother was a child,' said Tony. 'For it to work, we need satellite access.'

'Where can we get this satellite access?' said Kate.

'We can't,' said Don. 'Satellites are another thing of the past unless, of course, one has access to military resources.'

'Could we call the Canadians?' said Tony. 'It's their equipment, after all.'

'One thing at a time,' said Don. 'Let's focus on the assembly for now. That will give me time to think through our options.'

'Alright then,' said Tony. 'Let's get to work.'

It took the best part of half a day as Don had predicted. His engineering experience was essential. He was an expert with screwdrivers, power drills, lathes, and fusing rivets. He used much of the equipment that hung from the walls of the workspaces where they had been stored with great care by their previous users, including himself. In between breaks, they discussed Ruth Henry, her legacy, and the many woes that had befallen Iceapelago.

The end product stood proudly under the eaves of Hangar 3. Ready for use, but not quite yet.

'Have you a solution to the satellite issue, Don?' said Tony.

'It's worth a try. How about we try to make a connection with the Canadians using the Cork Airport radio?'

'That makes sense,' said Tony. 'Where's the radio room?'

'Atop the air traffic control tower over there. As with all the other buildings on the complex, I'll have to reconnect it to an electricity source. But that won't take too long.'

It took ten minutes to climb the two hundred steps to the top. A vast room opened before them. Unlike the other storm damaged buildings in the airport complex, the triple glazed windows were still closed shut. The rank smell of unused air was nauseous.

'Get a few windows open quickly,' said Don. 'We should be able to breathe once the wind blows this smell away, or at least dilutes it.'

Don, once a regular visitor to the tower, busied himself. He observed straight away that the tower area had been systematically and carefully closed down. He reversed the functionality of the parts of the tower they needed. While he was getting on with the practical side of restoring power, Tony and Kate sat at the main radio communications console, again hugely aware that their grandmother had used the same equipment decades earlier. She managed and controlled radio communications across Iceapelago from this very spot.

'See here,' said Kate. She removed a plastic coated board from the side of one of the radio receivers. It was covered in dust. She removed a layer of the dirt.

'What's that?' said Tony.

'It's a sheet with all the call signal codes they used, and the corresponding codes from all the centres they were in touch with,' said Kate. 'Here's one that's underlined and says Canadian Johnny. I assume that was an operator's name.'

'Show me,' said Tony. He took the clipboard. 'It's a list of the call signs of all the Iceapelago Sixes.'

'Can we call Jon?' said Kate.

'First things first, shall we?' said Tony. 'Don, when we will be online?'

'Wait just a minute. A few more adjustments.'

Don's magic hands again did the business. The lighting in the tower was turned on, and the radio control panel lit up with buttons of various colours and sizes flickering. In a short while the system completed its reboot.

'Shall we start with Canadian Johnny?' said Tony.

'I'll show you how,' said Don.

He entered the call sign provided. The console in front of him instantly flashed Canadian Johnny.

'Once I press the radio transmission button on my hand-held microphone, we can start. Canadian Johnny, Canadian Johnny, this is Cork Airport. Can you hear us? Over.'

There was no response.

'Canadian Johnny, Canadian Johnny, this is Cork Airport. Can you hear us? Over.'

The same. Don tried ten times.

'The signal is emitting, it's just not being received. Sorry, Tony.'

'Can we now call Jon?' said Kate.

'Why not,' said Tony.

He turned the dial and typed in the access code for Malahide Castle Island – 450459 – and pressed the transmission button.

'Malahide Castle, Malahide Castle, this is Cork Airport. Can you hear us? Over.'

They waited expectantly, and somewhat nervously.

There was no response.

Tony put his finger on the redial key. There was an instant reply.

'Cork Airport, this is Malahide Castle. It has been a very long time since we last heard from you. This is Veronica speaking. Please identify yourself.'

Tony, Kate, and Don felt a surge in their inner emotions. They never had a radio in the Old Head of Kinsale that would have allowed them keep in contact with other communities. They began to understand the full power and potential of this medium.

'Veronica, it's Tony, I'm with Kate and Don from Kinsale Head. We were nearly your dinner guests the week before last.'

'I remember well. Orla told me you were heading to Cork Airport. I trust you got there safely?'

'Yes, it's a long story, a very long story for another day. How are Orla and Jon?'

'There're busy, and that's why I'm on radio ops duty. We've been attacked by that renegade Captain da Gama, or whatever he calls himself. I told our Six she made a big mistake inviting him to Iceapelago.'

'We know about the attack. What's the latest?'

'It's been more than two days since they tried to blow open the front door. They carried off their dead and wounded. Nothing since. Jon and Orla are on high alert. As far as I know, they are monitoring the channel that leads to the marina. We are expecting more trouble. The community here doesn't have a stomach for a fight. We're too old for that sort of thing. I really don't know what to say. But it's nice to hear from you.'

'Please tell Orla and Jon that we have opened communications. Let's keep in contact.'

'Really nice to speak to Cork. The last time I did so I spoke to your grandmother.'

'She's here with us, Veronica, believe me.'

Kate closed the radio circuit to Malahide.

What a day. Tony, Kate and Don sat side-by-side watching the flickering lights of the radio console. Silently, they watched the sun set over the hills of East Cork from their elevated and unique point atop the control tower. The fringes of the Celtic Sea were in the near distance. The tip of the lighthouse at the Old Head of Kinsale could just about be seen in the far horizon. No doubt Tony and Kate's mother was still pining for her lost children, while getting on with her daily chores.

'You thought today was eventful, wait until tomorrow,' said Don.

'The priority is to get the hoverbike working,' said Tony. 'I've seen an instruction video on flying the hoverbike on Grandma's laptop that made little sense until now. Helping you assemble the machine has given me a much better understanding as to what it is capable of.'

'That's for tomorrow,' said Don. 'We need rest, otherwise mistakes will be made. Mistakes mean accidents.'

They walked in the direction of the staircase. Don turned off the lights. Then descended the first step.

The silence of the control tower was suddenly disturbed.

'Cork Airport, Cork Airport, this is the Canadian Air Force. Can you hear me? Over.'

Tony rushed back to the radio console. He pressed the receiver switch. 'Cork Airport receiving.'

'Good to hear from you. Can we be of assistance?'

Given his level of over-excitement, Tony went into a long diatribe about how happy he was to make a radio connection.

'Slow down! I am having trouble understanding your rich Cork accent,' said Bill, who identified himself as the radio operator based at the Canadian Air Force Ops Centre high atop the Baie Verte peninsula on the north coast of Newfoundland.

'We've not heard from Cork Airport in a long time, or indeed from anyone in Europe, so it's nice you made the connection.'

'Thanks, Bill,' said Tony. 'Before we explain what's happening here, could you give us a heads-up about the climatic conditions in your part of the world?'

'There's really been no change. For reasons of personal safety primarily, civilians continue to live in military camps. For example, we have a population here of five hundred. The conditions are very rudimentary. There's been no fossil fuel for decades, and that means no flights, which is a bit tough for an air force. No cars or trucks, which is a total bummer for us Canadians. Electricity in Canada was for the most part generated by fossil fuels. The tankers that brought us the golden barrels stopped when they ran out of marine diesel. The refineries have long processed their last consignments. Anyway, it's all changed, utterly changed.'

'Do you have renewable energy?'

'Nothing like the level needed to compensate for the absence of fossil fuels. The climate changed so quickly and with such ferocity that nobody had time to build out sufficient capacity. At Baie Verte we spend most of our time trying to keep the solar panels working. The on- and offshore wind turbines were blown down long ago. To be honest, I think everyone has gotten used to the Ice Age conditions. Nobody complains any more. Another Canadian tradition gone down the toilet.'

'How bad was the climate damage?' said Tony.

'We lost over ninety percent of the Canadian population within five years of what you call the Eriador Event. Subsequent storms have wreaked havoc on an ongoing basis. If there is a positive, all our remaining dwellings are now relatively sturdy, dry, and well insulated. In common with dozens of other communities scattered all over Canada, we are self-sufficient. Nobody starves. There is plenty of fish and game. But do not get sick. That's a sure way to you know where.'

Tony was enjoying his chat with Bill who clearly was not in any way discreet.

'What about America?'

'Yeah, what about America? The east coast took a total hammering when the La Palma tsunamis hit. The combined Greenland and Antarctic ice melts raised sea levels to heights nobody had predicted. Even the most eager of the climate scientists were taken by surprise. Places like Florida and the big cities of Washington, New York and Boston have been under water for, what, forty years? I never hear from anyone down south. No doubt isolated communities exist but they are not on our radar. So much about this side of the pond. All is well in Iceapelago? Long time, no hear. Why did you make contact by the way?'

Tony's patience as a listener had been put to the test. Bill was a natural chatterbox. It was time for the business side of the conversation to begin.

'Bill, you may not be aware, but decades ago the Canadian Air Force sent a troop of army rangers to Cork.'

'They did? That is news to me. Long before my time.'

'Well, they left some military equipment in our safe-keeping, and that's the reason I'm calling.'

'Not one of our nuclear things?'

'No, thankfully.'

'Thank goodness for that.'

'We have two military drones. One is a hoverbike, embossed with the colours of the Canadian Air Force.'

'And the point is?'

'I need your help to provide us with satellite communications.'

'How did you know we had satnav comms?' said Bill.

'Because when we used the drones back in 2091 you provided us with the necessary communications links.'

'That's a bit above my pay grade, Tony. Hold on a while. I will have to get one of my IntelSig colleagues. Nice to talk to you. Hold on for a few minutes.'

Tony put the microphone on the table. 'What do you make of that?'

'Canada appears to be in the same state of dilapidation and distress as Iceapelago,' said Don.

'That's not a positive thing,' said Kate. 'I would have assumed they had far more resources than we have.'

'What everyone forgot going back a century, is that Mother Nature does not filter out the rich and the well-prepared for special treatment,' said Tony. 'She strikes in a random manner. Canada is as banjaxed as Iceapelago. But let's hope we get help.'

The radio crackled back to life. 'Who am I speaking to?'

'My name is Tony Henry, and I'm talking to you from the control tower at Cork Airport Island in Iceapelago. And who I am speaking to please?

'General Peter Collins of the Canadian Air Force here.'

'Nice to talk to you, sir,' said Tony.

'Tony, are you by any chance a relation of Ruth Henry, the Commander of Iceapelago?'

'Actually, I'm her grandson, and her granddaughter Orla is also with me on the call.'

'Well, I never,' said the general. 'Your grandmother was a hero, did you know that?'

'Yes, we know all about her. Have you visited Iceapelago by any chance?'

'Sure did. I was one of the rangers that flew to Cork years back. I was a young sergeant then.'

'Did you meet Grandma?'

'A sight to behold. Yes. She was a pretty one, with a sharp tongue and a sharper sense of humour. She out-talked everyone effortlessly. I reckon every soldier fell in love with her, but only one was lucky in the end. Your grandmother's love life is off limits, I suppose?'

'You guessed right,' said Kate.

'What did you do while in Cork?' said Tony.

'I was a qualified hoverbike pilot. Your grandmother took a huge interest in the capability of the machine, which I gather you have reassembled. Is that right?'

'We have. I guess we are talking to the right man, then?'

'What exactly are you planning?' said the general.

Tony gave the general a briefing about the pending attack on Malahide Castle, and the rationale for the Portuguese climate refugees' interest in Iceapelago.

'I intend to pilot the newly assembled hoverbike to Malahide Castle. Based on what we find out, I will deploy the firepower of the hoverbike to destroy the attacking forces.'

'It would be much better if you got some feedback from the ground before you commit resources over Malahide,' said the general. 'If I recall, Malahide Castle has a radio centre.'

'And we've been in touch, rest assured,' said Tony. 'As of an hour ago, the admiral's fleet was still at anchor. Once they move, we will get a signal.'

'Is that blackguard Rory still in charge at Malahide?' said the general.

'Yes, in fact he's the current Commander of Iceapelago. He took over from Grandma. His wife Veronica, who is doing the radio operator job at Malahide Castle, says he has just landed with some reinforcements from Howth Head.'

'When you see him, tell him Peter Collins said "Hi". He and I did a lot of verbal arm wrestling during our down time. We also shared the occasional bottle of whiskey, I'll reluctantly admit. He was a great support to Ruth.'

'Let's catch up with the nostalgia later,' said Tony. 'Time is not on our side.'

The general paused his story about his friend Rory knowing the young man he was talking to was in a hurry. Just like his grandmother had been.

'I need to get the hoverbike in the air pronto,' said Tony. 'General, I understand that the hoverbike's rockets only work if they are laser guided to a target, and to do that, we need access to satellite communications. Can you help us?'

'Yes, is the short answer. First of all we need to open and check the satellite's systems. We have had no reason to use it of late, so that will take an hour or two. When I tell you, you will need to power up the hoverbike. Once that is done, it will seek out our communications satellite because it has been preconfigured to do that. I will give you the passwords. You then need to reboot the machine, and you should be ready to go.'

'That sounds simple,' said Tony.

'Hoverbikes may be complicated in many respects, especially the one you intend to fly, but their electronics are quite basic. I am assuming you've no experience in piloting a drone?'

'Actually, no,' said Tony. 'Though I have seen the instruction video.'

'Use the time over the next few hours to get in some practice,' said the general. 'A word of caution, do not fly the hoverbike until the batteries are fully charged. With a payload of 300 kilograms, including munitions, I estimate you will have ninety minutes in the air, no more. It's about seventy minutes to Malahide provided you don't meet a headwind so those ten remaining minutes over the target area will be precious. Also, you'll need to land, so factor that into your plans.'

'Thanks, Colly,' said Tony.

'Colly? I've haven't been called that since I met your grandmother.'

'I know. You get a few special mentions in her private diary.'

'Good ones, I hope?'

'Of course. Very friendly references, in fact.'

'Nothing too indiscreet, I trust?' said Colly.

'Not to my reading,' said Tony.

'That's a good lie,' said Colly. 'I'll radio you when we have matters sorted here.'

With that the radio signal went dead.

'What did you make of that?' said Tony.

'Apart from the fact that Colly may have been your grandmother's much talked about beau, we're lucky that the hoverbike will be synchronised with the Canadian satellite,' said Don. 'What concerns me more is your total inexperience in flying one of these things. The hoverbike should have a fully-charged battery by now, so let's practice flying it around the airport.'

Back at the hangar, Tony strapped himself onto the hoverbike's saddle seat with a safety harness and put on a safety helmet. The lightweight aluminium frame that looked like a conventional motor bike was positioned above four independent spinning rotors. He sat upright with the oblong dashboard panel at chest level. The hand controls were similar to those on the handlebars of a motorcycle. Stability was provided by two long parallel skids. Between the skids, it had been possible to bolt on a 70 mm bracket that could hold three armed projectiles.

Once he switched on the ignition the dashboard lit up.

'That's the navigation feature,' said Don.

Standing astride the bike's frame, he pointed to the map at the centre of the console.

'Once the satnav is sorted, you'll be able to pre-programme it to fly direct to Malahide Castle.'

'What's this?' said Tony touching the red button on the top of the left handlebar.

'That's the rocket firing button,' said Don. 'And there's another one on the right that is a trigger for the machine gun. They won't work because we haven't yet attached the weaponry pods.'

'OK, step back everyone. Let's try and get this machine in the air.'

Over the following ninety minutes – the life cycle of the battery – Tony carefully worked the controls. He started with the vertical lift and landing features which he mastered quickly using the joystick that was located on the centre of the control panel. He practiced rising and lowering the hovercraft by two to three metres at first and once he got the knack, admittedly after a shaky start, he uplifted the hoverbike to an elevation of a hundred metres. Moving forward at elevation was more problematic. He was beginning to get a better feeling for the controls to fly the hoverbike vertically. However, as he soon discovered, it was more complicated to steer the hoverbike sideways.

He landed with a bump outside the hangar.

'I've spoken to Colly while you were up there, messing about,' said Kate. 'Their satellite will be available from oh six hundred hours our time tomorrow. He suggests you should practice flying with the full weapons' payload before you head to Malahide Castle.'

'That makes a lot of sense,' said Don.

'You'll be glad to know that Colly will be able to talk to you during the flight using the radio receiver built into your helmet. He'll be your co-pilot.'

'I'm glad to hear that,' said Tony.

The enormity of the task and associated risks of flying a military drone into battle over Malahide Castle had finally dawned on him. He was nervous, very nervous.

'Also using the helmet radio,' said Kate. 'Colly will support Don who will need to assemble and load the Hydra 70 rockets and the ammunition belt for the machine gun.'

'I'll need to talk through what's involved. It has been a long time since I handled munitions,' said Don.

'And I've also spoken again to Veronica,' said Kate. 'The admiral's ships are still at anchor. They do not expect any engagement until the morning. We've agreed that we'll speak on the radio immediately before you set off.'

She did not mention that she and Jon also had a long chat. Their personal chemistry was sparking.

CHAPTER 17

Avanti

Jon and Orla were hidden within deep bushes at the water's edge near the end of channel that linked the marina to the open sea. They were about a kilometre from Malahide Castle. This viewpoint gave them a full line of sight across the water. All of the admiral's fleet were in view. A ship flying the colours of the Principality of Ria Formosa was approaching under half-sail. They had been monitoring it since it appeared on the horizon from the direction of Howth Head Island. It was sailing close to the coastline, and well away from the rest of the fleet.

'There's something unusual going on,' said Jon. 'It's flying the duke's colours. There are grenadiers on board, or at least people in grenadier uniforms. But there are also a lot of young people wearing working clothes not unlike our regular attire. Look at the girl in dungarees standing on the bow. She's not a grenadier.'

'Let it get closer,' said Orla. 'In about ten minutes, it will have to drop sail as it approaches the entrance to the channel. Like the rest of the fleet, it doesn't have sufficient displacement to go any further.'

And that is what happened in slow motion.

Orla raised her hunting rifle.

'Don't shoot, hold your fire,' said Jon.

With a lot of shouting and noise, *La Santa Fabio* dropped two heavy anchors in an almost perfect position at the middle of the mouth of the channel about a hundred metres from the sibling's hiding spot.

'That's good seamanship,' said Orla.

She and Jon were now in a much better position to study the ship in more detail.

Jon took out his father's binoculars from his hunting jacket pocket. Almost a hundred years old, and with low-light optical technology, the set was lightweight and compact. He adjusted the lens to get the best magnification. Once that was done, he pointed the binoculars in the direction of the cockpit at the stern of the ship where the huge wooden steering wheel was located. He did a final adjustment to get the clearest perspective.

A man dressed in a full captain's uniform waved at him.

'Orla, we better move,' said Jon. 'We've been spotted.'

'Stop panicking. Give me the Zeiss. Let me see.'

She put the binoculars to her eyes. She did not see a captain waving at her. It was her grandfather.

'Grandad!' she roared across the water. She stood up. Jon remained crouched. 'Jon, you idiot, it's Grandad.'

Jon slowly raised his head above the cover of the bushes. His eyesight did not lie. It was true. His grandfather was on the deck waving furiously. Actually, the entire crew, including the grenadiers or whoever they were, were waving, and shouting.

It was hard to hear anything at a distance of one hundred metres, but Orla and Jon did not need to be told, help was at hand.

A rowboat was soon in the water. It reached the rocky crag after a few minutes of hard pulling by a clearly inexperienced crew.

Orla and Jon approached the visitors.

'Look at you,' said Orla. 'You look like a stuffed rooster.'

'How dare you, minion!' said Rory. 'If you must know, this is the ceremonial uniform, goose feathers and all, of a Second Captain of the fleet of the Duke of the Principality of Ria Formosa. Captain Rory at your service.' He bowed and doffed his hat to his granddaughter.

'Oh Grandad, it is so good to see you,' said Orla. She fell into his arms.

Jon was two paces behind her in the rush to greet their grandfather.

The Howth Head volunteers gave the family time to hug and cry.

'How did you escape?' said Orla.

'Where should I start?' said Rory. 'In a nutshell, after I was taken away from you on *La Santa Maria*, you went in one direction, and I went in the opposite direction. I was on Howth Head Island no more than two days before I made my escape on *La Santa Fabio* with the help of my new friends. I discovered that the admiral has summoned a large fleet of Ria Formosa climate refugees to Howth Head, and they will arrive within days. It appears the Ria Formosa people have been evacuated off their lands and are on board ships in harbours around Quinta do Lago awaiting instructions as to where they should land in Iceapelago.'

'It's Malahide Castle's turn next, isn't it?' said Orla.

'It was until you gave them a bloody nose,' said Rory. 'By the way, who shot Captain da Gama?'

Rory looked at Jon and got no reaction. He looked at Orla, who blushed. She could not tell a lie, and he knew it.

'He's alive, rest assured,' said Rory. 'I suspect once recuperated he'll be back to making a nuisance of himself.'

'What can we do to defend ourselves?' said Jon.

'I brought you some firepower from Howth Head.'

Rory did not think it opportune to explain the terms and conditions. The Malahide Castle elders should be told first. Whatever happened was their decision.

'Once we keep the castle's walls intact, we now have enough manpower to mount a solid defence.'

'What do you think the admiral will do?' said Orla.

'Once he confirms orders to the fleet offshore Quinta do Lago to sail towards pre-determined locations in Iceapelago, we will get his full attention. He is probably talking to his boss, the Duke of the Principality of Ria Formosa, as we speak. Nothing happens it appears unless the duke says so.'

'So Admiral Rodriguez is not really in charge?' said Orla.

'I'm afraid he is as far as we are concerned. His job is to secure land and accommodation before the climate refugees leave their lands around Quinta do Lago. And Malahide Castle is his primary target. The ships' captains across the bay are awaiting his command. They will not take the initiative. Nothing will happen until the admiral gives a direct order. That's why we sailed unchallenged past everyone. We took precautions admittedly. But a single ship sailing direct from Howth Head to Malahide Castle should have been spotted and stopped.'

'Why don't they all settle in Dundrum Island? Wouldn't that be the easiest and obvious solution?' said Jon.

'Great idea, but for the fact that a yellow fever contagion has rendered Dundrum off limits, at least until its effects pass. The admiral and the duke see Malahide Castle as their new centre of command, and the location for one or even two thousand climate refugees.'

'This is on the Richter Scale of the unimaginable given Iceapelago's history and legacy,' said Orla. She did not get a chance to vent her anger any further.

'Look,' said Jon.

He pointed his arm northwards. In the far distance around the Lambay Island anchorage, the mainsails of several ships unfurled at the same time.

'We must defend Malahide Castle to the last otherwise we are all doomed to exile,' said Rory. 'You best make your way back to the safety of the castle.'

'What will you do?' said Orla.

'I've a plan. But I must get back to *La Santa Fabio* now. My crew and I will be at the front door of the castle within the hour, well ahead of the fleet getting here.'

Orla and Jon headed in the direction of the castle.

Back on board, Rory gave the instructions he had briefed his crew about earlier – to scuttle the ship in the shallowest part of the channel, and in doing so, they would prevent any of the admiral's ships getting within a kilometre of Malahide Castle. Once the already loosened bungs were furthered removed, seawater filled the lower decks, and the ship soon touched the sandy bottom of the channel with a soft bump. *La Santa Fabio* was a replica of most of the other ships in the fleet. It had a displacement of two metres. The channel was four metres deep at low tide. *La Santa Fabio* settled upright across the width of the narrow channel.

Rory viewed his handiwork from the safety of a rowing boat.

The job done to his satisfaction, he turned to his volunteers. 'Six of you should row to the bank where Jon and Orla were hidden. There's good cover there, and along most of the seashore. The rest of us will reinforce the Malahide Castle garrison.'

'What will we do if the grenadiers land near here?' said the leader of the small group.

'Use your initiative. Try to avoid a direct confrontation as the grenadiers will be heavily armed. However, if they land any cannon, and I expect they will, I'll be relying on you to do your best to destroy it. The only way we will lose the castle is if cannon fire breaches the walls. If you have to retreat, use the treeline that will take you to the northern shore.'

'You can rely on us, Rory, rest assured.'

'Stay safe,' said Rory.

He looked seawards. There were six ships under full sail. Six ships meant at least ninety grenadiers. More ominously, the flagship *La Santa Jorge* was also on the move. That worried him. He had seen its mobile heavy artillery. This suggested the admiral could deploy weapons other than the two-hundred-year-old cannons that were from a different era altogether.

'*Avanti*,' said Rory.

The Howth Head volunteers were welcomed with cheers at the main entrance by the Malahide Castle residents. The first thing the volunteers noticed was the age profile, and how few they were in number. While Rory had explained the situation before they left Howth Head, seeing such a small group did not give them confidence despite being forewarned.

While they were being fed in the banqueting hall, Veronica took the opportunity to catch up with her husband. 'You won't believe who I spoke to yesterday!'

'Captain da Gama?' said Rory.

'No. Don, Kate, and Tony were on the radio from the air traffic control tower at Cork Airport.'

'That place brings back memories. Goodness, how did they get there? The last time I met them they were prisoners on *La Santa Maria*.'

'Well, they escaped, didn't they, just like our grandchildren. It appears Don floated the abandoned cruiser near the graveyard and motored it to Cork Airport Island in quick time.'

'Don is a genius with his hands. We could do with him here. Did they have any news?'

'None other than they wanted to speak to Orla and Jon.'

'I'm guessing they won't have time for casual conversations for a while. I'll call them after sunset. The admiral is unlikely to do anything until the morning.'

CHAPTER 18

Tunnel

'THAT IS ONE OF our ships,' said Admiral Rodriguez. 'What is it doing there, blocking our way?'

The captain of *La Santa Jorge* had no idea how, or why, *La Santa Fabio* was scuttled in the near perfect position to block access mid-channel in the shallow water. There was no way to get around it. The last time he saw the ship, his ship, it was heading to Howth Head. He was confused. One thing was for certain, the fleet could get no nearer to the marina close to the main entrance of Malahide Castle.

'We will have to anchor here, sir,' said the captain. 'There is no other option.'

'That is ridiculous. From here, Malahide Castle is out of range of our cannons. Get them ashore and quickly.'

'That is going to take time and effort, sir. The guns have to be disassembled, transported ashore, and reassembled.'

'I do not care. Make sure the cannons are positioned as close as possible to the rear wall of the castle. Ideally, at a range of two hundred metres.'

The other ships in the fleet faced the same fate. They all anchored at the end of the channel leading to the Malahide marina. The admiral's master plan had been foiled. With great effort, two cannons were loaded in pieces from *La Santa Jorge* onto two of the larger rowboats that could get within a few hundred metres of the marina at high tide. The castle walls would then be within range. In position, the idea was to pulverise the rear wall area and once the brickwork was breached, companies of grenadiers would charge the castle.

Neither the admiral nor his senior officers were aware that Malahide Castle had been reinforced with armed volunteers from Howth Head. The basic assumption was that a handful of lightly armed, elderly residents stood in their way.

Rory knew that to mount a successful attack, the grenadiers would have to manhandle two heavy artillery pieces off the ships, and land them close to the castle. He correctly assumed based on Captain da Gama's intelligence that the admiral's primary target was the rear wall. It was much lower than the wall at the front and was not as thick.

Rory had to decide when it would be best to counterattack. Because once he committed his defenders against at least sixty grenadiers, he would have practically no reserves. It was a win it or lose it gambit.

Veronica came into the room as he was plotting with an open map of the castle grounds in front of him on the banqueting table.

'You'll never guess who I've been speaking to again?'

'Tell me.'

'You remember the hoverbike that the Canadian rangers used decades ago to repel General Gove and his Welsh mercenaries?'

'I do. A great invention with smart technology was the hoverbike.'

'Don has reassembled one at Cork Airport and plans to attach a rocket pod to the underside. It also has a high calibre machine gun attached.'

'What's the relevance, Veronica? I'm busy deciding how best to deploy our defenders in a way that the fewest get killed.'

'Tony says he will fly the hoverbike to Malahide Castle and expects to be here before eight o'clock tomorrow morning.'

'Are you serious?'

'That's what he told me. He wants to talk to you before he leaves.'

'Great. But he will need satcoms. That technology doesn't exist anymore.'

'A call to Canada has sorted that out. Tony will explain it all when he speaks to you on the radio.'

'That changes things. Could you please ask Jon, Orla, and Mary from Howth Head to join me? By the way, what time is it?'

'Five thirty in the afternoon.'

Ten minutes later the young folk joined Rory who briefed them about Tony's planned sortie.

'What are you seeing?' said Rory.

'All the rowboats from the ships have been launched,' said Jon.

'Where are they heading?'

'Half contain the parts of a large artillery piece.'

'What about the second one?'

'I'd imagine it's too troublesome to land and assemble a complicated piece of equipment, they decided to prioritise only one gun.'

'That's what I would have done,' said Rory. 'Where will they locate it? Close to the rear wall?'

'Yes, that's what it looks like,' said Orla.

'The gun will be well guarded,' said Jon. 'I expect at least half the grenadiers will protect the artillery piece, while the rest will head for the marina and will be at the castle any moment now.'

'Let me think,' said Rory.

'Can I say something?' said Mary. 'The castle is impenetrable, am I right?'

'That's the assumption,' said Orla. 'Unless the walls are breached.'

'And we expect a full frontal assault?'

'Yes, that seem likely,' said Rory. 'I'm not going to allow anyone leave the safety of these walls to challenge the admiral and his mercenaries. It's far too risky. I'll not be responsible for an unnecessary loss of life.'

'Orla told me you have a tunnel under the castle that runs to the seashore to our north,' said Mary.

'For someone who has just arrived, you're well briefed,' said Rory.

'What I'm proposing is that I take my group and once through the tunnel, we will manoeuvre to behind where the artillery piece is being set up. Under cover, we will fire at those assembling the gun. If we are lucky, we'll pin them down for an hour or so.'

'Enough to delay the full assembly of the gun before it gets dark?'

'Exactly. We'll retreat back to the tunnel as soon as it is safe to do so.'

'That's a great plan, Mary, but with two changes. Firstly, Orla will join you. Secondly, we'll provide covering fire from the castle's rear walls to keep the grenadiers pinned down.'

'I'll take charge of that,' said Jon

'That's agreed then,' said Rory. 'If we pull this stunt off, and if Tony gets here in the morning as planned, we may drive these climate refugees back to where they came from.'

Orla and Mary left to gather a few defenders.

Jon took another armed group to the top of the rear wall.

As this meeting broke up, the admiral landed ashore not five hundred metres away. He had decided not just to lead the assault but to be seen to be leading. He reckoned the risk of getting injured was very low.

He rasped instructions as teams of grenadiers attempted to lift the heavy parts of the artillery piece out of the row boats, up the stony bank onto the grass margin. It took two hours to get all the pieces ashore. It took another hour to haul the parts into what the admiral determined was the preferred attacking position; behind a large mound some three hundred metres directly opposite the rear wall of the castle.

He was so busy shouting and cursing at his subordinates that he did not notice Jon and other defenders take up positions. Atop the wall, they had an uninterrupted view to where the artillery piece was close to being fully assembled. Jon noticed several grenadiers lugging artillery shells and placing them close to the gun.

On cue, the sky was lit up with short bursts of automatic fire from behind the artillery piece. Work assembling the gun stopped immediately as everyone took cover. Jon put his binoculars to his eyes to survey the damage.

The first thing he noticed was the admiral's very discernible hat with its white ostrich feathers. He was hidden behind the mound but exposed to Mary's group firing.

'OK, let's give them what they deserve,' said Jon.

He raised his body above the protection of the rear wall and commenced firing on the grenadiers who were in the open, no more than three hundred metres away. Several bodies dropped. Others scattered for the treeline beside the channel as it afforded some protection. Jon's group stopped firing as did Mary's. It then became a game of cat and mouse. As soon as any of the attackers moved in the direction of the gun, the shooting resumed with a fury. The admiral and his grenadiers were pinned down as night fell.

Meanwhile, beyond the oak tree at the front of the castle, unseen, Captain da Gama spoke to his trusted troops, his personal unit of ten experienced grenadiers. Unknown to the admiral and against the advice of the medical orderly, he left the ship and landed by rowboat to the east of the castle. He was disguised as a grenadier so as not to attract attention. His right shoulder was heavily bandaged to the point it was unusable.

The noise of gunfire at the rear of the castle was sporadic as dusk settled.

'Listen up,' said the captain. 'I know there is an escape tunnel from the castle to somewhere on the northern seashore. We need to find the exit and when we do, it is our way into the castle.'

'Will it be defended?' said a grenadier.

'Probably not, as there are only a handful of people capable of fighting in the castle, and they all seem to be at the rear wall.'

'We will start over there,' said the captain, pointing to a gap in the trees. 'That leads to a secluded cove about five hundred metres away. We will spread out and walk long the seashore until we find the tunnel's entrance.'

Mary and Orla started to withdraw from their positions and retreat back to the tunnel at nightfall. Before they did so, they blasted the area around the artillery piece for one last time. Lines of tracer fire lit up the sky. As soon as it stopped, Jon and his team opened up again. That gave cover for Mary, Orla, and the defenders to move back to the stone track at the seashore that led back to the tunnel.

As they approached the tunnel, they heard loud noises in the distance coming towards them also on the same track.

'Speed up,' said Orla in a whisper. 'The entrance is just a few metres away.'

Her group did what they were told.

'They're trying to find the tunnel,' said Mary.

'They'll regret that,' said Orla to Mary. 'Let the others return to the safety of the castle. You and I can take positions inside the tunnel and surprise these fools.'

Minutes later and protected by an alcove about a hundred metres inside the tunnel, Orla heard voices. She saw light from their torches. The lead invader held a torch in his left hand as he walked fearlessly up the tunnel at a fast pace. Portuguese voices came within earshot.

'It's Captain da Gama,' whispered Orla. She immediately raised her rifle and inserted a bullet.

The captain did not hear the click of the bullet loading until it was too late. The shot caught him in his mid-chest. His body rocked back with the force of the bullet entering his body. It exited, winging the grenadier who was immediately behind him. Mary broke cover and rattled the tunnel walls with a burst from her semi-automatic.

Two sounds could be heard. The scuttling noises of those exiting the tunnel, and the groans of those who had been shot. Orla approached her victim cautiously. The captain was lying mortally wounded on the flat of his back. His good hand lay over where the bullet had entered his body. It was soon sticky with a flow of deep red blood.

'You deserve this,' said Orla. 'Attacking a defenceless Malahide is outrageous and unjustified. It's a pity I didn't finish the job the last time you were here. Die peacefully.'

As blood filled his lungs, Captain da Gama gurgled his last words. 'At the end of the day, we are all climate refugees.'

Orla and Mary walked away from him, up the tunnel towards the castle.

CHAPTER 19

Hoverbike

COLLY WAS ABLE TO communicate with Don using the headphone set embedded within Tony's helmet, which lay on a work bench. With the speaker on, they could all talk easily to each other.

Following Colly's precise and somewhat rushed instructions, Don fitted the launch pod for the rockets under the base of the hoverbike. It was like a big assembly kit. He found the right grooves and counterparts and screwed everything tight with a wrench. He then carefully primed the three rockets with Hydra 70 warheads. They weighed twenty kilograms each. That task completed, he fitted and secured the machine gun unit at the side of the bike's fuselage. Again it was a click and fit arrangement. He loaded the huge heavy calibre magazine clip into a deep hopper above the unit. Don grunted and cursed as he carefully completed the jigsaw puzzle of armoury parts and ammunition.

He inspected his handiwork. 'They're loaded and it's all yours,' said Don.

'Great work,' said Tony. 'You really used your engineering skills and physical strength to great effect.'

'Let's recap, Tony,' said Colly. 'I estimate the payload is close to three hundred kilos. On that basis, with the batteries fully charged, you will have ten minutes maximum over Malahide Castle before you will need to land. So use the time over the site to good effect. *La Santa Jorge,* which is anchored close to the northern seashore is the primary target for the first two rockets. The ship's coordinates have been fed into the satnav system. The cannon that Admiral Rodriguez intends to deploy is the target for the third rocket. We also have its precise location, again thanks to the information that Malahide Castle gave you earlier. How and where you use the machine gun is your business. You have enough ammo for four maybe five short bursts. Don fixed a five hundred bullet belt meaning the effect will be devastating within your chosen firing zone.'

'That sounds simple,' said Tony. His nerves were even more intense as the time of departure approached. Outwardly he appeared calm. However, his stomach was in a knot and his eyes twitched uncontrollably, a sure sign of stress. His deep breaths helped keep him focused.

'Let's test the readiness of the system,' said Colly. 'Put your helmet on.'

Tony did what he was told.

'Press the *Test* and *Load* button please.'

'It's lit up *Ready*,' said Tony.

'Good,' said Colly. 'When you are over the target, you only need to double press the same button to launch a rocket. If you double press immediately afterwards, the second rocket will launch. Now turn it off.'

'Done,' said Tony.

'It's the same routine for the machine gun,' said Colly. Tony completed the test.

'Finally, I should tell you that when the rocket is launched, it will jolt the hoverbike backwards, so make sure you stabilise it before firing the second rocket. And when you fire the machine gun, you should also anticipate that it will also rock the hoverbike. That is why short bursts are best. Understood?'

'You're a great teacher, Colly,' said Tony taking off his helmet. 'Thanks for all your help and giving me the confidence to fly the hoverbike.' He stepped out of the cockpit with a stern countenance.

Once she saw that his instructions were complete, Kate approached her brother and gave him a warm hug. 'You take care of yourself. Don't do anything stupid.'

'I'll do my best,' said Tony. 'I plan to land in the castle's grounds once my job is done.'

Kate stood apart, quietly sobbing as Tony bade his farewells.

'Don, thanks so much for all your help,' said Tony.

'It's you we should be thanking,' said Don. 'If I was your age, I would be doing the exact same. You are certainly brave, but no heroics please. Promise?'

'Sure,' said Tony. 'Can you help me with the jumpsuit?'

They buttoned up the protective suit. When his hiking boots had been laced up and his helmet secured, Tony remounted the hoverbike. He sat into driver's seat. Once comfortable, he clipped on his safety harness. He turned on the radio, then the ignition. The console before him lit up.

'Engine on,' said Tony.

'Let's do a pre-flight check,' said Colly over the radio. 'Battery level?'

'Full. Ninety-five minutes estimated flying time.'

'Satnav?'

'Locked on coordinates 53.4446 degrees north and 6.1655 degrees west.'

'That's Malahide Castle. Once you arrived overhead, you will need to turn off the satnav and free fly towards *La Santa Jorge*.'

'Understood,' said Tony.

'Munitions?'

'Both indicators show they are full.'

'Great. You are ready to go. Once you are airborne, we can talk en route. I'll keep you company during the flight.'

Tony pulled the visor of his helmet over his eyes, and gently lifted the joystick. The hoverbike responded instantly. Despite the additional weight, it rose vertically some five metres off the ground. He then pressed the joystick upwards and forwards. Soon the hoverbike was heading out in a north-easterly direction over the airport's long disused runway.

Don was in awe as the hoverbike accelerated and rose under Tony's control.

Beside him, Kate was feeling a different set of emotions. She was crushed and sobbed uncontrollably, fearing the worst for her brother.

Tony's nerves settled as the automatic pilot kicked in. The hoverbike rose to one thousand metres. He clicked on the radio.

'Colly, I'm up and flying.'

Silence.

'Colly?'

More silence. Tony turned off the radio, and then turned it on again. The reception light was green.

'Colly?'

He tried several more times to no effect.

On his own over ground and travelling at a speed of one hundred and ninety kilometres an hour, he took in his surroundings as dawn was breaking.

There was a low cloud ceiling and little wind. The features that dominated Iceapelago were there for him to see. Large green and brown land masses were everywhere, surrounded by water. Destroyed buildings lay scattered in all directions. At higher levels, he could make out the outline of old road networks, now overgrown. The sun rose from the east, casting rays of light across the land and seascapes below. He could not discern any habitable housing nor people, nor did he see any animals or birds. Abandoned onshore wind turbines dominated the skyline. There were thousands of them. Once a renewables lifeline; now broken and useless. The hoverbike shuddered gently as it sped on its journey in a north-easterly direction over Iceapelago. After an hour, he noticed the eastern coastline in the distance. As he approached the Dublin Bay area, he could see what he assumed were the tall apartment blocks of Dundrum Island close to the seashore. Offshore arrays of wind turbines cluttered the eastern seaboard east and south of Dublin Bay. In the distance to the west lay Howth Head Island. The red and white tops of the twin towers of an old electricity station told him Malahide Castle was not too far away.

He tried the radio for the last time. No luck.

The hoverbike had performed as expected. As he got nearer to his final destination, Tony's nerves returned. He tried to remember what Colly had told him. He needn't have worried so much. As it approached the target, the hoverbike slowed speed and dropped altitude. In the near distance, he could see the high walls of Malahide Castle. In no time, he was directly above the castle. Colly had said the automatic pilot would disengage immediately. Anticipating this, Tony let go of his grip of the hoverbike's handlebars and had the sense to take control of the joystick. The hoverbike dipped a few metres before he used the joystick to fly in the direction of the biggest ship located near the coastline.

'What the hell is that?' said the admiral, reacting to a loud noise above him. He turned to see some sort of flying apparatus heading out to sea. He was only momentarily distracted. 'On my orders.'

The grenadiers responded immediately. The cannon spat out a mortar round that blasted into the middle of the castle's rear wall. It did not collapse but large blocks fell to the earth. Clouds of grey dust filled the morning air.

'Reload. Fire!'

The second attempt was more successful. The mortar hit the same area with huge explosive force. The rear wall cracked, a large hole appeared. Even more dust and detritus was generated.

'They've breached the wall,' said Jon.

He needn't have bothered speaking. The defenders who had taken up positions away from the wall itself within the courtyard could see for themselves that while their delaying tactic had worked, now the admiral's grenadiers would surge through the gap. They were too preoccupied to notice the passage of the hoverbike overhead.

At the same time, Tony turned the hoverbike towards *La Santa Jorge*. As instructed by Colly, he opened the aperture of the firing button for the first rocket. A *Ready* sign flickered.

He pressed the button.

Nothing happened.

Tony was stricken with panic.

He rapidly turned off the firing button and restarted it immediately. He pressed button even harder. This time the hoverbike shuck violently as a rocket left its launcher.

Tony was flying over *La Santa Jorge* as the missile struck. He avoided the heat and the smoke of the blast. He could not see the damage he had inflicted on the flagship.

'Reload. One more shot should finish it,' said the admiral.

Behind him a loud explosion told him something was wrong. He turned to see *La Santa Jorge* in trouble. The main mast was on its side and flames covered the ship's stern. Crewmen, some with their uniforms ablaze, were jumping overboard.

It suddenly dawned on him that the object that had flown overhead had caused the explosions. He tried to find it. He could see it was turning out at sea to make another run at his ship. The admiral knew he could do nothing but watch.

Tony decided that he should use the second rocket to finish the job. He would attack the cannon later. At a distance of five hundred metres, he unclipped the firing button. He could see the first rocket had almost destroyed the stern section. He took aim for the midship and pressed the firing button.

He was over and beyond *La Santa Jorge* when the second rocket struck midship. His helmet dulled the noise of several smaller explosions as ammunition caught fire.

He decided to leave *La Santa Jorge* to its fate. He manoeuvred the joystick, flying the hoverbike in the direction of the castle. He could see the rear wall had been shattered.

'Fire!' roared the admiral.

The mortar round blew open the rear wall, exposing the courtyard.

Tony could see the source of the blast and took aim.

The admiral was torn between the loss of his flagship that was burning out of control some hundreds of metres away and the opportunity to order his grenadiers to advance.

Flying overhead, Tony saw that a large group of grenadiers was preparing to attack. At the same time he saw the battery light on his console flashing red. He guessed he would have just one short opportunity. He decided not to use the last rocket. He moved the joystick and turned the hoverbike around to position himself for an attack. He hovered in a stationary position a hundred metres off the ground. He unclipped the button connected to the machine gun. Colly had told him to fire in short bursts. Seeing the grenadiers break cover and run to the breach in the wall, he lowered the hoverbike to fifty metres above ground, firing as he shimmied the hoverbike slowly from left to right. Because he nearly emptied the magazine, the outcome was deadly. On the ground lay dozens of corpses and badly wounded.

Tony then rotated the hoverbike towards the cannon and pressed the trigger. He fully emptied the magazine. The bullets twanged off the metal cover and surrounds with a fierce grating noise. The cannon was rendered useless. Bodies fell everywhere. Two large explosions followed as the gun shells exploded.

The admiral from behind the rocks, observed all of this destruction in a growing state of shock. This flying machine that had appeared out of nowhere had destroyed his flagship and was now decimating his grenadiers, never mind the cannon. His anger grew. He was beyond furious.

'Give me your rifle!' He snatched the weapon from a grenadier, expertly raised it to his shoulder, taking aim at the hoverbike that was stationary off the ground less than one hundred metres away. He could make out the shape of a person in the centre. He took a shot.

Tony felt a searing heat at the back of his head. The admiral's bullet had ricocheted off the rear fuselage and entered above the neckline of his protective suit and, critically, just below the rear rim of his helmet. He did not die instantly, but passed out when the bullet struck his windpipe. As he collapsed and lost consciousness for the last time, his grip on the hoverbike's joystick loosened. The hoverbike plunged to the ground. It landed in an upright position with a thud against the broken rear wall of the castle. Tony's limp body fell towards the control panel, suspended by his safety harness. He died moments later.

The dynamics of the situation changed in an instant.

Dozens of grenadiers had been killed or injured. Those at the rear of the castle retreated to the safety of the shore-line, out of range. The admiral let them. He knew the balance of the battle had shifted.

Inside the castle, the defenders did not see the downing of the hoverbike as it was obscured from their line of sight. However, as Jon led the advance towards the shattered walls, he saw the broken fuselage and its dead pilot.

'What happened?' said Rory. He advanced towards Jon under cover.

'The flying machine, I think it's called a hoverbike, has destroyed *La Santa Jorge*. Look.'

In the distance, the flagship was an inferno. The flames engulfed the main mast. Bits of the sails floated high above the decking that was also on fire. A loud explosion under the bow section split the ship in two. In slow motion, the rear section sank like lead into the shallow water. The main deck lasted somewhat longer. When the masts collapsed, their weight pulled *La Santa Jorge* into her final resting place.

'The pilot also destroyed the cannon, killing dozens of attacking grenadiers,' said Jon. 'What timing. This action saved us, for sure.'

Rory could see a line of grenadiers running towards the northern seashore. He knew from Orla that the troops in front of the castle had also dispersed once the attack on the tunnel was foiled. A full retreat was underway. Malahide Castle had been saved.

Rory stood up to get a better view. Corpses and dying bodies lay in all directions in front of the rear wall. Smoke was seeping from the catastrophic wounds of the cadavers.

The area where the gun had been placed was flattened. Rory scanned the horizon for any sign of life. He saw the tips of the admiral's ostrich hat feathers hidden behind a mound at a distance of two hundred metres, a safe distance from the carnage in front of him. Rory broke cover. He walked slowly towards his enemy with a loaded pistol in his right hand. Jon and his defenders fell in behind him.

'Admiral, this is Rory. It is time to parlay. And come alone. Your grenadiers should drop their weapons and tend to the wounded.'

On hearing the offer, the admiral rose from his protected position to face the voice that came from the direction of the castle's destroyed rear wall. He waved his hand and walked in the direction of Rory, his enemy.

As he did, Jon noticed the downed hoverbike, and splitting from the group, he ran towards it. The pilot who had saved the day was motionless. He knew Tony was dead judging by the blood flowing from the back of his neck. Jon gently removed the bloody helmet from the shattered head. Amid the mess, he instantly recognised the facial features. Stunned, he looked at the body of his fallen friend. Unclipping the safety harness, he took Tony's body in his arms, lying him on the ground. He stood still over the body.

'You saved us all, Tony. But did you have to die?'

Orla arrived. She put her hand around Jon's waist as she tried to control her emotions.

'I liked him, you know? I really did. I never told him, and now look.' She burst into tears as the first fledging love of her life lay motionless. Her body shuddered with grief. Jon held her more tightly.

'He was a hero, Orla, and we'll remember him as such,' said Jon.

The siblings stood silently over Tony's body, each processing their feelings. Orla knelt down, and kissed Tony's forehead.

'I best tell Kate,' said Orla. 'She must have known there was a risk in flying the hoverbike over this battlefield. She will miss Tony desperately.'

Along with supporting hands they placed Tony's body on a blanket and moved him indoors.

Unaware of what his grandchildren were doing, Rory had his own hands full.

'Follow me, please,' said Rory. He turned to the admiral as he clambered over the ruins of the rear wall. 'We have matters to discuss.'

Other defenders emerging from their positions around the courtyard watched as Rory walked through the rear entrance door with the admiral four paces behind him. The few remaining grenadiers had enough sense to stay at a distance far away from the castle. Seeing the admiral surrender, they tended to their wounded and covered their dead.

Rory did not want an audience. He decided he should speak to the admiral in private. The best place to do this was the small library room above the main entrance. This room had history. When the admiral entered, he shut the door while signalling to his fellow residents that they should remain outside.

'Sit down,' said Rory.

The admiral did what he was told. He knew the cards were stacked against him. Losing so many grenadiers did not bother him as much as losing his command ship with its supplies, and most importantly, its radio.

'What's your name?' said Rory.

'Admiral Martin Rodriguez, Head of the Navy of the Principality of Ria Formosa.'

'From Portugal?'

'What was Portugal, yes.'

'I'm Rory…'

'I know,' said the admiral, 'the Commander of Iceapelago.'

'I said we should parlay,' said Rory.

'What are you proposing?' said the admiral.

'Let's talk first.'

This was not what the admiral was expecting. He knew his life was at risk. If the tables were turned, he would have no hesitation in executing his defeated opponent.

'You are climate refugees,' said Rory.

'We are.'

'Remind me. How many were you planning to transport to occupy Iceapelago?'

'Originally, about seven thousand. But many have died in the past months as conditions deteriorated throughout the Principality of Ria Formosa. I have some five thousand men, women and children cramped on a fleet of ships at a place called Quinta do Lago awaiting my orders. Some have already set sail for Howth Head and Cork Airport Island.'

'How long will it take them to get here?'

'Where are you going with this?'

'Let me ask the questions. You are in no position to bargain but to cooperate. Understood?'

'With good winds, the first group could be here within days.'

'And to Cork Airport Island?'

'At least a day sooner.'

Rory paused and sitting directly opposite his foe said, 'Order them all to sail to Cork Airport Island.'

'What! Are you serious?'

'I haven't been more serious in a long time, I can assure you.'

'Cork, why Cork?'

'It's unoccupied. It's a much larger island than either Howth or Malahide, and the airport complex with its hangars can shelter the numbers you are talking about until permanent accommodation can be built.'

'I do not understand,' said the admiral.

'Let me put in this way,' said Rory. 'There are several Iceapelago situations across the planet. What we have learned over the past fifty years, at great cost I should add, is that communities can survive provided they are self-contained and self-governed, and most importantly, they respect their neighbours. I'm giving you and your people that opportunity. Mother Nature almost destroyed us. And if we continue to fight each other, we will do Mother Nature's work for her. My mission is that my people can live and survive in peace. That should be yours, should it not?'

'That is a very generous offer, Rory,' said the admiral. 'Your view of the world and that of the Duke of the Principality of Ria Formosa is very similar. He wants security in a safe and sustainable location for his peoples. For that reason, he will be on the first ship that lands at Cork Airport Island. He will want to meet you.'

'My proposal comes with certain conditions, of course.'

'Obviously,' said the admiral. 'What do we have to do?'

'Remove any temptation that you or your leader will re-attempt the troubles you have already inflicted on Howth Head and Malahide Castle.'

'What do you mean?'

'You'll travel from here to Cork Airport Island in one ship only for starters. The remainder of the fleet will be scuttled off Lambay Island.'

'But…' said the admiral.

'No buts. Listen carefully. You'll also disarm all your remaining grenadiers. Order them to leave their weapons at the rear of the castle before you depart. You are also to tell the duke to throw all non-essential weapons off his ships before they land.'

'I cannot do that. We would be defenceless.'

'Against whom?' said Rory. 'You can keep some weapons as you will need them for hunting.'

The admiral took a deep breath. 'Anything else?'

'Yes. You, on behalf of your duke, and I agree the people of Ria Formosa will not leave Cork Airport Island without my express permission. You may eventually trade with the adjacent Iceapelago communities, but will need my authority to do so.'

'How will I get such an instruction?'

'By radio. Iceapelago's best radio set is atop the control tower at Cork Airport.'

'That is agreed then,' said the admiral. He extended his hand and Rory shuck it firmly.

'Come with me,' said Rory. He walked down the corridor to the radio room with the admiral and sat him in front of the set. 'I want to hear you give the order to your officers. Tell them to anchor their ships at the yellow buoy beside the steeple of St Sylvester's Church. You choose which ship will take you all to Cork Airport Island. Then radio the duke to let him know he is welcome to reside in Iceapelago.'

The admiral knew how to operate the radio. In short order, he made contact.

Rory stood over his shoulder.

He communicated as instructed to the officers who were surprised at the news, and the change in plan. They had expected to be shot or imprisoned.

'I will contact the duke now,' said the admiral.

'I'm listening, so be crystal clear about what we've agreed.'

The radio receiver was picked up instantly. 'Admiral, when do we set sail? I told you to get back to me last night. What is going on? Did I not give you strict orders?'

Rory took the microphone without giving the admiral any notice.

'Duke, my name is Rory, the Commander of Iceapelago, and resident of Malahide Castle. I want…'

'Why are you online? Where is the admiral? Put him back on. Now.'

'You can rant and rave all you want, but it might be better if you calm down and listen for a change.'

'What is going on?' said the duke. 'I demand an explanation.'

'It's simple, Duke. Your plan to take over Malahide Castle has failed.'

'What do you mean failed?'

'For starters, *La Santa Jorge* is sunk, most of your grenadiers are dead or wounded, Captain da Gama is dead, and Admiral Rodriguez and I have reached an understanding.'

'An understanding? I want to speak to Admiral Rodriquez.'

Rory handed him the microphone.

'Duke, I am sorry, but our plan failed miserably.'

'You can say that again.'

'The Commander of Iceapelago has made us an offer that I accepted in principle, subject to your agreement of course.'

'This better be good or you will be hanging from the nearest yardarm when I find you.'

'We have been offered use of Cork Airport Island.'

'But Captain da Gama told me it was long abandoned and required too much work to accommodate all our people.'

'He did, but the bottom line is that Malahide Castle and Howth Head Islands and indeed Dundrum, are off the agenda.'

'Put me back to the Commander,' said the duke. He then proceeded to ask a lot of practical questions about the suitability of Cork Airport Island. Rory responded honestly. When it became clear that the island and its airport infrastructure could accommodate all his citizens, the duke finally accepted the *fait accompli*. His over-arching priority was to leave the marina at Quinta do Lago at the earliest opportunity. At the end of the day, as long as he and his people could live in Iceapelago, he really did not care where exactly.

'What next?' said the admiral after the radio call ended.

'You leave this part of Iceapelago as quickly as possible.'

'That simple?'

'Get going before I change my mind.'

The admiral walked back to the library, ready to leave. The Malahide Six, Orla, Jon, and several other residents blocked his way. It was time for an explanation.

'I've an agreement with the admiral. He'll disarm and leave Malahide immediately,' said Rory. 'The people of the Principality of Ria Formosa will settle in Cork Airport Island. I've agreed this arrangement with the duke, who will become a Six. We'll trade with them eventually. But for the foreseeable future, their priority will be to set up accommodation and to make the best use of the island's fertile lands.'

'Peace in our time?' said Emily, the Malahide Six.

'Yes, and what's more, I've agreed with the elders of Howth Head Island that their community, one hundred strong, will move immediately to Malahide. We have plenty of space and more than enough resources. The most important thing for me is that it is better for our young people that we create a larger and viable community at Malahide Castle. Over dinner this evening I'll give you more details. But what's for sure is we've a good future ahead for the first time in decades. So please welcome our new neighbours with open arms.'

Spontaneously, the small group applauded. Rory's announcements made sense. It was totally unexpected after the drama of the past days.

The group stepped aside as the admiral walked out the door.

'Grandad, you need to contact Don urgently,' said Orla. She had tried to get to him for nearly an hour at this stage.

'I was planning to do so after I finished my business with the admiral.'

'Go back to the radio room,' said Orla.

Once there, Orla sat in front of the radio set. Cork responded almost immediately.

'Don, it's Orla here. I have Grandad for you.'

'Don, what's up?' said Rory. 'We've had more than our fair share of excitement here over the past two days.'

'I gather,' said Don. 'But I have other news, so please listen. I have been in regular contact with the Canadians since Tony flew to Malahide. They lost contact with him.'

'What are you talking about?'

'He flew a hoverbike to Malahide. Where is he?'

Rory turned to Orla. He had been so preoccupied with arresting the admiral that he was not aware of Tony's death.

Orla spoke. 'There's been an accident.' Her voice broke as she spoke.

'Is he safe?' cried Kate taking the microphone.

'There is no other way to say it, Kate. I'm afraid he died after he repelled our attackers,' said Orla. 'His bravery saved the Malahide Castle community.'

Kate's sobbing continued for quite a while.

The enormity of his heroics slowly began to register.

'He not only saved Malahide Castle,' said Jon, 'his bravery in seeing off our attackers will allow our communities to flourish. We will bury him with full ceremony. We will wait until you get here to wake him.'

'Thank you,' said Kate recovering her composure. 'I knew this adventure would be his undoing. What a waste of a young life.'

'Kate, it wasn't wasted,' said Jon. 'If Tony hadn't taken the initiative in flying the hoverbike to Malahide Castle, I and many others would be dead by now.'

'That gives me some solace,' said Kate.

'Get here soon, Kate. I miss you,' said Jon.

'Me too.'

Rory took the microphone. 'Don, there's been a major change in plan. I want you and Kate to come to live in Malahide Castle. Your community at the Old Head is also welcome. The more the merrier. I secured a peace deal with our failed invaders and offered them Cork Airport Island instead of Malahide Castle and Howth Head as a place to live. The basic idea is to bring back some life to Cork Airport Island after it being left unlived in for so long. We also need new blood in my community here. I hope you will accept our offer.'

'Yes, gladly,' said Don. Kate nodded her head. 'We've a few things to tidy up here but should be on our way in a day or two.'

'And there's another thing, before we sign off,' said Don. 'I've an important message for you, and the Malahide Castle residents. As you know, the Canadians have access to a communications satellite. In tracking the hoverbike they extended the field of search and found a series of radio signals to the north, northeast off Lambay.'

'What does that mean?' said Rory.

'You'll have company soon enough. The satellite picked up images of boats heading in your direction.'

'Hell, more climate refugees. Orla, run and bring the admiral back here. Don, I'll call you back once we sort out this problem. Please get here as soon as you can.'

CHAPTER 20

Swedes

RORY STOOD BESIDE THE admiral on the bridge of a ship of the fleet looking out over the leeward side of Lambay Island towards the hundreds of broken static wind turbines with their blades half-submerged.

The admiral's prompt action had resulted in the remaining five ships of the fleet being positioned in a line along the seashore at Malahide, opposite the area called the High Rock. Once the situation about the new arrivals had been explained to the admiral, he readily agreed to postpone his voyage south and cooperate. He guessed if he helped Rory, he might compromise on some of his conditions.

'What can you see?' said Rory.

The admiral put down his binoculars.

'There are fifty, maybe sixty, small boats at full sail coming in our direction from the northeast. As soon as they sail past the wind turbines, they will be at close quarters within the hour. It seems they haven't seen us yet.'

'What sort of boats?'

'I have not seen the type before, but the lead vessels are Viking longboats, similar to a Drakker judging by the way the main sail is rigged, with a number of other small craft at the rear.'

'Vikings?' said Rory. 'First Portuguese, now Vikings. Are we on a travel brochure or what?'

As the sailing boats got nearer, they finally spotted the admiral's line of ships. The lead longboat tacked, stopped, and the others behind it did likewise.

Through his binoculars, the admiral could see the person in charge of the lead boat shouting orders and waving their hands. In response, two smaller longboats came up alongside the lead boat.

'What's going on?' said Rory.

'It appears the fleet has pulled up and are treading water, waiting orders. Look.'

As he spoke, a large blue and yellow flag was raised up the mast of the lead ship.

'Swedes,' said Rory. He was still puzzled about what was unfolding a kilometre in front of him.

'The second longboat has been emptied of its crew and passengers,' said the admiral. 'Whoever is in charge, is on their way to us.'

The admiral's ships were much larger and taller than the smaller longboats and could easily ram them. The ships also had some cannons, but they were almost ineffective given their age and condition. But the Swedish travellers did not know that.

'The leader is not wearing a uniform,' said the admiral. 'He is dressed like a fisherman.'

As the longboat got nearer, Rory could see it was a

woman in charge. Her blond hair was covered by a beanie. She wore yellow dungarees and gumshoes like most off-shore trawler men had in the distant past. Her red life jacket completed her outfit.

As the longboat sailed closer, both parties got a better view of their opponents. Rory knew he had the advantage due to the size of the admiral's fleet, or for as long as the fleet remained under his command.

The longboat sailed within ten metres of the brigantine before it dropped sail. The leader stood up now that she was within speaking distance.

Rory noticed neither she nor her crew were armed.

'Welcome to Iceapelago,' said Rory. 'I'm the Commander in charge of the thirty islands that comprise Iceapelago. Who are you?'

'I am Bergit. I am the leader of the families from the Swedish Islands.'

'Greetings, Bergit. What brings you to our shores in such great numbers?'

'A mixture of famine and pestilence, to be honest,' said Bergit. 'We have been at sea for nearly three weeks and were hoping to find landfall here.'

'Landfall you may find, but not here,' said Rory. 'Come aboard, Bergit from the Swedish Islands. I find shouting across the water a bit difficult at my age.'

Bergit's crew nudged her boat alongside a ladder that was thrown over the guardrail. In short order, she climbed the steps and jumped onto the deck while discarding her life jacket in a practiced motion.

Bergit took in her surroundings with an observant eye once she put her feet on the main deck. There were many lightly-armed grenadiers about, but many were wounded. The cannons were rusty, as were the cannonballs. She also noticed that the other ships in line were the same. At a quick guess, the total combined crew were no more than eighty or maybe a hundred. She had nearly a thousand in her fleet of small ships.

Rory and the admiral stood opposite her. She scanned their faces, and correctly surmised that Rory was the person in charge despite his age. It seemed incongruous that the man beside him dressed in full military uniform in a style from at least two hundred years ago would hold a position of lesser authority.

They too observed Bergit's features. Once aboard she took off her beanie, letting her hair flow over her shoulders revealing a full pretty face. Her soiled, over-sized dungarees did not do her figure justice. She looked to be fifty, but they knew that Scandinavians hid their age well.

She knew she was being assessed, and let her opponents take time to absorb whatever they needed to see.

Unlike the admiral who had a roving eye, Rory did not care much for appearances. He just want some facts before he made a decision.

'Why exactly did you leave your lands?' asked Rory. Given what had happened in recent days, he had no time or tolerance for small talk.

'We were once on the fringes of the relatively temperate influence of the arctic weather zone. The past summers have brought the highest temperatures imaginable. When our crops totally failed for the third season and our animals started to die in great numbers due to the heat, we had no option but to set sail to find a new home.'

'Why did you not stop in Britannia or Cymru?' said Rory.

'We sailed through the midland islands but could not find a sign of life, neither human nor animals. The fields were barren and bleak. It looked like they had not been farmed or cultivated for a long time. We had heard first-hand reports that Iceapelago was in much better shape, so our final target was a landing somewhere on these shores.'

'How did you hear about Iceapelago?' said Rory.

'You had some trouble a while back? Am I right?' said Bergit.

'What do you mean?' said Rory.

He was puzzled by the question but did not show it.

'You exiled a Welsh mercenary called Gove.'

'That waster,' said Rory. 'He's nothing but a professional rogue. A modern-day pirate that I wouldn't trust as far as I could spit.'

'That rogue as you called him eventually sailed to Malmö where we come from. He told us all about Iceapelago and its riches.'

'Riches!' said Rory. 'I'll tell you something about riches, Bergit. The wealthiest thing we have is our lives. And I'm not letting you threaten us.'

'Who said I was threatening you?'

'I assume Gove is skulking aboard one of your ships, is he?'

'I would not lie, but he is. He is not the man he once was. For one he is much older, as we all are. All he wants is a roof over his head, a reliable supply of food and the comfort of good company.'

'Don't we all yearn for such bliss. You have come to the wrong place, Bergit. Malahide Castle and the neighbouring Iceapelago communities do not want to share what we have spent decades building with you or indeed any other climate refugees. Isn't that so, Admiral?' He did not wait for a response from Iceapelago's newest citizen. 'Between the Portuguese, and now Swedes, this area is far too cluttered for my liking,' said Rory. 'My guess is that you have over a thousand people on your longboats?'

'Nearly twelve hundred, including children,' said Bergit.

'Here's my proposition,' said Rory. 'You sail north for about ninety kilometres sticking close to the shoreline. From here you can see a mountain range called the Mournes. To the left is the abandoned and flooded town of Newry. It was evacuated a decade ago to my knowledge. There you will find some dwellings and large commercial units around the higher harbour area. There should be enough basic shelter for all your families.'

'Why was it abandoned? said Bergit.

'Pestilence,' said Rory. 'There was an unavoidable incident and let us leave it at that. While it killed most of the community more than decade ago, it is now a viable disease-free location. Look at the positives. What makes Newry attractive is that it has a hilly but fertile hinterland, lots of forests and importantly fresh water supplies. I suggest you make it your home.'

'Is that an offer or an order?'

'Both,' said Rory. 'As the Commander of Iceapelago, I have the authority to decide who lives where. As with all offers, there are conditions.'

'Please explain,' said Bergit.

'I want you to leave three of your longboats here with us at Malahide Castle, and their occupants of course.'

'I do not understand, Commander,' said Bergit who was quite taken aback with Rory's no-nonsense approach.

'You don't need to. Just see it as my insurance policy. I want forty of your youngest and fittest, including at least three full family units, to make Malahide Castle their home.'

Bergit had been standing on the deck for over twenty minutes during the exchange. Having sussed out the strength of the opposition, and its leaders as the conversation unfolded, she was mindful to continue with her original plan. A full attack on Malahide Castle. General Gove had explained in detail how this could be done with a minimum loss of life. Now she hesitated. Rory was not the impulsive renegade that Gove had described to her with florid language. He seemed to have an honest side to his stiff exterior. He knew what he wanted, and she could see the attraction of the deal that was on the table.

'We will be peaceful neighbours then?' said Bergit.

'I do hope so,' said Rory. 'The surest way to oblivion on Iceapelago is active aggression. We all need to survive, and to survive we must co-exist. That's why I'll be asking you to disarm, apart from personal weapons. We need a peaceful environment without heavy weapons. Isn't that right, Admiral Rodriguez?'

'Yes, sir.'

'I will send emissaries when you have settled with a written concord that we can sign. It's important that you know your rights and obligations.'

'And what might they be?' said Bergit.

'You are to elect a leader. We call that position the Six. Appoint a sheriff who will be responsible for upholding the law. Both will travel on a regular basis to Malahide Castle to meet your Iceapelago neighbours to discuss mutual interests, such as trading and sharing food and medicines.'

'That sounds like democracy, a long-lost ideal, some would say,' said Bergit.

'I don't care what it is called,' said Rory. 'When we work together, things get done. As we have experienced all too often over recent decades, when dialogue disappears, so does the rule of law.'

'That sounds very statesman-like,' said Bergit.

'It's not meant to be but remember, I'm the boss in these parts.'

'Is that all?' said Bergit.

'Yes, with two final conditions. You get yourself elected as the Newry Six. That way we will meet with each other on a regular basis.'

'Fine by me,' said Bergit. 'And the second?'

'Whatever else you do, do not let Gove off Newry Island. Find him a nice retirement home. There will be trouble if I ever hear he is starting any sort of agitation. Am I clear?'

'Yes, sir,' said Bergit.

She smiled and walking to Rory gave him a huge bear hug that took him by surprise. She stepped back. 'You're some man, Rory Commander of Iceapelago. Families from Malmö will sail to Malahide Castle as soon as I speak to them. I assume that they can visit us?'

'Yes, of course, Bergit, Commander of the Swedish Islands.'

Rory took her hand as she stepped over the side of the ship onto the guardrail. Her blond hair disappeared as she descended with ease.

The admiral had stood at a distance as Rory interacted with Bergit. He had initially seen Rory as a bitter foe. No longer. He did not find it difficult to admit that Rory was one of the most genuine and generous persons he had met. He knew already that transitioning from being a foe to a friend would be a seamless experience.

CHAPTER 21

Final Words

The remaining residents of Malahide Castle, and their new guests from Howth Head were gathered at Rory's request in the banqueting hall. It was hard to believe, but it was less than three weeks since Captain Vasco da Gama had walked through the door for a surprise, if pre-arranged, dinner. Tonight an air of calm and quiet reflection was evident. Small groups chatted in hushed whispers as all tried to rationalise the latest dramatic events that had befallen the castle's residents. Was there ever going to be an end to the turmoil, trauma, and tension?

Rory let the conversations flow for a while. He observed that nobody was angry. There were no raised voices. The lightly wounded boasted about their bandages but did not otherwise complain. The camaraderie that was so characteristic of what the castle residents had experienced in the past was very much in evidence.

The visitors from Howth Head were comfortable in their new surroundings. The castle represented security and safety. Something that had been missing from their lives to date. They mixed and mingled. Stories about the happenings of the past decades were exchanged, some exaggerated but most true.

The third generation of Iceapelago survivors, the Iceapelago 3 generation, wanted answers and only Rory could provide them.

The room hushed without prompting as he moved to the front of the table to assume his position.

'I've spoken to General Peter Collins. Now that our radio link has been reopened with Canada, we can keep in touch in case of emergencies. He told me the Canadian Rangers left a large cache of arms and ammunition buried at Cork Airport. Ruth Henry knew about the arrangement but told nobody, not even me. Don and Kate will transport the remaining boxes to Malahide. They are due here next week. The admiral, our new best friend, had no issue providing a ship. Suitably equipped, we will be able to better protect ourselves. This is an ageing community,' continued Rory. 'As we all know, and before recent events, I could safely say we were on a one-way street to almost certain extinction.'

'I wouldn't go that far, Grandad,' said Jon. 'Speak for yourself.'

'As part of the arrangement I made with the Howth Six and the Swedes, the future of this community is secured.'

'Less prevarication, Rory, please,' said Veronica. 'Get to the point!' She approached him, and gently put her hand on his shoulder.

'With full consent, our friends from Howth Head will become part of our family. The youngest members played a key role in repelling our attackers. For that, we are grateful. We are even more grateful that they want to work to build Malahide Castle as their new home. Forty young Swedes, all under thirty years old, including three families with seven young children, will also be making Malahide Castle their home. With the residents from Howth Head who will live here, we'll have the physical resources for the first time in decades to expand our crops and flocks, to re-build the parts of the castle's dwellings that have fallen into disrepair. I pray you welcome this new blood.'

'We surely will,' said Emily, the former Malahide Six who had accepted earlier that she was the primary source of the disturbances that had befallen the castle residents. She had willingly stepped aside to allow Rory assume the position of Six.

'And where do the Portuguese fit in?' said Veronica.

'I have a commitment from Duke de Sousa, in his capacity as the Cork Six, that his people will disarm, live in peaceful co-existence with their neighbours and join the Council of Iceapelago as a partner.'

The room applauded.

'Decades after the Eriador Event, one thing is certain,' said Rory. 'We are all climate refugees. If we do not have good neighbourly relations, while respecting everyone's right to self-sufficiency, we are all on a path to anarchy. I'll do everything, and have in fact done everything as Commander of Iceapelago, to allow us to live in peace. Admiral Rodriguez, Bergit and I have grown to appreciate that it is not just the best, but the only way forward.'

His final words to the group were interrupted by the rising tenor of children's excited voices.

The door to the banqueting hall was pushed opened. Seven young boys and girls made their way cautiously into the room with their parents close behind. They were clearly suffering the effects of being at sea for several weeks. Before introductions could be made, one of the youngest, a blond boy aged about five spotted a bowl of apples. He ran to the table, climbed a chair, snatched the brightest red apple and took a big bite out of it. With his mouth full of a long-forgotten taste, he looked around the room. Everyone's eyes were on him. And everyone was smiling.

EPILOGUE

Five Years Later

The Malahide Castle marina was overflowing with craft of all shapes and sizes that had arrived over the previous days from the four corners of Iceapelago and beyond. The visitors had all travelled for a special occasion – to celebrate the fifth anniversary of the arrival of the climate refugees from Portugal and Sweden.

The atmosphere in and around the castle complex was relaxed and good-humoured as everyone took full advantage of the residents' hospitality.

Led by their Sixes, representatives from the Iceapelago communities gathered on the lawn in front of the main door of Malahide Castle. The old oak tree was in full bloom, providing a beautiful backdrop.

At midday, the temperature was over twenty degrees with no wind – a positive example of improving climate conditions.

Everyone was dressed for the ceremony in the unique costumes of their community. Hats, robes, shirts, baggy trousers and vestons had been carefully repaired and restored by helping hands. The Duke of the Principality of Ria Formosa, the elected Six representing Cork Airport Island, stood out from the crowd in his splendid traditional dress adorned with a gold chain and medals.

Beside the flag of Iceapelago stood the pennants of the larger islands and those of the invited visitors from Britannia, Cymru and Canada.

Rory approached the podium and mounted the steps carefully. His knees ached. Despite being days short of his eightieth birthday, he had grown tolerant and accepting of such pain, and indeed of many aspects of life in Iceapelago. He had prepared a short speech, his last as Commander of Iceapelago, which he believed was fitting for the occasion. He took the script from his pocket and placed it on the lectern stand. He nodded to Don who, in turn, rang a bell softly.

The crowd silenced.

Rory began.

'You are all most welcome to Malahide Castle on this special occasion.

'It is appropriate that I start by remembering those close to me who have died recently.

'My wife Veronica passed suddenly three months ago. She was my constant companion. Her loss is great, beyond any words I can express. The only thing that keeps me going and her memory alive, are Jon and Kate's two children. My great-grandchildren are the fourth generation of Iceapelago survivors.

'Others too have passed. Old age creeping up on many, including Emily who was the Malahide Castle Six for over a decade. And in the recent past, my good friend the admiral sadly drowned while swimming at Garrylow Beach off the Old Head of Kinsale. Those who did so much for Iceapelago, and many taking personal risks, will never be forgotten.

'When I shared a draft of my speech with the Howth Six, she chided me for using the term survivor. And do you know what? She is correct. In the past years we've moved beyond survival. Within some Iceapelago communities, problems have arisen but peaceful collaboration, not conflict, has been the proven way for resolving disputes. At long last we are getting some things right.

'Everyone has at least basic accommodation. And housing renovation activity is evident everywhere I travel.

'We are totally sufficient in food and water, with all our communities trading their surplus products, as was our tradition before the Big Storm.

'Solar panels have been repaired. Every community now has at least one source of electricity.

'It is also good to see craft brewing has made a recent comeback to the delight of many.

'I am especially pleased that twenty cruisers have been fully restored and made seaworthy, under Don's guidance and tutelage. They, along with the Portuguese fleet and the vessels from Sweden, have resulted in a huge increase in inter-island travel. This is helping Iceapelago to integrate more quickly. It would not have been possible to set up the fledgling communities in Kilkenny, Athlone and Mallow without access to reliable transport. Everyone I talk to seems to be on the move. Don's new inn at Straffan seems to be a popular venue for short breaks.

'Our Portuguese friends have been more than generous in providing a team of doctors and nurses who travel on a regular basis across Iceapelago to meet with old folk like me who have aches and pains. They have saved many lives. The fact that we now have some basic medical services puts many a mind at ease.

'It is wonderful that strong friendships are developing.

'The Council of the Sixes has met every three months or so. There was an edgy start to our meetings as our new arrivals struggled to settle in. But to everyone's credit, when a call for help went out, the Iceapelago communities went to the aid of the Newry and Cork Airport Island communities. New enduring relationships have been formed. I want to acknowledge that Bergit and Duke de Sousa played a key leadership role in integrating their communities with ours. They have secured the future of their people and ours thanks to the goodwill and generosity of the citizens of Iceapelago. And we are all the better for having so many climate refugees among us.

'It is great to see a contingent here from Baie Verte in Canada with our old friend Colly in charge. He tells me that the North Atlantic below the Arctic Circle is now fully accessible to sailing boats, and several small communities in the southern and mountainous parts of the American landmass have been in radio contact these past few months. They too have had their woes and worries but seem to be recovering well.

'I can confirm that the spectacular *dhow* that arrived at Malahide marina last week came from the Atalaya region of Turkey. Their leaders wish to develop trade ties with us, and we welcome the setting up of a trading post, probably on Newry Island. With sea ice gone from the Mediterranean, we can expect more visitors from Asia, and maybe further afield.

'What satisfies me most of all is that our population is growing steadily. It has been a very long time since young healthy children have been running carefree around the Malahide Castle estate. How things have changed and changed for the better.

'As I start my well-earned and belated retirement, I was asked what will I be remembered for. That is a tough question to ask of an old man.

'Since Eriador Day, I have been at the centre of many traumatic events, and the cause of one or two rumpuses, I must admit. I have had a few lapses, but I have always sought to be honest in my dealings with friends and adversaries alike. Honesty with patience results in trust. When we trust each other, anything is possible.

'I have done my very best over the past five years to build bridges as we all sought to transition to a new peaceful way of life.

'Today's gathering is testimony to my endeavours, my legacy.

'While Iceapelago should not forget its tragic history, I believe it is time to look ahead, and to bring in a younger generation of leaders. That is why I resigned as Commander of Iceapelago.

'I am looking forward to the outcome of the meeting of the Council of Sixes this afternoon that will elect my successor.

'We are becoming stronger and more resilient, but we should take nothing for granted. There are many nations that will view the success of Iceapelago with envy. No doubt, we will have to greet and accommodate more climate refugees.

'My abiding wish is that Iceapelago thrives under the watchful eye of the new Commander and the Council of the Sixes.'

ACKNOWLEDGEMENTS

FERGIA MAC ANNA's SAGE advice again helped me shape and structure the storyline and develop the characters. I am indebted to Jean O'Sullivan who carried out a comprehensive copy edit. Kelley Garcia (Goodreads cli-fi group) also gave me good feedback.' Rebecca and Andrew Brown at Ardel Media got the book into production and published in their usual professional, low key but highly efficient and friendly manner. Fellow author Peter O'Neill was always to hand when I needed advice. My wife Margaret was so supportive of me in writing Iceapelago 3: *Merci Encore*. Thanks to Ger Nolan who created the map of Iceapelago. Finally, my sincere appreciation to everyone who read the first two books and provided such positive feedback. This motivated me to complete the trilogy.